FAIR DREAMS

Science Traveler Series

Book 16

FAIR DREAMS

Science Traveler Series
Book 16

J. L. Greger

Bug Press   Bernalillo, New Mexico

Fair Dreams

Bug Press
An Imprint of Ingram Sparks
Bernalillo, New Mexico 87004
http://www.jlgreger.com

ISBN (paperback): 9798989418466
ISBN (EPUB): 9798989418473
Library of Congress Catalogue Number: 2026906169

DEDICATION

To those who dream but mange to keep their feet on the ground.

CHAPTER 1: Welcome to the Kingdom of Camelot

Thursday

A fairy—all pink and sparkly—with her silvery wings bouncing on her back sprinted toward Sara Almquist. One of the fairy's large wings knocked the blue cone hat off the head of a woman in a blue brocade dress. The fairy didn't slow down. She trampled the gray silk scarf attached to the hat and shoved aside an elderly man in a red velvet doublet who tried to retrieve the woman's hat.

Sara Almquist stepped back, but her FBI partner, Jack Drum, reached out to slow the fairy. The fairy turned, and a wing made of coat hangers and lace hit his face. He groaned. "My eye."

The fairy gave a startled glance at Jack as she darted behind a peasant in a burlap tunic and leather britches. Sara lost sight of the fairy as she zigzagged through a group of women in a modern spandex leggings and sports jackets.

Sara grabbed Jack's arm and pulled him toward the booth labeled Guinevere's Hair Goods. "Let me look at your eye." She yelled to the uniformed Santa Fe police officer who had been leading Jack and her through the mass of peasants, nobles, and tourists meandering among the booths at the medieval fair. "Call the gate. They should question her."

The officer looked at Sara in disgust as he pulled his phone from his pocket. "She's just another crazy. I hate manning events like this."

Sara turned her attention to Jack. "Don't rub your eye."

Jack immediately dropped his hand to his side and waited silently as Sara gently pulled his left eyelid up and ordered him to look to the right, left, up, and down. "I don't see any foreign objects or cuts. Probably would feel better if you rinsed it with eyedrops."

"No time for that. The sergeant is waiting for us at the blacksmith's shop." The officer aggressively grabbed Sara's sleeve and swung a wooden cane back and forth like an angry blind man as he led the way to a permanent shed at the El Rancho de Las Golondrinas Living History Museum.

The crowd parted before him. Sara and Jack followed in his wake. The playful atmosphere of the medieval fair was broken by the yellow crime scene tape around the shed. A swarthy man in a shabby suit stood by the door to the blacksmith's shop and glared at the crowd.

The man in the suit greeted Jack. "Agent Drum? I'm Sergeant Miguel Roybal. I called the resident FBI agent in Santa Fe, Hank Snow, when the crew in the stables found two empty bank deposit bags this morning. The bags have the serial numbers of those taken in the heist at the Wells Fargo Bank on Route 528 in Albuquerque on Tuesday."

Jack nodded. "Hank called and said he'd have the bags delivered to the FBI offices in Albuquerque later today. But then…"

"The stable crew found human body parts in the straw as they mucked out the stables for the jousting horses. Hank came over immediately." Roybal looked toward the back of the blacksmith shop. "Hank is in the stable behind the shop now. He took one look at the scene and advised us to ask for you two." Roybal extended his hand to Sara. "He says you're only a science consultant for the FBI, but you're the best at cutting through red tape."

***

Roybal focused on the milling crowd for a few seconds. "I hate costumed events. They bring out the worst in everyone because people feel anonymous in a costume. But the mayor has already pointed out this new event will bring dollars to Santa Fe by starting the tourist season early in April." He pointed to a series of wood panels painted with trees. "The whole investigation was slowed because the mayor didn't want the crowd to see the vans of the medical examiner or of the Department of Public Safety Forensic Lab. We had to get those scenery backdrops from the Santa Fe Opera's prop room and to hide the action around the stables."

Sara didn't listen to Miguel's and Jack's continued conversation because she was watching a lanky man with a cowboy hat as he sauntered out of the stable.

Hank Snow pulled off his hat and scratched his thin, grizzled hair. "Howdy, Sara. It's been a year since we worked a case together in Santa Fe. 'Course, we're now in Kingdom of Camelot. What a lot of horse pucky." He spat in the dirt.

Same old Hank. "How's your wife?"

"About the same."

Sara thought she saw tears in his eyes. She wasn't surprised. Hank's wife had suffered a major stroke six months before and had made little progress in regaining her ability to walk despite intensive physical therapy. Hank had told Sara a couple of months earlier, "I could retire, but my wife says I have to go on as if nothing is different."

Time to change the subject. She turned on her phone to record the conversation—a procedure she'd started when she first began consulting. *It's not a matter of trust but a way to catch all details.* "What do we have here?"

Hank waved his arm toward the stable. "The ME's crew is almost through. They found a leg and the lower torso of a woman. Recently deceased."

"Might suggest the robbers are old school. They thought removal of the head and hands would prevent identification by fingerprints and dental records."

Hank put his Stetson back on. "Could also suggest the victim left the prison system before DNA analyses were used much—twenty years ago."

"Any other info about the victim?"

"Adult. No clothes or jewelry. Tattoos." He blew his nose in a large red bandanna. "Amazing how bad a body can look after horses trample on it in the straw."

"I thought horses avoided bodies."

Hank spat into the gravel. "They tried but couldn't get out of their stalls. Want to take a look?"

"No. I'll see the body at the autopsy. Jack…"

Hank snickered. "Everyone knows Jack fainted during an autopsy. But the rumor is he's crackerjack at tracing how money is laundered. That makes you two perfect for this case."

Sara winked. "Yeah, we're the ones you contact when a case looks weird." She paused. "Is this the second day of a five-day event?"

"Yep."

Sara sighed. "How do we need to interview by Monday morning?"

"Roybal sent me a list with fifty names, but I think there's more like a hundred-twenty vendors and employees here."

"Hope you don't have other plans for the next few days."

Hank spat again. "Couldn't come at a worse time. The other resident agent in Santa Fe is on vacation this week and next. And Roybal doesn't seem…." He didn't finish his sentence.

***

Sara and Hank gabbed a bit before they found Jack and Roybal standing at the entrance to the stables. "Guys, I've scheduled us to meet with the manager of this event at eleven. Let's coordinate first." She looked at Roybal. "What can you tell me about the blacksmith and the stable hands?

Roybal pulled out his phone and gulped repeatedly as he studied his notes. "I think six men."

Hank winked at Sara. "Four of the stablemen are itinerants. The blacksmith and one assistant are locals."

"Guess so." Roybal fumbled with his phone. "According to the manger, half of the crew at the fair are locals. Most of the vendors start their season in early April. They move east and north until September. Then they turn south and return to their permanent residences in Arizona and California in late October. He's not sure about their employees, but they appear rough and…"

Hank interrupted, "Many of those—at least the ones I talked to—appear to have no permanent home."

Roybal's face twisted in disgust. "*La gentuza.*"

He's just called them riffraff. It may explain why he didn't bother to talk to anyone but the manager.

Roybal continued, "Did any on the list of vendors I gave Hank have criminal records?"

Sara nodded. "That's one reason why Hank and I were slow to join you in the stables. We were reviewing the data."

Roybal's phone rang. He said, "Yes," twice and disconnected.

"Did the police catch the fairy?"

Roybal's lips tightened. "My men at the front gate stopped her. She claimed she was working at a booth called *Portia's Potions*, but her name wasn't on the manager's list."

Jack had been studying his phone. "I think the fairy is worth a serious interview. The blacksmith claimed she was watching the ME's staff as they pulled out a tattooed leg from the straw."

Sara was used to Jack's way of thinking. "You're guessing she recognized the tattoos and can ID the victim?"

Jack nodded. "Did you see the look on her face when she ran into me? She was scared. We need to talk to her. The ME's crew couldn't give me much on the victim. White female in her forties. Probably tall—about five-ten—and muscular. Their close-up shots of the tattoos on the leg and the buttocks of the victim are our best clues until we get DNA tests done."

Miguel snorted. "That's for sure. The crime scene investigators from the New Mexico Public Safety Forensic Lab didn't even try to collect DNA or fingerprints before they left." Miguel looked at his watch. "We'd better get to the manager's tent. Be warned. He's not very helpful."

He's not the only one.

CHAPTER 2: Introductions

Sara didn't know whether to be annoyed with or to pity the scrawny, red-haired man sitting behind a long table at the front of the main shed not far from the entrance to the fair. He looked like a student from one of the Harry Potter movies in his cheap black high school graduation gown and oversized black framed glasses. His name—Ron Weasley Engel—didn't inspire confidence either, even though the sign over the table where he sat said: CHANCELLOR OF THE EXCHEQUER.

"No one told me I had to verify the vendors' identities. How could I? They're all in costumes. Besides the Camelot Fair Enterprises doesn't employ most of them." He pushed his glasses up the bridge of his nose. "I was told to get their space rental payments before I let them set up their booths on Tuesday. The owner doesn't care if they use stage names."

Jack showed no emotions. "Let's try something simpler. How many attended the fair yesterday?"

Ron pushed back the black sleeves of his oversized gown and pulled out his phone. "I don't know. The gatekeepers couldn't get the turnstiles to work." He fiddled with his phone. "I only know we deposited two thousand from the till and a few credit card receipts in the bank deposit slot last night."

"How much in credit card receipts?"

Ron shrugged. "Bank hasn't told me yet."

Jack whistled as he played with his phone. "Let me get a few facts straight. Tickets for everyone over thirteen are fifteen dollars. Can we assume at least half paid with a credit card?"

"No idea." Ron didn't look apologetic, just bored, as he stared upward.

"My calculations suggest about three hundred adults and teens paid to enter yesterday."

"Not that many." Ron slumped on his stool. "The boss was disappointed at the poor turnout."

"The bank should have logged in your deposit by now. I want to see the bank deposit acknowledgment."

"I guess." Ron made no effort to check his phone.

Roybal whispered to Sara. "I told you he was an airhead."

Jack voice was deeper now as he stared at Ron. "I'm waiting. Call the bank."

Sara couldn't decide if Ron was dumb or had an attitude. *Probably both.* "Maybe we could get more info from your boss."

"Doubt it," Ron smirked. "He's in Nipton, California."

Jack cleared his throat. "Mr. Engel, this is an interstate business. So, you and I are going to review your accounts as soon as Dr. Almquist, Agent Snow, and several Santa Fe police officers begin to interview all the vendors and crew at the fair."

"You can't. They need to work their booths."

Jack smirked. "No arguments. Make it work. You know someone from the New Mexico Taxation and Revenue Department might enjoy working with you and me."

Ron looked ready to cry. "I'll try."

***

"Okay, we're all in agreement." Sara looked around the huddle of law enforcement officers. "This appears to be a slippery crew. The boss behaves like a defiant teen. Record everything."

Hank and five Santa Fe officers left to interview the staff at Portia's Potions and then other booths, while Jack and a Santa Fe police officer set up shop with Ron at the table at the front of the Chancellery of the Exchequer. Roybal and Sara found a nook behind a pile of boxes and crates at the back of the shed. They focused on the pink fairy: Hannah Merchant according to her driver's license.

***

Hannah's wings bounced as she pounded her fists on a crate. "Call me Crystal Star. Everyone does."

Roybal checked his phone. "Are you sure it isn't because you want to hide your police record? You've built quite an impressive one for your age. Arrests for petty thefts in two states while you were seventeen."

"Stupid clerks and overeager small-town cops."

"I'm sure there's more in sealed juvenile records."

The fairy jumped to her feet and fluttered her long, silvery eyelashes. "You can't hold my juvenile..." Her wings swayed as she spoke. "... experiences against me."

J. L. Greger

Sara stood and grabbed the edge of one wing. "Before we continue, let's remove your wings. They're almost lethal weapons."

"Must I?"

"Yes."

The girl unhooked the front closure on her sturdy pink vest. The wire wings, covered in silver netting and lace drooped, on her back before she slid them off.

Almost like the wings of a real butterfly when it lands on a flower. Kinda pretty. "Aren't you more comfortable now?"

Crystal rolled her shoulder repeatedly. "The wings are heavy, but I'll need help to put them back on."

Sara pointed at the girl's tousled long, pink hair. "Can you take off the wig, too?"

"What wig?"

Sara tapped her laptop sitting on a stack of boxes and pulled up a photo. "Your driver's license indicates you're a brunette."

"That's old. I've had pink hair ever since I joined this traveling medieval fair last year."

Roybal snapped a photo of her. "I've instructed the crew doing interviews to photograph everyone. Stupid costumes make driver's license photos useless."

The girl bounced into a chair. "My costume is not stupid. It's the real me. And I won't answer any more questions unless you call me Crystal."

Sara thought this thin eighteen-year-old looked like a flat-chested child in her pink leotards. Then she noticed the tears in the blue eyes outlined by the harsh metallic eyelashes and the way the girl chewed her lip. The girl was putting on a brave front, but she was afraid.

Time to try a different approach. "Living on the road is tough, especially if you're alone. Was the woman who was killed a friend of yours?" She pushed Crystal onto a crate, shoved her laptop close to Crystal's face, and flashed pictures of the victim's tattoos—a butterfly and stars on her rump and more stars on the back of the leg.

Crystal flinched as she saw each photo. "I… I… I don't know." She paused. "Tattoos look different on dead skin. Why is the skin blue and purple on one side of her seat and streaked on the leg?"

Sara guessed the lividity on one cheek of the buttocks and the leg suggested the body had laid on its side before being butchered. *No need to offer that tidbit.*

Roybal leaned forward. "You're saying you saw these tattoos on a live woman? Who?"

The young woman bent forward, put her head between her legs, and moaned.

Sara put her arm across Crystal's shoulders. "Look, it's all right to be afraid. Those pics are scary. We think the woman might have been tall, sturdy, and in her forties. Do you know anyone with the fair who meets that description?"

Crystal stopped groaning but didn't look up. "My boss. The manager of Portia's Potions—Portia Merchant."

Roybal typed rapidly on his phone. "Diablos! Don't any of you carnies use your real names." Finally, he muttered. "The manager of Portia's Potions is Anne Harper. At least she's the one who paid the booth fee to Ron Engel."

Crystal sat up. "That's what I said. Harper is the name of her current husband—I think soon to be ex-husband number three. Anne Portia Merchant was her birth name. She goes by Portia Merchant." The girl rubbed her right eye. "See what you've done. My eyelashes came off." She pushed Sara away and held up a silvery piece of metal foil. "It will take me thirty minutes to get myself back in shape."

***

Roybal pulled Sara aside when he re-entered the shed used by the Chancellor of the Exchequer. "I talked to the interview crew. They got nothing at the first three booths until they mentioned the victim might be Anne Portia Merchant Harper. Then everyone had a story. Seems she was bossy and secretive."

Crystal shrieked, "No, she was just protecting her products. She made her own stuff—soaps, candles, creams, and herbal remedies— during the winter months in Arizona. But sometimes, she had to make remedies while on the road. She didn't want anyone to steal the recipes that she got from her grandmother—a *curandera*."

Sara had to think a second before she remembered the word. *Curanderas* were women healers during colonial times in New Mexico and Arizona. They were sometimes accused of being witches, but they often provided the only medical care in rural communities in the Southwest until a generation before.

Roybal stepped closer. "Viv Lorenzo in the booth next to Portia's Potions—I think Treasure Chest—claimed Portia poisoned her crew. She said they got sick last night after they ate candies Portia gave them."

Crystal stood. "She's lying. Portia warned them not to eat the suckling pork from King Art's last night. She said the pork and turkey were leftovers from the show last weekend in Tempe. Viv and her crew didn't listen. That's why Portia gave the mints. She knew they'd need them."

Not a motive for murder but might be worth investigating. She turned to Roybal. "What type of symptoms?"

"Nausea, vomiting, diarrhea. That's why Viv was slow to open her booth this morning. She and her crew were sick."

"Did anyone else get sick?"

Crystal fluttered her eyelashes. One was her real light brown eyelashes; the other was a garish, silver foil fake lash. Sara managed not to laugh at Crystal's lop-sided face. Roybal turned his back to Crystal and coughed.

Crystal was unfazed. "Don't know." She paused. "Oh, I guess Weird Willie got sick. He stopped by my truck around nine last night to ask for antacids, but he seemed okay this morning."

I'm missing something. The fair was open last night. Lots of people should have been at King Arthur's Feast. "Did you eat together after the fair closed for the evening?"

"No. King Art's was closed to the general public."

"Why would King Arthur's Feast be closed on the first night of the fair?"

"Don't know. Probably because the head cook—Art Last—didn't think many would attend the Baroque musical concert last night on the center stage. Portia thought he wanted to get rid of the leftovers from last week."

"Seems odd Portia ate there."

Crystal shrugged. "She didn't want to waste time over supper and only ate a hot dog. She muttered something about making a mustard plaster for the horses."

Looks like those in the horse barn and the food stand need to be questioned again. "When did you last see Portia?"

"When we walked back to her camper and truck after supper." She must have noticed Sara's frown. "I have a bunk and shower closet in the truck, which we use to store and transport supplies. Willie has a separate entrance to his space in her camper. Otherwise, the camper is Portia's bedroom and our kitchen and dining space. It's where we eat breakfast most days. It saves money."

Odd a single young woman was left alone in the truck. "Why didn't Willie sleep in the truck instead of you?"

"Portia is often noisy when she works in the kitchen. I'm a light sleeper. Also, I have more space in the truck. Well, if you don't mind using boxes as tables. I sew little bags to hold some of the soaps. Customers pay more for soap in drawstring purses, and Portia lets me keep a dollar for each purse sold."

"Hmm. So, you're busy most evenings."

Crystal nodded.

"Did you work on the purses last night?"

"No. I'd had a couple of long days. We'd driven from Gallup on Tuesday and had to finish our set-up yesterday before we could open." She bounced in her chair. "The first day of the fair in a new site is always a busy time."

Crystal seems to be honest and has no way to leave the complex unless she steals a vehicle. Better talk to Willie and the horse wranglers. They may be more mobile.

"Two more questions. Are you related to Portia? You both have the last name of Merchant."

Crystal looked down. "Portia gave me her last name and raised me after the commune broke up."

Better have analysts back in the FBI building check out Portia's and Crystal's backgrounds. "Were city health officials notified about the food poisoning?"

Crystal frowned. "I hope not. We showmen don't bring in officials unless necessary. The cook at King Art's would be mad if we shut it down." She smiled at Sara. "That's all officials do: hurt business and call us carnies. We are artisans and showmen not carnies."

CHAPTER 3: Confusion Reigns

"Food poisoning is not a motive for murder." Roybal glared at Sara. "We've got enough problems here without adding health officials. They'll close the fair down. Then our witnesses and suspects will disappear immediately."

"They'll only close King Arthur's Feast." *Bet Roybal's main worry is not the closure of a food booth but the bad press it will generate.* "Maybe you or your boss should call the mayor and warn him of the problems."

"Diablos." He pulled his fingers through his sleek, black hair. "Who do you think kept interrupting me?"

"Look, the health workers will talk to the last people to probably see Portia alive—those eating at King Arthur's Feast last night." She snickered. "After they're grilled about their bowel movements by the public health workers, they'll think our questions are pleasant."

He stroked his carefully trimmed black beard. "You might be right."

Roybal was an enigma. *Very polished and sleek. His nails are even manicured and glisten a bit from clear polish. But his suit is old and grungy. Let's see if I can get him to loosen up.* "You don't have to be polite and proper around me. None of my FBI colleagues are." Without a pause, "I need to check signals with Jack before we interview the horse wranglers even though I don't think Portia was killed and cut up in the barn."

"But there was blood in the straw."

"Not enough." Wait! What about other garbage? "Did the CSI team from the New Mexico Public Safety Forensic Lab inspect other garbage besides the straw on the floor of the barn? It would be easy to stash body parts in discarded boxes and crates." Sara stopped. "When did the truck pick up garbage from the fair this morning?"

"Diablos." Roybal rapidly typed on his phone, groaned, and made a call. "Stop the garbage truck that left the medieval fair an hour ago. Everything in it must be examined for body parts." He listened for thirty seconds. "Don't give me excuses. Your team was so hot to get out of here this morning, they did a sloppy job. Blood and body parts could be inside the garbage."

As he reprimanded someone at the forensic lab, Sara thought about the fair. *The vendors don't own the land on which they are parked.* When he completed his call, she asked, "Does the city own Los Golondrinas?"

Roybal shook his head. "No, a historical society does. Why do you ask?"

"I think we can check the liquid waste tanks for each vehicle parked here without a warrant." She frowned. "But maybe we should get permission from the owner of the land."

"What?"

"It will be like examining items set out on the street as garbage." She stood. "I bet we'll find evidence of excess amounts of blood or at of least hemoglobin residues in the tank and disposal hose for at least one of the booths or campers parked here."

***

"Ron, you're doing it again."

"What?"

"Lying. It's a crime to lie to law enforcement officers. This isn't a game." Jack tapped his fingers on the table. "I checked. The turnstiles at the gate didn't break yesterday until five. The women at the gate were sure the two turnstiles had recorded the entry of over four hundred and fifty fair goers." Jack leaned closer to Ron. Their noses almost met. "You said less than three hundred entered."

Ron squeaked. "The two women at the gate were new. They read the meters on the gates wrong."

Jack leaned back. "I doubt your answer. The crews in several booths have told my friends the crowd was decent yesterday. They guessed at least five hundred."

Ron blinked.

"Did you lie to your boss and steal part of the entry fees? Or did your boss instruct you to underestimate the take?" He turned to a woman Sara didn't recognize. "This lady from New Mexico Taxation and Revenue Department takes a dim view of businesses that cheat on their taxes. When she's annoyed, she calls her friends at the federal level—the IRS."

The woman stopped texting and flashed a broad smile at Ron.

Ron shook a bit.

Sara enjoyed watching Jack in action. She had watched him develop from a hesitant newbie to a skillful FBI agent. It was unusual for a science consultant like herself to be asked to train a new agent. However, Carbonne—the special agent in charge (SAC) of the Albuquerque office

J. L. Greger

of the FBI—had not wanted the first Black agent he had recruited to Albuquerque to be hazed by senior agents. Sara knew Carbonne had a reason to be worried. Several of the senior agents based in Albuquerque had repeatedly displayed contempt for minorities and women. That was a problem in a state in which more than ten percent of the population was Native Americans and almost fifty percent was Hispanic. Sara guessed Carbonne trusted her to mentor Jack well because she had been his partner on several major cases before he was promoted to the SAC position.

Wonder if Jack would like my help. "Ron, did you forget what you told those eating at King Arthur's Feast last night?" She frowned. "I think you bragged that you were able to hire two women who had manned the gates at the New Mexico State Fair for years."

Ron's Adams apple bobbed in his neck and a pink glow rose from his neck to his face. "Er, er, I guess..." He suddenly smiled. "I forgot I put a thousand dollars in a jar around four and stuck it in a box in back. I didn't want anyone to steal it."

"Tell Dr. Almquist where to find the money."

Ron gulped. "Why did you bring a doc along? Is she the one who ratted out King Art's? It's not easy for food stands at fairs to make much money. Who knew suckling pork and turkey legs wouldn't store well in the refrigerator for a week?"

Glad I had my recorder on. Guess that proves the food vendors for this fair take shortcuts. And the management condones it. "Are you sure you didn't stash cash in more than one jar?"

Ron jumped from his chair and scurried to a box in the pile behind him. He pulled a jar filled with cash from the box and handed the jar to Jack.

As Jack counted the twenties and fifties in the jar, Sara pulled the box out again and opened it. There was a white legal envelope in the box.

"What is this?" She waved the envelope.

"It's private." Ron lunged for the envelope. It ripped. Cash and slips of paper fell out. "Some vendors can't pay their fees until they get the first day's receipts. I didn't have a chance to deposit these yet."

The woman from New Mexico Taxation and Revenue Department snickered. "I'm learning more about your operation today than I expected. Weren't you in Tempe last week? Maybe, I'd better talk to my friends in Arizona about you."

Jack finished counting the cash. "One thousand, three hundred." He looked at his notes. "The bank said the credit card receipts and cash deposited last night came to four thousand, eight hundred. That means the gate from Wednesday was six thousand, one hundred dollars." He scribbled on a page. "If the entry fee was fifteen dollars each that suggests four hundred and six attended the fair on Wednesday. The women at the turnstiles said four hundred and fifty entered before five. I think a lot more would have entered the fair after five last night. Where's the rest of the cash?"

Ron shook his head. "That's all I have. The only show we had last night was a concert of Baroque music. Jousts only occur on Thursday, Friday and Saturday nights."

"Who's your second in command?"

"Why?"

"He's going to have to man this desk while you answer questions at the Santa Fe Sheriff's office. You'll be able to think more clearly when you aren't distracted by the background noise of the fair. It will also be easier to do a video conference with the woman your boss in Nippon sent to speak to the police. She's on his way to the sheriff's office for San Luis Obispo County now. Your boss must really be annoyed with you."

Ron turned icy white. "I might have hidden a little more cash around six."

***

"Diablos. We'll soon have more state and city officials here than fair goers." Roybal loosened his tie as he listened to someone on his phone. Occasionally, he said, "Yes, sir."

Sara studied the thirty-something sergeant. She noted the smoothness of his neck when he loosened his tie. *Looks like he waxes his neck even though he has a beard.* His right ear was either scarred or pierced. His eyebrows had been artfully plucked to prevent a unibrow. *Odd, a man who's so fastidious wears such a dirty, ill-fitting suit.*

He disconnected and swore as he either texted or wrote himself a note.

She stepped closer to get a peek at his phone. "You seem like a fish out of water today. Petty larceny and food poisoning are regular parts of fairs."

He snapped, "Ron went way past petty larceny. Originally, he only admitted to about two thousand from the gate yesterday. We now know it was about seven thousand."

"It's not unusual to have to sort through a lot of chaff in a murder investigation." Sara shrugged. "Ron's part of the chaff—a grifter. Jack thinks Ron will buckle quickly when sheriff's deputies grill him, especially if they can threaten him with major larceny charges."

J. L. Greger

"Diablos, you don't understand."

"I understand that you don't usually wear an old suit to work. I'd guess you might do undercover work as a slick operator." She put a hand on his shoulder. "How did you get stuck at the fair? Did you annoy your bosses? Or were you at this fair for another reason and stumbled onto the murder?"

"Diablos, you're here to investigate a murder and a bank robbery not to investigate me."

"I can't trust my coworkers if I don't know their agendas."

"I'll be in the barn when you stop analyzing me." He stalked away.

CHAPTER 4: Jack's Observations

Jack and the woman from the state taxation office stopped interviewing Ron when they heard Roybal's raised voice behind the wall of stacked boxes. Jack became alarmed when Roybal stalked out of the building. A minute later Sara followed.

"You'd better check," said the taxation officer.

Jack stood at the front door of the shed. Sara was trailing after Roybal as he almost loped toward the horse barn. She seemed in no hurry and stopped to fumble with something in her purse.

Jack's phone vibrated. He read Sara's message:

Roybal is at the fair for something besides this murder investigation. Most likely, a long-term undercover project. Defensive unnecessarily.

Poor Roybal. Doesn't know what he's up against. Jack smiled and remembered being mentored by Sara. She had taught him two main things. One was the importance of details. The second was to know your colleagues and suspects well. He coughed. But she'd never revealed much about herself. He had noticed she occasionally consulted for the State Department and other agencies on scientific issues. He'd assumed some of her travel was related to her significant other—Eric Sanders. He had also sensed that Carbonne trusted Sara implicitly and didn't treat her like the usual FBI consultant. He assumed it was because she had been his partner.

Jack realized Sara had a higher security clearance than anyone else in the FBI office in Albuquerque, except Carbonne, only recently. It was after Sanders had been appointed the Director of the Bureau of Intelligence and Research for the State Department with the title of Assistant Secretary of State. Moreover, he'd learned Carbonne had served as an operative for Sanders when Sanders directed intelligence collection for the US in Cuba.

The sooner Roybal gives in and reveals his secrets, the sooner she'll concentrate on the murder and bank robbery.

"Agent Drum, come back inside," yelled a Santa Fe County sheriff's deputy. "Searching these boxes was a waste of time. Mainly we found packing materials. My boss, the Sheriff of San Obispo County, and this lady…" He pointed at the tax official. "…are eager to begin interviewing Ron by video conference in our offices. We don't need you as much as that Santa Fe police sergeant needs help." He guffawed.

***

"Why don't I get an FBI CSI team to help the state forensic lab sort through the material collected by the garbage truck?"

"Fat chance of that type of cooperation," snapped Roybal. "No one willingly sorts garbage."

Sara gave a knowing smile. "I think I can get them here in an hour."

Hank took off his hat and scratched his head. "Roybal, don't be a fool. Take her offer. One of the men in the FBI CSI unit—Winslow Red Feather—is like a bloodhound when tracking evidence. He'll do it for Sara. They're both into DNA and weird science. Kinda strange when they get brainstorming together."

While Sara made the arrangements, Hank, Jack, and Roybal analyzed the results of the interviews with staff from the various booths. It appeared sixteen people had eaten at King Arthur's Feast the previous night: Portia and her crew—Willie Shakes and Crystal Star, Viv Lorenzo and the two men who worked in her booth, the two cooks and three wait staff at King Arthur's Feast, Ron Engel, and four horse wranglers. One of the wait staff had seen Portia and Willie walk from her camper to the horse barn after supper. Several noted that Willie was weird but wouldn't define what they meant.

Accordingly, Hank, Roybal, and two Santa Fe officers began to question all the men who worked in the stables again. Jack and Sara went to look for Willie Shakes.

***

"Willie, everyone else in the fair caravan left Tempe around nine on Monday morning and went straight to Santa Fe. Why did Portia stop off in Gallup?"

Willie gave Sara a blank look with his mouth hanging open. "Don't know." He folded his hands so that his index fingers formed a steeple while his other fingers were pointed down with his thumbs together in front of his steeple. He almost sang, "Here's the church."

Sara ignored his hand game. "You worked for Portia during the last three fair seasons. You told us during the off-season from November through March, you lived near her and did odd jobs for her. What kind of odd jobs?"

Willie moved his thumbs apart to show his wriggling fingers. "Open the doors and see all the people." He giggled and brought his thumbs together. "The people all go home." He stared at Sara. "Portia made soap, lotions, and candles in the off season. She needed help. Then too, I worked in her dairy, making cheeses. Some have blue streaks."

Sara pushed her hair back from her face and bit her lip. "Okay. Did Portia sell those items in Gallup?"

Willie stared at her.

"Why did she stop in Gallup?"

Jack forced himself not to laugh. *Willie is trying Sara's patience. Wonder who'll win this battle of wills.*

"Well, her old man—Bodet Harper—lives in Gallup. Expect she wanted to see him." Willie shook his head. "They should never have married. Argued all the time."

One point for Sara. She learned something potentially useful. Time to try to help. "Willie, why didn't they get a divorce?"

Willie looked puzzled. "Would ruin their partnership."

Sara's voice was sharper than usual. "Partnership for what?"

"Don't know. Portia sold stuff for Bodet."

"Like what?" Sara frowned. "Drugs, maybe?"

Willie continued to play his church game with hands. "Not drugs. Portia was a good woman. A healer. She'd never used drugs. Didn't even drink much."

"Did you ever help her load stuff from Bodet?"

"Sometimes." Willie grinned every time he parted his thumbs to show his wriggling fingers. "Bodet is an artist. At least he thinks he is. She delivered his paintings to buyers, I guess."

"Was she going to make a delivery in Santa Fe?"

"Don't know. Portia never took me along when she delivered Bodet's paintings."

"Did she take Crystal along?"

Willie shrugged. "Doubt it."

Jack noted Sara was frantically typing on her laptop. *Time to distract Willie.* "Will Bodet join the fair caravan anytime during the season?"

Willie didn't stop his hand game. "Portia didn't poke her nose into my business. I didn't put my nose into her stuff."

"You had to notice something. You said they argued a lot. When will Portia and Bodet get together again?"

"Maybe in Michigan in July."

"Why then?"

"We do a fair in Ann Arbor in July." He grinned.

Sara seemed to have finished her emails and smiled at Willie. "Did Portia stow Bodet's paintings in her truck or in her camper?"

"Don't know."

"You must have some idea."

"Well, Portia took the truck somewhere on Monday evening. Never saw her move anything from the truck to the camper after she came back." He created the church steeple with his hands again. "You done with me? I got to help Crystal manage our booth. Portia always said the booth would be ours if anything happened to her. I sure like working in the booth better than working in the dairy."

Jack whispered in Sara's ear. "Is that a motive for murder?"

***

Winslow's thick braid swung from side to side as he got out of FBI's CSI van. "Sure, was glad Sara arranged for the other FBI van go to the garbage sorting site. But I'm not clear what we're looking for here."

Jack laughed. "I'm not sure either. Sara thinks human blood or blood residues will be found in the waste disposal tank and the flexible hose to the tank for one of the campers or booths."

"And that will indicate the murder site." Winslow sniffed. "Sounds logical, but it will be a stinky, miserable job. What am I looking for in the victim's vehicles?"

"Maybe paintings. Certainly, blood and prints on the paintings and their cartons if you find them. Otherwise, I think fingerprints and DNA collection will be a waste of time. I hope you'll find cash from the robbery. Sara's hoping for traces of drugs."

"Where's Sara?"

"She's in the Portia's Potions watching two—I don't know what to call them—suspects, witnesses, or victims. Both Crystal and Willie are eager to continue the victim's business. They claim the booth is now theirs." He shook his head. "I guess you're also looking for documents, like a will."

"Guess I'd better get started."

Jack knew he didn't want to stick around. "I think I can be more useful helping to interview the horse wranglers and the riders for the joust in the barn. Come get me or Sara if you need help."

Winslow nodded. "Has Sara offered any theories yet?"

"Well, she thinks most of the vendors in the fair have side hustles. We both think Portia was killed because she knew too much about one of these side hustles." He started to leave. "She also thinks Sergeant Roybal of the Santa Fe PD is too slick to be a beat cop who worked his way up to being a sergeant."

***

Two hours later, Winslow rushed into the stables where agents and police were still interviewing the riders for the joust. "Jack, come look at what we've found in the truck. Portia's side hustle might have been stolen art. We found three boxes with framed pictures. The top painting in each frame is an oil cowboy scene signed by B. Harper. What's underneath is more interesting."

Roybal stood as Jack did. "I'd like to see what you found, too."

As the men approached the truck, they saw Sara examining art on a portable table behind the truck. Winslow pointed at Sara, "I got her first because she likes Southwest art. She suggested Sergeant Roybal probably would be interested in the art, too."

Roybal reddened. "Why?"

Jack felt annoyed. *Sara summoned me to bait Roybal. Oh well, now she'll settle into looking for the bank robbers and the murderers.*

Sara glanced at Roybal. "You looked too slick underneath that rumpled, old suit to be someone who came up through the ranks and still worked the streets. The only thing I could see you investigating was illegal sales of art and antiquities. I figured the police might have an art expert on staff because of the large art market in Santa Fe. Was I right?"

"Diablos." He grimaced. "What did you find?"

Sara pointed to several lithographs of Navaho women. "R. C. Gorman signed these." She waved her hand across three prints of Navajo scenes. "Old prints by Harrison Begay." She stared at Roybal. "It's quite possible Bodet Harper acquired these prints legally through yard sales or charity auctions. What do you think? But why were they being transported in such a clandestine way—underneath these tacky oils?" She motioned to oil paintings signed by Harper.

Roybal leaned over the artwork. "The galleries in Santa Fe hire hack artists, like Harper, to locate valuable, re-discovered pieces. Unfortunately, they've been burned lately because several re-discovered pieces were stolen from major collections." He smirked. "Bad publicity for them and the Santa Fe business community. I asked to be assigned to work this medieval fair because two of the gallery owners had been alerted to expect a shipment of re-discovered art on Sunday. Then the body parts showed up."

J. L. Greger

Sara touched Roybal's hand as he studied Harper's work with a magnifying glass. "So will another sergeant be assigned to the murder case now that you've accomplished your goal?"

She was less sarcastic than I expected considering Roybal wasn't honest with her about his background.

Jack decided to appease Roybal. "I hope Sara is wrong. I think you're an asset to these intertwined cases."

Roybal glanced at Jack. "You don't need to apologize for your partner. She's right. This fair scene is too gritty for my taste. But Sara is in for a surprise." He turned to Sara. "Bodet is quite talented. What you called 'tacky oils' are apt to interest a segment of the Santa Fe art community who like cubism applied to Western scenes."

Jack stared at the barely recognizable men on horses. He agreed with Sara. *Bodet's art was weird. Maybe as weird as Willie.*

Sara didn't even blink. "Okay, what do you plan to do?"

Roybal gave a triumphant smile. "I think I can lure Bodet here with the help of one or two of the galleries. He's apt to know a lot more about Portia than the two airheads she hired to work in her booth and the illiterates in the stables."

Jack saw Winslow was already walking away. "Where's he going?"

"To King Arthur's Feast." Sara looked up from the art. "I forgot to mention. We're pretty sure it was the murder site. There was a lot of blood residue in the waste discharge hose and the effluent in the waste tank. I convinced a judge the amount or residue was more than would be found in tanks with only meat juices from a kitchen."

Jack shook his head. "Glad I didn't have to do those calculations. How did he find it so fast?"

"It was the first unit he checked. I convinced him it was most the logical murder site."

"Why?"

"An institutional kitchen is the perfect place to do a messy murder. It's easy to clean."

CHAPTER 5: Hidden Treasures

"It's four now and we're…"

"Nowhere," said Roybal.

Wish Roybal wasn't so negative. "Not true." Sara put her phone in her purse. "The sheriffs of Santa Fe County here and San Luis Obispo County in California have agreed Ron should he charged with grand larceny for the attempted theft of about four thousand dollars from his employer, Camelot Fair Enterprises. They'd like to arraign him tomorrow. But both sheriffs think Ron might not have acted alone. He could have been acting under his boss's directions to hide gate receipts and thus cut taxes."

Jack looked up from his notes. "Why are they suspicious?"

"The woman came to the sheriff's office quickly demoted Ron to the job he held last year as a juggler, but the owner refused to file charges against Ron. That means the sheriff can't arrest him. So, I did some checking. Seems Ron is the grandson of the owner of Camelot Fair Enterprises. The new manager, who arrives tomorrow, will have to make the final decision on whether to charge Ron with larceny."

Jack slapped Roybal on the back. "You're right. Most of those associated with his fair are grifters or weirdos. And we've made no progress on identifying the murderer or bank robbers."

Negativism is contagious. "Not true. We've tentatively IDed the victim and the murder site."

Jack looked at his phone. "I skimmed Winslow's report. He said the kitchen had the cleanest counters and floor he'd seen, but the insides of the refrigerators were filthy."

Sara bit her lip. "True, but he found a few traces of blood in crevices in the kitchen and lots in the drain outlet. The lab should be able to ID the DNA in the blood traces." She nodded to Hank. "He says police and agents have interviewed the staff in more than twenty booths and everyone who worked in the stables. That's progress."

Hank drawled, "Hard to see how any of them could do anything as complicated as a bank robbery." He cleared his throat. "But a couple may have perfected the art of acting dumb. At least two seem contrary enough to have killed Portia for not much of a reason." He spat on the ground. "Sure, hope you can get analysts to do thorough background checks tonight, especially of Weird Willie, Viv Lorenzo, the head cook at King Arthur's Feast—Art Last—and the guy wearing red in the joust tonight. His driver's license lists him as Earl Scruggs, but he calls himself the Red Earl."

"Analysts are already doing the background checks." Sara's phone pinged. She read the text. "I guess this is good news. The teams at the garbage site have found a woman's head wrapped in a bloody shower curtain inside a box shipped to Viv Lorenzo."

Sara was surprised when the three men didn't respond to her announcement. "I think at least two of us should go to the garbage site. And one of us should stay with Winslow and his team. They still have a lot of work to do. And we all should get something to eat first because we won't feel like eating after we go to the garbage site."

Jack eyed her silently for thirty seconds. "What haven't you told us? Usually, Winslow and his team can search a whole house in a couple of hours, especially with your help."

Sara swallowed hard. "We had several problems today. Luminol is usually used to screen for blood at a crime scene, but the kitchen of King Art's Feast reeked of chlorine bleach."

"So?"

"Luminol reacts with chlorine bleach and gives false positives for blood. So, he had to use DCFDA instead."

Jack shook his head. "That doesn't explain his slow progress."

"Our assistant prosecutor was worried a defense lawyer could claim the residue Winslow found in the waste discharge tank from King Arthur's Feast was not unusual. He wanted Winslow to check several other food stands." Sara swallowed hard.

Jack choked. "He's more persnickety than you. That's a first."

Sara continued. "And the volume of stuff packed into Portia's camper and truck was unbelievable. Winslow doubts he's found all the secret compartments. I wanted to take both vehicles back to our building in Albuquerque for a more thorough search but that would leave Willie and Crystal homeless."

Roybal shrugged. "That's their problem."

"Not entirely. The assistant federal prosecutor thought Crystal and Willie had cooperated and allowed us to search the vehicles and the booth. He thinks making them homeless tonight could make a jury think we targeted them. Well, if they ever are charged with anything. He wants them handled with kid gloves for now."

"What?"

Sara pursed her lips "He's more nervous than most prosecutors."

Hank scratched his head. "They had to comply. You had a warrant."

"Yes, but I got the warrant before I saw Portia's will. Both Willie and Crystal provided me with copies of it. Everything here is theirs now—sorta."

Jack rolled his eyes. "Strange they could find their copies of the will so quickly. And the property isn't theirs until Portia's estate is probated."

"But they can claim their personal items in the camper, truck, and booth are private. I had to amend the warrant twice."

Jack sighed. "You're saying these two airheads know a lot more about the law than typical suspects. And we've got a gutless assistant prosecutor on the case."

"Yes. Fortunately, the assistant prosecutor thinks we made no mistakes and everything we found is legal."

Jack stood and patted Sara on the back. "You had a hard day. I'll treat for supper. Would anyone mind if we went to a local MacDonald's or Burger King rather than eat fair food?"

Roybal coughed. "Did you forget I interviewed the men who ate at King Art's last night? You couldn't pay me enough to eat at this fair. They were sick—violently sick."

Hank put on his cowboy hat. "Stop yapping and let's get some grub. We'd better go in separate cars. I'll bring food back to Winslow and his crew."

***

The stench from the parking lot behind the Santa Fe police garage wasn't as bad as Sara expected. The last time she and Jack had supervised a search of garbage had been on a hundred-degree summer day. She handed Jack and Roybal masks anyway and put on her own mask as they approached a table in front of the garbage piles.

A lieutenant in the Santa Fe PD pointed to two men who were shoveling trash from the largest pile into a dumpster. "We've sorted through most of the loose wastes." He pointed to the FBI's second CSI team who were unpacking cardboard boxes. "They've been a Godsend. The state forensic team that services the Santa Fe PD aren't used to this type of search and couldn't get organized. Your team thought it was easy."

The leader of the FBI's CSI team at the site—Sara thought his name was Tom—yelled, "Found the other hand." Bloody blobs lay on a pink plastic shower curtain. He waved to Sara. "Dr. Almquist, glad to see

J. L. Greger

you. Whoever did this was crazy. Look at this hand. Someone slashed it with a knife repeatedly." He pointed to the woman who sauntered over to the table. "We called the ME's office when we found the head. They decided they wanted staff here for recovery of body parts."

The woman from the ME's office made a clucking noise as she looked at the hand. "Our pathologists will love this. The other hand was the same way. Looks like someone took a meat cleaver and chopped the hands, particularly the fingers."

Roybal suddenly raced to the edge of the parking lot and vomited. The lieutenant turned from the table and raced after Roybal.

Jack gulped. "I don't think you need my help." He walked over to the crew who were shoveling garbage into the bin.

Sara couldn't believe what she was seeing. She thought about her conversation with Hank. "Was the head hacked like this?"

"No"

Hank was right. "Tell the ME the fingerprints may be important. Perhaps the victim was convicted of a crime or was in the military twenty or more years ago under another alias. Then DNA analyses wouldn't have been done. Only fingerprints. Hence, the killer tried to destroy the fingers."

The woman from the ME's office photographed the hand before placing it in a bag in an ice chest. "The pathologist will want you to be present at the autopsy." She glanced at Roybal and then the lieutenant. "I doubt the Santa Fe PD will want to be present."

Sara pointed to the pink shower curtain. "What color was the plastic around the other hand and the head? Were they new?"

"The head was wrapped with a blue plastic curtain." Tom closed his eyes and seemed to be trying to remember the scene. "Don't know for the other hand."

"Blue and pink shower curtains aren't apt to have been ripped off from a hotel. I don't think most of the campers have showers with curtains. The killers appear very well organized and came prepared. Not what you'd expect from someone who was crazy."

Tom waved the two other members of his team to join him. "Sounds right to me."

"Would used shower curtains have mineral deposits that might indicate their origin? Could they have fingerprints from past use." Sara paused. "I assume the killer or killers wore plastic gloves last night. Were any discarded gloves found in the garbage?"

The CSI team whispered among themselves. Tom said, "We saw no plastic gloves in the boxes. We'll talk about your questions tomorrow at our lab meeting before we begin work on the samples."

Sara pointed to the cardboard box which had contained the second hand. "I was told the first box had been shipped to Viv Lorenzo. What about this one?"

One CSI member examined the box. "Don't think you're going to be lucky. This one was shipped to Portia Merchant."

Another CSI team member said, "I think the other hand was in a box shipped to Portia Merchant, too."

The killers were too careful about details to be sloppy in the choice of boxes. Probably. "Please check for fingerprints and DNA on the boxes which contained the body parts." Sara looked around the lot. "What happened to the state forensic CSI team?"

Tom grinned. "The lieutenant forced them to shovel the garbage. He said we could leave as soon as all relevant evidence had been documented. They'll finish the cleanup."

***

Winslow was depressed when Sara and Jack returned to the fair. "I checked Portia's truck and camper thoroughly. Only the few traces of blood I told you about earlier. No gloves—plastic or otherwise. But I found something odd. Magnets on the inside fenders of the truck. Couldn't figure out their purpose. Then I found a meat cleaver lying on the ground under the fender. Obvious blood on it."

Sara gave Winslow a hug. "I'm too tired to discuss this case more, but it looks like the lab will have plenty to do tomorrow."

CHAPTER 6: Data Galore

Sara guided Bug, her black and white Japanese Chin, into Carbonne's office and plopped on a chair near her boss's desk. Bug more daintily walked in a small circle before he lowered himself to the floor.

Carbonne didn't look away from his computer. "I doubt you came to socialize at seven-thirty in the morning. Is Sanders coming this weekend?"

"Yes, but we haven't made plans yet. If I'm not worn out, we may have you and your family over tomorrow night for a casual dinner, but it all depends."

"What went wrong yesterday besides what you wrote in your emails?"

Sara sighed.

"It was unfortunate Sergeant Roybal wasn't honest with you from the beginning. Hank even emailed me late last night."

"Oh?"

"Yeah, Hank never talked much. Since his wife's stroke, he communicates mainly by one-line emails. He was effusive last night—five lines. Complimented you for keeping your cool with the 'Dour Dud.' That's what he called Roybal. Guess he doesn't trust him either." Carbonne finally looked at Sara. "Hank cc'd the mayor and the chief of the Santa Fe PD. Not like him."

Sara fed Bug a treat so Carbonne wouldn't' see her smile. *Guess Carbonne doesn't know Hank and the mayor of Santa Fe have been friends for years.* "Sorry, we had to take the lead for the murder at the fair. But…"

"Stop." He reached into the under-the-counter refrigerator by his desk, pulled out two diet colas, and handed one to Sara. He popped the tab and sipped. "We were played yesterday by the Santa Fe PD. They knew Roybal couldn't handle even the investigation of the art thefts without the help of the FBI, especially since the art was moved across state lines."

Sara sipped her cold drink. "And we were there anyway for investigation of the bank robbery."

Carbonne nodded. "Hank even chided the mayor for supporting the medieval fair. Called it a farce run by low-grade hucksters." Carbonne printed a copy of the email and handed it to Sara.

Sara glanced at the short email. *Thank you, Hank.* "So, who's my primary contact in the Santa Fe PD?"

"The mayor must not like Roybal either. He told me you 'could use Roybal anyway you wanted.' If Roybal resisted, you should call him. I emailed you the mayor's number."

"Good. Hank supervising Roybal and four Santa Fe police officers can finish questioning vendors and performers at the fair today. I need to work with the lab and the ME. Although it is likely King Arthur's Kitchen was the site of the murder and dismemberment, the evidence is slim until the lab finishes several analyses." She didn't pause. "And Jack wants to check serial numbers on cash circulating at the fair and in Santa Fe and relook at tapes from the robbery before he returns to Santa Fe."

"What are you leaving unsaid?"

Carbonne knows me too well. "Jack and I talked as we drove home last night. He thought one of the robbers on the bank robbery tape might be a man he interviewed yesterday. Since the robbers wore ski masks, it's iffy."

***

The chief of the FBI lab intercepted Sara before she reached her office. The tiny, middle-aged woman sniffed when she saw Bug. "I assume you'll be around the building much of today because you brought your dog to work."

Even her voice sounds grouchy. "He's a big help when I interview children, hospital patients, or emotionally distressed victims."

"Whatever." The lab chief sniffed again and pulled her gray hair behind her ears. "My staff may need to consult with you today."

Nothing unusual. Sara nodded politely.

"Much of the lab's work today will be related to processing all the material retrieved from the fair." She cleared her throat. "It's not fair of you to monopolize the resources of the lab."

"I didn't create the mess in Santa Fe. I only investigated it."

The lab chief's scrawny neck turned red. Her lips trembled.

Better add an apology quickly. "I'm sorry to have used so many of your resources yesterday, but the medieval fair in Santa Fe is a nightmare of petty grifters, sloppy cooks dispensing dangerous food, misfits who don't fit in anywhere, and probable killers and bank robbers."

The gray-haired woman adjusted her glasses. "All my crew—not just Winslow—like you." In a lower tone, "They couldn't stop talking about your ideas." She started to walk away. "But I wish you could have forced the state forensic lab to do their fair share of the work."

"I do, too. Let me know if you need anything from Santa Fe. I don't want to send our CSI teams back up to the fair."

"Good. Remember not to bring your dog into the lab."

She can insult me but not Bug. "I never do."

The woman turned her nose upward and paced down the hallway.

Wonder what I did—besides the obvious—to annoy her. She figured she'd find a clue to the lab chief's annoyance among her emails.

She opened a preliminary report from the Bureau of Biological Sciences in the New Mexico Department of Health. They had found two reasons people had become ill after eating at King Arthur's Feast.

The first Sara expected. The Bureau had found *Salmonella* bacteria on the turkey they collected at King Arthur's Feast. The report noted:

> *We checked the turkey wings and drumsticks. They were contaminated with Salmonella. This most likely was due to cross contamination from surfaces used to cut raw turkey to already cooked meat and then inadequate refrigeration.*

> *Although the diarrhea and vomiting induced by Salmonella infections of the gut can lead to dehydration, patients generally require no treatment after 24 hours. No follow up with these patients is needed.*

Sara was surprised by the second reason for illness among clients at King Arthur's Feast:

> *Clostridioides difficile (C. diff) infections have in the past have been associated with poor sanitation and the overuse of antibiotics in clinical settings, e.g. nursing homes and hospitals. However, recent research suggests pork, particularly improperly cooked suckling piglet, is a major source of C. diff infections. Our immunoassays indicated C. diff was present on pork in the refrigerator of King Arthur's Feast. This is a serious infection and needs to be monitored in all those exposed. Those who eat infected pork can become carriers of the infection even if they aren't ill themselves.*

Accordingly, the Bureau wants to interview and collect fecal samples from all staff and guests who consumed the suckling pork from this booth. Can the FBI help us?

We're willing to send staff to the fair on Friday morning or Saturday morning. At that time, we must interview the staff of King Arthur's Feast and will deliver notice to the owner of King Arthur's Feast—Camelot Fair Enterprises—that this booth is closed for the rest of the event. We will also notify public health officials in Texas of our findings. They will want to recheck the kitchen and employees of King Arthur's Feast before they allow it to open in Texas.

Sara checked notes from the police interviews. It appeared four men working in the stables, Viv Lorenzo and the two men working in her booth, and Willie Shakes had admitted to eating the pork on Wednesday night or had complained of gut distress on Thursday. *No way will those guys cooperate willingly. We don't want to be involved.*

Then she realized three of the men Jack and Hank thought were most apt to have participated in the bank robbery were on the Bureau's list. *Perhaps, this is an opportunity to question those three more thoroughly.* She emailed the names of all those who worked at King Art's Feast or complained of GI distress to the food safety inspectors. She cc'd Jack and Hank.

She opened her next email. The ME had scheduled the autopsy of Portia Merchant for nine. Sara was pleased for two reasons. She had worked with this pathologist previously and enjoyed his relaxed style. The nine o'clock appointment guaranteed she would not have to go to Santa Fe this morning.

The next emails from CSI team members explained the bad humor of the FBI lab chief. They had enjoyed their discussions with her yesterday. *That's pathetic.* Agents rarely solicited opinions from the lab crew or suggested ways they could be creative. The net result was the lab crew were eager to tell Sara about their ideas for identifying the source of the shower curtains. *Most of the ideas look half-baked. Probably because my initial suggestion was poor.* She emailed them encouragement anyway. *I don't have any better ideas.*

***

The pathologist looked at the body pieces on his stainless-steel table. "Our killer or killers appear to have wanted to do my job."

Sara forced a smile at his lame joke. As usual, she elected to watch the autopsy from an observation room adjoining the autopsy suite. In this room, she could talk to the pathologist and see all his actions but miss the olfactory clues that accompanied most autopsies.

"The technician has x-rayed the body parts. No bullet wounds. No evidence of broken bones in the torso or arms. The left leg was broken years ago and mended normally. Nothing useful could be gained from the x-rays of the minced hands."

"Can you tell how she was killed?"

The pathologist winked at Sara. "The decapitation makes it difficult to be sure. There is deep cut on the neck that looks pre-mortem. There is also a contusion on the back of the head with signs of internal bleeding. Most likely she was stunned by a blow to the head with a heavy flat object and had her throat cut. The stab wound in the back is superficial and missed vital organs. I'd guess more than one person was involved." He shook his head as he studied the hands. "The hands were cut—more like chopped—with probably a high-quality steel knife or meat cleaver. Seems like obsessive compulsive behavior." He pointed at the technician. "She'll use the computers to try to assemble the pieces into pictures of the hands. Sort of like doing a jigsaw puzzle."

The technician sighed. "I'll do my best, but there are hundreds of pieces."

The meat cleaver, which Winslow found under the Portia's truck, may be important. But why would the killer hide it there. Was it a memento?

The pathologist made the standard Y-shaped incisions across the two pieces that had been the woman's chest and abdomen. After fifteen minutes, he said, "The victim was a healthy woman in her forties. Looks like she had given birth at least once."

He rubbed the butterfly and star tattoos on the woman's legs and rump. "I want to examine the tattoos under the microscope. They remind me of tattoos I've seen on women who have been in our state prisons." He pressed harder on several spots. "I think she later decided to disguise the crude originals with bigger professionally done tattoos."

"How can you tell?"

"Pigments provide color in professionally done tattoos. In prison, the ink is produced by mixing soot, produced by burning hair, grease, or melted plastic, with water or shampoo." He stared at Sara. "What do you know about the victim's past?"

Sara read notes from the analysts assigned to the case. "No indication of a police record or military service." She scanned her laptop. "Lived in a commune in the Tucson area during her childhood. The commune property was purchased by Herbert Engel twenty years ago. The victim gained sole ownership of it almost fourteen years ago and has lived there since operating a successful sheep farm and dairy." She paused. "This is interesting. She was an active volunteer for the Tucson Boys and Girls Club. I'll have to ask the analysts to get a list of teens she interacted with and for details on Herbert Engel. He may be the owner of the fair company." She paused. "Her apparent daughter—Crystal Star—claimed Portia was a curandera."

"Wow. Was she into black magic or just a healer?"

"Don't know."

He pointed to one of the tattoos. "Perhaps she got her original tattoos in the commune, not prison."

Sara nodded. "Hank Snow and I wondered why the killer mutilated her hands. We wondered if she had been fingerprinted for a crime twenty years ago before DNA analyses were common. And the killer didn't want us to use her fingerprints to learn her alias."

"I think you're overthinking this case."

Sara nodded. "Probably. There are no time gaps in her bio."

The pathologist entered the observation room. "I think this autopsy tells you more about the murderer or murderers than the victim. They have some knowledge of biology or at least anatomy. The body was butchered logically, not with wild slashes, except for the hands. Thus, I doubt they were high on drugs or hallucinating, but they were angry with the victim." He pointed to the technician cleaning up after the autopsy. "I'd give the technician a five percent chance of being able to reconstruct the fingers enough to get usable fingerprints. You should get a tox screen on the blood, vitreous humor of the eye, and liver in about a week."

CHAPTER 7: Jack Scores

Jack leaned toward the analyst's computer screen. The video from the camera located by the door of the bank showed a big man—about six feet tall and about one hundred, ninety pounds—and a shorter, thin individual enter the bank. Both wore black knit ski masks, which hid their hair and faces, and dark hoodies.

"Switch to video from the second camera and stop it when the big man reaches to collect cash from the teller. Then enlarge his hand."

The young, dark-haired analyst nodded. When the man reached out his hand, she froze the frame and enlarged it. "The man wore clear plastic gloves like those used in food service operations."

Jack nodded. "Progress until we get an image of the black pattern on the back of his hand."

The analyst progressed the film slowly and stopped it. "Is this what you want?"

The black pattern looked like a spiky flower. She enlarged it more. It looked like a spider in a web and must have been at least an inch across.

"Print it and send pics to all tattoos shop in New Mexico and Arizona. Maybe someone will recognize their work. I might have seen something like it."

The analyst glanced at Jack. "You think? I'd be sure if I saw such an ugly tattoo. Only a wacko would want a spider on their hand."

"I don't know if Art Last, the head cook at King Arthur's Feast, is psychotic, but he fits the general body type." Jack looked at his notes. "Now I'd like to look at the footage from the parking lot."

The next footage was even of poorer quality than the interior video. The camera shots seemed to sweep along the drive-through lane at the ATM on a slow cycle. Shots of the rest of the lot were incidental.

Why do billion-dollar corporations scrimp on security cameras?

After several minutes, Jack agreed with the analyst's earlier assessment. A white pick-up truck, three gray minivans, one white car, one white commercial van, and a red car were in the lot during the robbery. There were no shots of men with black ski masks leaving a vehicle before the robbery or entering a vehicle afterward.

Photos of the lot afterward showed two vehicles missing: the white pick-up truck and a gray minivan. Police at the scene had determined the owners of the remaining vehicles were customers or personnel in the bank at the time of the robbery.

Jack pointed to the screen. "Let's focus on the white pick-up truck and the missing gray minivan."

"I've tried already. The camera missed any views of the license plates or stickers on these vehicles' front or rear windows. The white pick-up truck most likely was a couple years' old Ford Ranger. The gray minivan looks like a couple years' old Honda Odyssey. Hard to trace."

"Maybe not." Jack handed her list of the those interviewed at the fair. "See what vehicles these individuals own ASAP." He looked at his list. "I guess I'd better check with the lab for information on the deposit bags."

"Wait." The analyst typed rapidly. "The lab chief sent me information on the bags this morning. Here it is." She pointed to her screen. "The bags were wiped to remove all prints and smelled of chlorine." She turned to Jack. "Now that's strange. Who uses chlorine bleach outside the kitchen or bathroom?"

"A cook might."

***

Jack read Sara's email. *I should thank her, but I won't.* The list of those who had to be checked for a *C. diff* infection included the best candidates for the bank robbery, but he dreaded spending much of the day with inspectors from the of Bureau of Biological Sciences in the New Mexico Department of Health. He'd found most health inspectors grooved on the grossest biological details and had no sense of humor about their work.

He arranged to meet the inspectors and Hank at the closed King Arthur's Feast at noon. Roybal claimed he had to meet with the new manager at the fair. *Whatever. Roybal wasn't that helpful.*

When he tried to talk to Winslow about evidence in Portia's truck and camper, the lab chief shooed him out of the lab. "The lab is closed to agents today. CSI team members will contact you or designated analysts when they have something to share. We can't waste time on chatter."

She's grouchier than usual. Sara had proven to Jack that discussions with the lab crew, particularly Winslow, were seldom a waste of time. *No need to get into a debate.*

He checked his emails.

Winslow's message offered little that was new:

J. L. Greger

I found a copy of a will with all the right stamps in Portia's files. It looks like the original of the copies Crystal and Willie showed you. Portia left her truck, camper, booth, and inventory in the vehicles to Hannah Merchant and William Shakes. Bodet Harper gets most of her other property, which is considerable.

I suspect the magnets inside the fenders of the truck weren't strong enough to hold the meat cleaver. The blade was poorly cleaned. We found specks of blood in the wood handle. We also found specks between the wood handle and the blade of one of the knives in the kitchen. Haven't done DNA analyses yet.

The analyst's message was more interesting:

One of the men working in the stables—Alonzo Wilder—lives in Albuquerque and owns a 2022 white Ford Ranger. No other direct matches.

Shakes is an unusual name. So, I did a wider search. Ellie Shakes of Gallup owns a 2024 gray Honda Odyssey.

***

Jack stopped at Alonzo Wilder's house on the north side of Albuquerque before he headed for the fair. No one was home. A seesaw made of wood scraps behind the small, decrepit adobe house suggested Wilder had a family. The ramshackle shed in back indicated he was handyman and was hard-up for cash. The house was less than two miles from the bank that had been robbed.

As Jack drove to the fair, he carried on a one-sided conversation on the phone with Hank. *No wonder the agents in Albuquerque called Hank "the silent cowboy."* Hank said only "yep," "good," and "nah" in response to most of Jack's questions.

However, it was clear Hank had been busy. He had forced Roybal and four other officers in the Santa Fe PD to begin work at seven. They had already finished interviewing the vendors in the remaining "original" booths this morning.

Hank seemed excited when Jack asked, "Is there anything new at the fair today?"

"The fair is 'bout twice as big today. New booths with pottery, knives, and junk. The center stage is spruced up. The acts change hourly. Saw an axe throwing demonstration and a weird act—pirates dueling on a plank suspended over two horse-watering tanks. Like the rest of this fair—hokey."

I asked the right question. Sara's right Hank is a much better agent than those in Albuquerque admitted. "What caused the changes?"

"Two rumors. Local vendors are only willing to work the fair on the weekend. And the new manager arrived last night."

"I don't think we need to interview the newcomers."

"Good."

"Can you get us on the new manager's schedule today?"

"Roybal already did. Seems the new manager wants to prove Camelot Fair Enterprises is not just a front for riffraff."

Before he signed off, Hank said, "Have you talked to Sara today?"

"Not much."

"Oh." Hank sounded disappointed.

"I forgot. She told me to thank you." *Didn't say for what.* "She's with the ME now."

"Good."

Then he remembered Sara had spent almost a half-hour with Carbonne early this morning. *Obviously, I'm not a member of the old-timers' club.*

***

The two women food safety inspectors from the Bureau of Biological Sciences were like drill sergeants with those on their list. They herded the eleven men and two women into the trailer formerly used by King Arthur's Feast and called them: "*C. diff* survivors." They warned that they would be unable to work in any restaurant in New Mexico or Texas until they proved they were free of *C. diff* bacteria. Then the inspectors gave the "*C. diff* survivors" laxatives and proceeded to interview them while they waited for them to produce fecal samples.

Hank poked Jack. "Let's leave."

"Good idea. Sara says patients with *C. diff* infections suffer from gas. The smell in this trailer suggests it might be true. Besides I want to follow up on a new lead: Alonzo Wilder. He's a local who serves as an extra in the jousts."

***

Hank and Jack found Alonzo in the stables currying a large, gray Percheron horse. The horse was so large, Alonzo could barely look over its back.

He's probably about five-eight. He could be the second man in the robbery video. "Alonzo, you look too small to handle a horse that must weigh a ton."

"Betsy and I grew up on my parents' farm near Gallup. She'll do anything for me." Alonzo slapped the horse playfully on its rear. "But you're right. I serve as a squire during the joust and hand the big guys their weapons."

"Isn't it dangerous?"

Alonzo laughed and walked to the wall and removed a six-foot-long, two-inch thick, gray rod with a point at one end from a rack. "Not when the lance is made of foam." He handed it to Jack.

Jack whistled "It's light. Don't they break easily?"

"That's the idea. I put a half-inch dowel rod in the middle of a swimming noodle, add a wooden cone at one end, and paint it gray. Then I have lance fit for a knight in a Camelot Fair Enterprises joust. Betsy and I don't do the full circuit. Just fairs in New Mexico and Texas. But I make enough lances for the whole season. It provides me a little extra income and isn't hard on old Betsy."

Jack leaned closer to Alonzo. "Are the guys who do the jousting good riders?"

"All hat, no cattle." Alonzo shrugged. "What can you expect from men who muck the stables and show off in a fake joust a few times a week? That's why I didn't bring Betsy until this morning. I'll stay at the fair with her during the next two days. I don't trust them to care for her properly."

He's the most likable man I've met at this fair. I hate to start the tough questions. "Alonzo, what were you doing on Tuesday around eleven?"

The man frowned as he placed the lance back on the rack with five other lances. "I ran errands."

"Did you stop by the Wells Fargo Bank just off Route 528?"

The man frowned. "Yep. I stopped but then found I forgot the checks I wanted to cash."

"Did you see anything unusual?"

"Nah, but I had my five-year-old-daughter with me. Don't notice much when your kid is screaming."

"Are you sure?"

Alonzo scratched his head. "Are you accusing me of robbing that bank?"

"The bank's' camera showed a white Ford ranger—like yours—in the lot."

Alonzo blanched. "Damn. I… I… I didn't even get out of the truck."

"You could have been casing the lot for the robbers or driving the get-away vehicle."

"Are you kidding? My daughter was with me."

Hank finally spoke. "Farmers were hard hit last year. Cash is tough to come by. An extra hundred dollars for being a look-out might be what your family needed."

Alonzo reddened. "I may be poor and associate with carnies at fairs, but I'm no crook." He thought a bit. "I can prove I picked up a can of gray paint for the lances at the nearby Walmart less than fifteen minutes later. The receipt is on my desk at home."

"I believe you. But that doesn't prove you weren't abetting the bank robbers. We're also interested in the driver of a gray minivan. Did you see a Honda Odyssey in the bank's parking lot? It was probably idling with someone waiting inside."

"Nah." A tear rolled down the man's cheek. "I need this job. Give me a break." He thought for a second. "I guess I need a lawyer."

"Fine. Don't leave the state. We will talk more later."

***

As they walked away, Hank said. "He had motive and means. I hope he didn't do it."

Jack nodded. "Now we go for bigger fish. Two extra agents arrived with a warrant while we were talking to Alonzo."

"Sara's work?"

"Of course. She can get a warrant faster than any agent. Not worth my time to even try. The backup agents are waiting outside the King Art's trailer. I hope the health inspectors were able to detain Art Last?"

Hank spat on the packed dirt. "I introduced myself to those two already. Art's no match for them."

As Jack and Hank entered the trailer, Art pushed a white, plastic carton, presumably with a fecal sample, across the stainless-steel counter to one of the health inspectors. "Did I label it right this time? Can I go now?"

The inspector glared at Jack and Hank. "The agents have finally arrived. They want to talk to you now, Mr. Last."

Art groaned. "What about?"

Before Jack could speak, the two women health inspectors had pushed the rest of the men out the back entrance to the trailer. "Art Last, show me your right hand?"

East looked ready to run but he must have noticed Hank had a gun in his hand. "What's this about?"

"Put your right hand on the counter."

"I don't want to."

J. L. Greger

"This isn't a request. We have a warrant for your arrest."

Art leaned forward and put his beefy right hand on the stainless-steel counter. A black spider sitting on a web was tattooed on the back of his hand.

"You are being arrested for robbing the Wells Fargo Bank on Route 528 in Albuquerque on Tuesday at eleven. Photos of the crime scene show a man of your build with a spider tattoo on his right hand."

"So what?"

"The federal prosecutor has authorized me to tell you your sentence might be reduced if you name your collaborators." Then Jack read Art his rights.

"I want a lawyer."

"Fine. My colleagues…" Jack motioned to the two other agents who had entered the trailer. "…will transport you to the FBI building in Albuquerque. You can have a lawyer meet you there."

CHAPTER 8: Jack Meets a New Regime

The warm-up act for Merlin the Magnificent was two jugglers. The young woman in a striped purple and pink leotard twirled flaming batons while a young man in a matching outfit juggled three balls flashing pink and the purple lights. Pathetically, the scrawny redhead dropped the balls several times.

Hank poked Jack. "Ron?"

Jack squinted at the juggler. "Doesn't look like he's much better at juggling than at managing this fair."

The two jugglers concluded their act by tossing their batons and balls into a large, black cauldron at the center of the stage. Pink clouds rose from the cauldron and an eerie voice announced, "Merlin is here." A figure all in black strode onto the stage as the two jugglers bowed to him.

"Another phony." Hank pulled Jack to a tent nearer to the gate. "I want to show you something at one of the new booths before we meet Carolyn Taft." He pointed to a sign: DRAGONS' DOMAIN. "Someone went wild with a 3-D printer and made hundreds of dragons." He pointed at articulated dragons in all colors and varying from a foot long to three-feet long. "Wonder if my three-year-old grandson would like one."

Jack picked one up. Each dangly segment was about an inch wide and long. *A kid could destroy this in five minutes.* "Better talk to his mother first."

Hank sighed sadly. "She says I buy too much junk for the boy." *Hank's becoming talkative.*

***

Jack couldn't believe the changes in the front shed. The wall of boxes and the stupid sign—CHANCELLOR OF THE EXCHEQUER—were gone.

Now the front of the shed looked like a candy shop. One young man wearing a long-pointed cap with bells on it and red tights with a purple tunic weighed chocolate-covered raisins and dried fruit on an old-fashioned balance scale. Two young women, dressed similarly, handled the sales at the counter. *I didn't think Europeans enjoyed chocolate in the Middle Ages. Guess the new management isn't worried about historical authenticity either.*

As soon as Jack showed his ID, he and Hank were waved into the space behind a divider covered with fair posters. The woman at the desk made no pretense to look medieval. Carolyn Taft was a California girl—blonde, tanned, and poised. Her smile revealed a set of perfect teeth. Her denim pant suit showed her curves discreetly.

"Gentlemen, you're right on time. I want to assure you Camelot Fair Enterprises is a responsible business, not the disorganized mess you saw yesterday." She waved to two chairs and waited for Jack and Hank to be seated. "I've just finished discussions with representatives of the New Mexico Taxation and Revenue Department and the mayor's office. What can I do for you?"

Better start with a compliment. "We're pleased that the guards are now checking everyone at the front gate to see that their knives and swords are peace-tied. The previous manager didn't seem to know how to use a zip tie to guarantee a sword or knife couldn't be pulled from its scabbard."

Carolyn sighed. "There are a lot of things Ron was taught but seems to have forgotten."

Now down to business. "We were surprised to see Ron trying to juggle at the center stage. We hoped your company would charge him with attempted larceny."

Carolyn gave a stained smile. "He's only working today to earn enough for a bus ticket back to California tomorrow. My grandfather has decided not to file embezzlement charges against him since we were able to find all the cash he hid and tentatively satisfied the New Mexico Taxation and Revenue Department." She smiled knowingly. "I suspect he'll wish he was in jail rather than with our grandfather next week."

Why is she so eager to get Ron out of the state? "We'll want to talk to Ron more before he leaves. I can't help but think he knows something about other questionable activities at the fair. Doesn't Camelot Fair Enterprises own King Arthur's Feast and some of the horses and gear used in the jousts?"

Carolyn's arched brows almost knit together. "Why do you ask?"

"We just arrested the head cook at King Arthur's Feast—Art Last—for a bank robbery in Albuquerque last Tuesday."

"He couldn't be involved. He was setting up the kitchen here that day."

Why is she so ready to argue? "We have photo evidence of his presence at the bank. My colleagues have checked with all the kitchen staff. No one saw him on Tuesday until after two. Most assumed he was sick because another member of the kitchen staff was experiencing gut distress."

Carolyn blinked twice. "I was told people got sick from eating at King Arthur's Feast on Wednesday evening. How could someone be sick already on Tuesday morning?" She must have noticed Jack's frown. "Aren't officials from the state's department of health examining those suspected of having gotten some sort of infection at supper on Wednesday?"

She's awfully well informed after being here less than a day. "Yes, but it's likely Art and the other employees in the kitchen had the infection already on Tuesday. Several may even be asymptomatic carriers of the infection." *Glad Sara updated me on details about C. diff this morning. I'd never have pulled off the bluff otherwise.*

Hank finally spoke. "One of his coworkers spotted Art getting out of a blue minivan at the gate on Tuesday at two. She figured he'd spent the night with a local woman." He turned to Jack. "Sorry, I forgot to tell you. I talked to the two women working at King Art's this morning. Something about their story yesterday seemed strange. Seems Art liked to rough up women."

Good old Hank. He's a stickler for details. No wonder he and Sara get along.

Carolyn shivered. "I won't put up with employees who abuse other employees. Has Art been arraigned?"

"Not until tomorrow."

"Will you detain him tonight?" She frowned. "He's a flight risk."

Jack managed not to grin. *She doesn't want him back at the fair.* "Are you saying you know his coworkers are telling the truth?"

"No, but I know this isn't the first time women employees have felt threatened by him."

"Show me what you've got on him." Jack handed her an arrest warrant for Art Last and a search warrant for where he slept, worked, and kept his possessions. "I think my colleagues can convince a judge that Art should await his arraignment in the ABQ detention center."

"Good. I'll process his termination papers immediately."

"Fine. You'll note the warrant allows us to search his quarters?"

She bit her lip. "He shares a converted semi-trailer with nine other male crew members. That warrant gives you no right to search their berths. Are we through?"

Hank chuckled. "Sergeant Roybal tells me you asked a lot of questions about the art the Santa Fe Police confiscated yesterday from the murder victim's truck. Why?"

Carolyn glared at him. "Give me a break. I got here at nine last night. I've worked almost continuously cleaning up this place. I'm tired of being polite. I want the facts. Roybal was almost as secretive as some of the crew here when I asked about the items confiscated from Portia's vehicles."

Hank stood. "I'll talk to Roybal while Jack explains a few legal details to you."

She stood. "I'm an attorney licensed in California. I'm aware of what you two might try to do next." She focused on Jack. "Remember many hard-working people depend on this fair for income. I want as many of them as possible to move on to Texas on Monday morning."

Jack wanted to say, *Cool it.* He said instead, "That's what the FBI wants, too. But the property and staff of King Arthur's Court and the jousts are not apt to be in your caravan. We'll also retain the property of the late Anne Harper, alias Portia Merchant, until we locate Bodet Harper and resolve estate issues."

"What about Willie Shakes and Hannah—I think she calls herself Crystal Star?" Carolyn looked at paper notes stuck on the edge of her computer screen. "Vivian Lorenzo and her crew are also afraid of being detained."

"Well, at least we agree on the problems."

"You're not funny."

Jack whistled. "Murder seldom is, and the murder of Portia Merchant was particularly gruesome. You don't want anyone associated with it to tour with your caravan. They could act again."

"I know. What do you suggest?"

"Have your grandfather press charges against Ron. The woman who spoke to the San Luis Obispo Sheriff said your grandfather wanted to protect Ron. That's too bad. Ron knows a lot more than he's admitted. Once he's charged, my partner can get warrants to search his belongings."

She nodded toward Hank who was talking to employees at the front of the shed. "You mean the old cowboy?"

"No, a woman back in Albuquerque. Sara's not here because she spent the morning watching the autopsy of Portia Merchant."

Carolyn tapped her carefully manicured pink nails on her desk. "I don't know."

"Your grandfather is not doing Ron a favor. If the robbers and/or killers suspect Ron knows anything, they will track him down and may kill everyone near him."

"Okay. What else?"

"I'd like to see your files—contracts, personnel matters, complaints—on everyone associated with the jousts, King Arthur's Feast, and Vivian Lorenz's and Portia Merchant's booths."

"Just because they all ate together on Wednesday night?"

"No, because several other vendors made it clear they avoided being around them. Several called Willie Shakes, Art Last, and the stable crew 'weird' or 'spooky.' Many thought Portia was 'witch' and considered Crystal Star and Vivian Lorenzo 'conniving fakes.'" He sighed. "And the agent you called the old cowboy is convinced the whole kitchen crew knows a lot but are afraid to talk. We need your help."

"These people have Fourth Amendment rights. I can't turn over their files."

"You have a temporary employee in the barn who might be willing to talk about a conversation he overheard in the stables. Sara can then get a warrant for the property of the stable crew."

"Then do it. I'll talk to my grandfather about Ron."

***

Jack and Hank retreated to the FBI car Jack had driven to the fair. "What's up with Roybal?"

Hank looked at notes on his phone. "He and the mayor's rep thought they saw pictures of the prints we found in Portia's truck on Carolyn's computer screen."

"How?"

"They got to the appointment early. She excused herself to go to resolve a dust-up at the front of the building."

Jack rolled his eyes. "They arranged the diversion and snooped. We can't use the evidence. Besides it could be a coincidence."

Hank shrugged. "One of the pictures looks like a print stolen from a collector in Scottsdale last week. That's twenty minutes from Tempe—the fair's location last week."

"Could be a coincidence." Jack looked at his phone. "Explains Sara's email." He handed his phone to Hank.

Guys, you have a choice. I can stay in Albuquerque cranking out warrants and running searches or I can join you in Santa Fe. What's your choice?

The resident agents in Gallup should execute a search (with a warrant) of Bodet Harper's home—a trailer—in the next hour looking for stolen art.

J. L. Greger

The lab found enough blood on the meat cleaver that they could do a quick DNA test. They found Portia's and unidentified DNA on it. I've requested a warrant to get a DNA swab from everyone who ate at King Arthur's Feast on Wednesday night and employees in all other food stands at the fair. It's iffy but I hope the judge believes no one has access to a meat cleaver, except kitchen staff. And no one hides a meat cleaver unless it was used for criminal purposes.

"Hard choice." Hank scratched his head. "Tell her to get on the road. The women in the kitchen will talk more to Sara than to us men."

CHAPTER 9: Slower Than Molasses

Sara listened to the lead agent who had searched Bodet Harper's trailer as she drove to the fair.

"Bodet wasn't home. When we first entered his trailer, we thought the search was bust. The only furniture was a bed, a table, and one chair. Then we found almost a quarter of the trailer was a closet."

"Oh dear."

"No problem. Your warrant specifically listed computers, phones, records, safes, and any art. We opened the closet. Bingo!"

"So?"

"We sent photos of several of several signed lithographs and other art to the galleries on the list you prepared. One of them immediately identified a piece as theirs."

"Did you confiscate all of the art as potential stolen property?"

"Yep. Took the computer and files, too. We left a copy of the warrant and a receipt for the property confiscated, but we doubt Bodet Harper will claim his stuff. Doesn't matter. We attached a couple trackers to the trailer. We'll know if he opens the door of the trailer or tries to move it."

"Great. Santa Fe Police also identified one of the signed prints in Portia's truck as stolen, and a witness indicated Portia picked up art from Bodet on Monday. So, I can request a warrant for Bodet Harper's arrest for possession of stolen property that crossed state lines."

"Not robbery?"

"So far, we only know he had possession of stolen property, not that he stole the pieces. Hopefully that warrant will be enough to start a discussion with him. And I should have the warrant for you yet today."

"Is that all you need?"

"Can you check on an Ellie Shakes of Gallup? She owns a gray Honda Odyssey that may have been used in a bank robbery in Albuquerque on Tuesday. Her brother was in Gallup on Monday and is one of our suspects."

"Sure, but we might not get to it until this afternoon."

***

The number of cars in the parking lot for the fair was at least triple of what Sara had seen on Thursday. Hank was waiting at the gate.

He tipped his Stetson. "Agents have already arrested Art Last. The inspectors from the Bureau of Biological Safety are almost done with interviews at King Art's. Thanks to your new warrant, Jack is interviewing staff at the other food stands."

"What?"

"He's not collecting samples just interviewing them. He'll join us at King Art's if we need help."

"Good. We also have a warrant for the arrest of Bodet Harper."

Hank stopped walking. "For what?"

"At this point, just receipt of stolen property."

"Roybal will be pleased."

"Yeah, if we catch Bodet Harper when he returns to his trailer in Gallup." Sara sighed. "I wouldn't bet it'll happen."

Hank resumed his rolling gait and led her to the back door of the kitchen trailer of the closed food stand. The trailer reeked of chlorine bleach.

Hank pointed to a young woman washing the inside of an empty refrigerator. "Elu Dosela." He pointed to an older woman of Native American heritage—at least judging by her facial features—washing the insides of the cabinets. "She's Tallulah Dosela. They are withholding info. First, let's settle more urgent business."

The scene was quieter than Sara expected. Besides the two women, one inspector was directing the backup cook and a male clerk as they loaded food from another refrigerator into garbage bags. The other inspector was pecking at her laptop as she questioned a man. It was obvious the inspector was in complete control. The man said, "Yes, Ma'am" frequently.

Hank grabbed Sara's elbow. "See that beefy guy with the interviewer. He's one of the *C. diff.* survivors." He chuckled. "That's what the food safety inspectors called everyone who ate pork at King's Art's. This one is Earl Scruggs who jousts as the Red Knight. I asked the inspectors to interview him last. I thought—was hoping—your warrant request would be okayed by now. I thought the unidentified DNA on the meat cleaver might be his."

"Why?"

"Bad temper when I interviewed him." He shrugged. "A feeling he could butcher someone and not flinch."

Sara studied the man. Fortyish, tall—maybe six-foot—with broad shoulders, and a florid, blotchy complexion. *He'd was probably handsome* when he was young but looks too angry to be considered attractive now. She remembered the analyst had noted he was the only stableman with a record of violent crimes. "His DNA is already on file. The unidentified DNA on the cleaver isn't his."

Hank sighed, "Shoot," and walked over to the inspector doing the interview.

Sara tapped Elu on the shoulder and whispered, "We know you haven't told us everything you saw and heard on Wednesday night."

Elu shook her head. "Not now."

"Art Last will not move on to Texas on Monday. You might not be allowed to move on either." Sara smiled. "Unless you tell me everything you know."

The pupils of the woman's brown eyes enlarged as she grabbed Sara's arm. "You agents and inspectors talk big but don't care about us." She almost spit at the nearest inspector. "Our backup cook argued with Art about the pork before supper on Wednesday. Art cursed him out. None of us working at King Art's ate it." She leaned forward into the refrigerator.

"I think you know more."

Sara saw Jack wave to Hank from the back door of the kitchen. Tallulah must have seen him, too. She backed away from the counter and looked ready to run.

Sara stepped back a pace to block the woman's potential path. Then Sara led both Elu and Tallulah to a front corner of the kitchen.

"This is your last chance to stop me from arresting you for abetting criminal activity."

Both women looked confused.

"Look Elu, you didn't tell me anything new. You saw the FBI arrest Art Last. The food safety inspectors have made it clear to everyone that the pork and turkey served Wednesday night weren't safe to eat."

Tallulah looked down at the floor. Elu looked defiantly at Sara.

"Let's start with something easy. Which one of you told Hank— the agent with the cowboy hat—that Art roughed up women."

Elu didn't change her position. Tallulah didn't look up but squeaked, "I did."

"Which one of you told Hank you saw Art arrive at the front gate at two on Tuesday."

Tallulah squeaked. "I did."

Elu snorted. "Auntie, why?"

"We want to know who killed Portia. It's likely the murderer or murderers ate at King Arthur's Feast on Wednesday night. Please help us. Did anyone argue at supper?"

Tallulah shook her head. Elu stared at the ceiling.

"What did people say?"

No response.

"Who left first? Where did they go?"

"Portia." Tallulah frowned. "Crystal ran after her. I thought they went to Portia's camper."

Crystal said Portia was making mustard plasters for the horses. "Had Portia talked to any the men from the stables?"

The women looked at their hands.

Okay, let's try something less threatening. "Tell me about your housing situation."

"In the women's camper, there's Auntie and me and three empty beds until last night. Then new women moved in. I think they're going to work in a new candy booth."

"Where do the men stay?"

Elu stuck out her lower lip and looked like she was pouting. "Much nicer space. They sleep in a converted semi-trailer. It has beds for the three men in our food stand, four of the men working in the stables, and Ron."

Tallulah added, "You forgot the two who work in Viv's Lorenzo's booth also sleep in the dorm."

Elu glared at Tallulah.

Tallulah ignored her and added, "I don't think Art stayed there Tuesday or Wednesday night."

"Why do you think that?"

"Our back-up cook complains he can't sleep when Art snores, but he didn't complain on Wednesday or Thursday morning."

"Tell me about the backup cook."

The women looked at the floor.

That's it. I'm out of patience. She winked at Jack. "Jack, come help me."

Jack pulled handcuffs from his jacket's pocket as he sauntered past the counter.

Good. He's playing his role to the hilt.

"Ladies, you'd better cooperate or we'll take you to Albuquerque."

Tallulah whispered so softly Sara could barely hear her. "We can't talk when the men are here. We don't want to be here."

***

Sara looked around the small conference room. *The FBI didn't waste money on its satellite office in Santa Fe.* She wondered whether the women had information worth the effort.

Jack and Hank had devised a complicated way to extract the women from the fair and disguise their location for at least a day. Jack had talked to Carolyn Taft while Hank confiscated all of Elu's and Tallulah's property from the sleeping camper. Both Jack and Hank had told anyone who asked that the women were being taken to the FBI offices and then probably detention facilities in Albuquerque. They had made a big show of escorting the women to an FBI-marked car and driving south down I-25. But Jack had taken the second exit and doubled back to deliver the women to the FBI satellite office in Santa Fe.

In the meantime, Sara had gotten Carbonne to send two more agents to the fair. They were dressed as typical fairgoers in jeans and t-shirts and could hopefully monitor the activities of the *C. diff* survivors, especially the backup cook and male clerk from King Arthur's Feast.

***

As soon as the two women, Jack, and Hank were seated at the conference table, Sara began the interview. "Okay ladies, you got what you wanted. None of your colleagues at the fair knows you are here. It's time for you to talk. After Portia and Crystal left supper on Wednesday night, what happened next?"

"Art left with Willie and the stablemen. The backup cook helped Auntie Tallulah and me clean up and close the stand. Then we went to the campers provided by the fair."

"Who does your backup cook hang around with?"

"He tries to avoid Art and the stablemen. He…"

Tallulah interrupted. "He's a good boy. That's why he helped us clean up."

Elu giggled.

Bet Elu and the backup cook would like to be an item. Interesting but not worth the time now. "What about the male clerk?"

"You mean Emmet Ant?" Tallulah leaned forward and studied Sara. "He's a snitch. Reports everything to Ron. No one talks to him."

Hank suddenly opened his eyes. "Wait a second. We know Art wasn't with you Tuesday until after two. Were any of the other men on the King Art's crew missing?"

"No. The four of us set up the kitchen on Tuesday. We didn't miss Art because he's never useful. Just bossy."

"Did you have visitors?"

"No, everyone was working too hard to gab."

Sara noticed Jack was typing furiously on his phone. Her phone pinged. The message had been sent to the two new agents at the fair. Sara and Hank were cc'd.

Ron Engel, Vano Georgescu—one of Viv Lorenzo's employees, Willie Shakes, and Emmet Ant—a clerk at King Art's—are all about the same size: five-eight to ten and thin. Any one of them could have been the second man in the photos at the bank robbery.

I just remembered the second man in the photos of the bank robbery wore a silver ring on his right hand. I enlarged the ring in the attachment. Check whether any of these four men is wearing a silver ring with a wide band.

Sara will get a warrant if you spot this ring on any of these men. Alonzo Wilder, a local guy working in the stables, can be trusted, maybe. See if he saw such a ring.

Sara noticed Tallulah and Elu were staring at her. *Must have studied my phone message too long.* She asked the women when they first had had seen each of the four men Jack had mentioned on Tuesday.

"They all appeared as soon as we closed to the public." Tallulah frowned "Except Vano. He and Viv were late to supper and were arguing when they arrived."

"What about?"

"Not sure. Viv kept saying, 'I depend on you.'"

Consistent with him not being around Tuesday morning to set up the booth but proves nothing. She texted Jack and the other agents:

A wide band, silver ring is common. Not enough for an arrest warrant but enough for a search warrant of the trailer bunkhouse. I'll prepare the warrant request.

Sara only half-listened as Hank and Jack checked their notes and barraged Elu and Tallulah with questions trying to verify or negate comments made by others. Nothing clicked, except both women admitted Art had hit them several times when he was annoyed.

These ladies have perfected the art of acting dumb. Time to be more direct. "Ladies, why were you so willing to leave the fair? If you don't cooperate, we could dump you back at the fair, instead of putting you on a bus to Taos."

Tallulah slumped in her chair and began to whisper to Elu. After a minute, she cleared her voice. "I wake up early many mornings. On Thursday I was walking around the fair before sunrise." She bit her lip. "I saw Earl Scruggs standing near the front of Portia's truck. When he saw me, he scowled and walked away."

"Is that all you saw?"

Tallulah looked at the ceiling. "No." She swallowed hard. "I left the parking lot with the campers and walked among the closed booths. It's quiet then. You can hear some of the items—especially the jewelry—on racks in the booths tinkle with the breeze. Pretty. When I returned to the lot, I saw a man with a navy hoodie leaning against Viv's trucks."

"How big was the man?"

"Bigger than me."

That doesn't prove much. Tallulah was probably five-three. *Wait.* "What color jacket did Earl wear?"

"Black."

Navy and black are easy to confuse in dim light. "Anything else? Did Earl talk to you on Thursday?"

Elu rubbed her aunt's hand. "Earl said to me around noon, 'Tell your aunt that sleepwalking can be dangerous.'"

Sara noted Jack was almost bouncing in his chair before he ran out of the conference room and could be heard giving orders to someone. Sara read the message from the agents at the fair to Jack and cc'd to her and Hank.

None of the men are wearing a silver ring with a wide band.

Alonzo said when the stable hands played craps last night in the barn, the Red Earl won a silver ring from Vano.

Hank rushed to join Jack.

Guess they expect me to handle the paperwork. "Ladies, we've recorded everything you said. An analyst in Albuquerque is preparing a written transcript for you to sign that summarizes your comments." She noted the women were fidgeting. *They won't talk unless I relax them.* "Why don't I order some food, and we can talk more while we wait for the statement to be prepared."

Elu whispered to Tallulah and then giggled. "We don't have a decent Chinese restaurant in Taos. Can you order Chinese for us?"

"Done." *This interview was slower than molasses in January and a whole lot less tasty.*

CHAPTER 10: Unknowns

"Ellie Shakes denied seeing her brother on Monday or Tuesday."

"Well, that kills a good lead." Through the open door to the conference room, Sara watched Elu and Tallulah eat. She'd ordered four entrees, thinking she or the agents might like some food. She doubted anything, but rice would be left when Elu and Tallulah finished.

The lead agent in the FBI's Gallup field office snorted into the phone. "We didn't believe her. We also noted her gray Honda was parked in a car port not a garage. So, we walked over and talked to her neighbors."

The second agent in Gallup said, "Three neighbors were clueless or at least silent. One finally admitted her car wasn't in its usual spot on Tuesday morning when he left for work."

The lead agent continued, "We went back and…" He coughed. "… politely confronted her. Amazing how stupid people think we are. Anyway, after a song-and-dance, she admitted her brother Willie was dropped off at her house by a young woman driving a camper on Monday afternoon. Seems he'd agreed to drive his sister in her own car to appointments at the UNM Comprehensive Cancer Center on Tuesday morning."

Darn. That negates Willie's claim to have seen Portia drive off with the truck in Gallup on Monday night.

A woman's voice could be heard in the background. She was obviously angry and yelling obscenities.

The second agent took over the report. "Another happy client." He coughed. "Ellie claimed they ate breakfast at Weck's in Albuquerque together on Tuesday before Willie dropped her off at ten for appointments. He picked her up at two. She drove home alone to Gallup. Neighbors confirmed her car was back in the carport on Wednesday morning. We didn't check out her story with the cancer center. Figured you could do it. This has been one of those days here."

"I understand and appreciate your help. I'll talk to the UNM Cancer Center. Did she say anything about her brother?"

"Yeah, he's—and I quote—'sweet but often confused.' Sounded like he was slow in school and couldn't keep a job, except with Portia

Merchant. Ellie thought Portia was a talented medicine woman. We didn't tell her Portia was dead."

"Could Portia had supplied herbs to Ellie for her cancer?"

"Don't know. That's beyond our scope. You're the one who'd have to extract that kind of info from her. Better do it soon. Ellie looks bad. A scarecrow with only wispy hair."

Gives Willie a motive. "I understand and will follow-up. Thanks."

***

Sara read Jack's message from the fair:

> *Can't find Vano or the silver ring. How much latitude do I have*
> *in searching for it?*

Sara looked over her amended search warrant requests and the resulting warrant. The judge had accepted her two main points: 1) Those who killed Portia and cut her up were apt to have blood stains on their clothes and jewelry. 2) All those present at supper King Arthur's Feast on Wednesday night were logical suspects. Thus, the judge had approved a search of semi-trailer used as a bunkhouse by the men, the women's camper, Viv's truck and camper, and Crystal and Willie's compartments in Portia's vehicles. The judge specifically noted an FBI's CSI team could confiscate any navy or black hoodies or jackets and all clothes with any sign of blood stains when viewed with a high intensity ultraviolet light. He also allowed the CSI team to search for articles attached outside the semi-trailer, campers, and trucks, i.e. more objects like the meat cleaver attached to the fender of Portia's truck by a magnet. *The warrant should be enough for us to confiscate the ring if we find it.*

The judge had not thought Sara had provided sufficient evidence to swab the cheeks of all food service workers at the fair. DNA could only be collected from those who worked in the kitchen of King Art's. She knew the judge was right. Besides, Winslow could get DNA from the containers of fecal samples the health inspectors had collected. *Of course, DNA extraction from a cheek swab is more pleasant.* It meant she could get DNA of all the suspects but Crystal.

Sara glanced at her next email. She'd received a polite note from the lab director:

> *You promised no more field trips for my lab crew for your*
> *investigation. You were wrong. However, they fought to be*
> *included on the team. Winslow will head the three-person team.*
> *They've left already.*

Sara thanked her profusely and thought the woman had reason to be grouchy. *This investigation is out of control.* She texted Winslow:

Don't forget to check the clothes and jewelry on all the suspects. They're a dirty bunch who might not have bothered to hide blood-stained clothes.

The two women from King Arthur's Feast are with me at Hank's satellite office. I'll keep them here until you arrive. If you prefer, I can join you for the searches and get Hank to monitor the women.

The response was immediate:

Prefer you to be present for the searches.

She emailed Jack and Hank:

Got a revised warrant. Winslow will head up a 3-person CSI team. They will search for the ring and clothes with bloodstains in the men's bunkhouse, the women's camper, Viv's vehicles, and Willie and Crystal's compartments in Portia's vehicles.

The judge didn't buy all my arguments. Winslow can only collect DNA with mouth swabs from those working in King Art's.

Winslow wants me to help him. Hank, can you come back to your office to monitor the women? They're becoming more talkative.

While she waited for Hank, Sara tried to learn more from Tallulah and Elu about the crew. "How did you get to know each other so well in only a week?"

Between mouthfuls of food, Tallulah said, "The crew is almost the same as last year, except for Elu."

The women's assessments of their coworkers varied. Elu thought Vano was handsome but felt Willie was weird. She wished she was as beautiful Crystal in her pink fairy outfit.

Tallulah was convinced that Willie didn't deserve the title of weird. "He's smarter than he acts." All Tallulah would say about Vano and Crystal was "bad vibes."

Elu considered both Portia and Viv to be "bossy, old witches."

Tallulah was more expansive. "Both Viv and Portia are curanderas. But Portia was a good woman. She prepared creams using the herbs grown in the Arizona desert to lessen the pain in my hands. Viv makes fake love potions for silly girls, like Elu. She also gives Ron pep pills. His boss expects too much of him. So, Ron sleeps only a few hours each night."

Sara pondered Tallulah's last comments. *Had Ron's grandfather set him up to fail? Need a background check on Camelot Fair Enterprises.*

Then she assessed Tallulah and Elu. They didn't know enough to be placed in protective custody by the FBI. *No. that isn't true.* They hadn't admitted enough knowledge to be granted protective custody. But Tallulah had seen a lot as she roamed the fair in the early morning. *Maybe enough to be in danger.*

Sara believed they would be safer in their native community than traveling with the fair. She called the chief security officer for the Taos Pueblo and explained the situation.

He noted two points. Tallulah is a "good woman." Elu is "boy crazy" and has "a chip on her shoulder."

CHAPTER 11: The Situation Worsens

"This place stinks almost as much as the stable."

Winslow pulled out a duffle bag from a shelf over the bed at the front of the trailer. "What do you expect? This is a dorm for ten men and has only one small bathroom."

He spread the clothes in the duffle bag on the bed and flashed a high intensity ultraviolet light across them. He pointed to white, fluorescent spots on the pillow and then on the sheets. "Probably saliva and semen. I see several dark patches indicating blood on this shirt's long sleeves, but nothing on the rest of the clothing or bedding." He pulled shoes from under the bed and checked them. "No signs of blood."

Sara looked at the name on the duffle. "That is the bunk of the backup cook. He could easily have blood from meat on his cuffs." She stuffed all but the shirt back into the duffle and put the shoes back under the bed. "Am I right that the UV light is like luminol in that it can't distinguish between human and animal blood?"

"Yep. This site with all its food stands and barns is a nightmare." Winslow followed the same process with the clothes and shoes at the next two bunks and found nothing interesting. Sara repacked everything at the second bunk, except a navy hoodie, into a tote labeled with Emmet Ant's name. She kept nothing from the berth of the third man—a clerk in Viv Lorenzo's booth named Tony Marin.

"The next bunk might be more interesting. It belongs to one of the horse wranglers."

Large spots on the clothes and boots of the man using the fourth bunk glowed yellow under the UV light. "Lots of horse urine I suspect." Winslow studied the dark spots on the jeans and one shirt. "I should check them more but it's not as much blood as I'd expect if you butchered a woman."

"I think some blood spots could be due to routine cuts on the horses and men as they pretend to joust and fight." Sara packed the man's gear, except a black jacket, stained jeans, and stained shirt, in a backpack and pushed the boots under the bed.

The clothes and shoes of the rest of the horse wranglers were like those of the first one. Certain pieces merited further study but weren't exciting, until Winslow inspected the soles of the last pair of shoes. The soles of the shoes were almost totally dark. "He stepped in blood. And a lot of it."

"Those shoes belong to Earl Scruggs—one of our best suspects. Funny his clothes had so little blood." Sara repacked his duffle. It was half-empty. "Wonder if he discarded some clothes. Where?" She thought a second. "The others had some sort of jacket in their kits. He doesn't."

Winslow directed the UV light to the floor. There were a few dark smudges at the doorway only. "Looks like someone cleaned the floor, or he took his shoes off when he stepped inside."

"Doubt the latter. He's not the sort of man who takes his shoes off at the door."

The bunk of Vano Georgescu was uninteresting. Sara rechecked his bags for secret pockets that might contain a ring. She found nothing.

Sara expected the bunk of Art Last would be uninteresting, too, because Tallulah had noted he had not slept in his bunk on Tuesday or Wednesday nights. However, the odor of chlorine bleach wafted through the trailer as Winslow unfolded what appeared to be a freshly laundered shirt, black fleece jacket, and jeans from Art's bag. He flashed the UV light. No dark spots. "I think he did a good laundry job." He checked the shoes. Not just the sole but the laces and tops were dark. "Now this is what I expected."

"He's in the ABQ detention center awaiting arraignment for bank robbery because a judge at a preliminary hearing an hour ago thought he was flight risk. I bet I can get a judge to rule tomorrow that he stays in jail until his trial because he now appears to be either a murderer or at least someone who helped dispose of a body."

Sara ignored Winslow as she talked by phone to the agents who had taken Art to Albuquerque and the assistant federal prosecutor. They suggested Sara could modify Art's arraignment documents when she got back to Albuquerque.

Her conversation was interrupted by Winslow. "Surprise. We've got a winner."

Sara stared at the dark spots all over the jeans and black robe on the last bunk. "Oh my, I thought Ron Engel might be an embezzler, but I never dreamed he might be involved in the murder. No wonder he wanted to go back to California tonight." *At least, now the agents in Albuquerque have no choice but to rewrite the documents on Art. I'll be busy following up on Ron.*

She called Jack. "We've got to stop Ron Engel before he leaves the fair."

***

Jack ran faster than Sara and was talking to Carolyn Taft in the fair's main office when Sara arrived. "When was the last time you saw Ron?"

"Well hello to you, too." Carolyn frowned. "I guess when he reported in after the magician's act ended on the center stage around eleven."

While Jack questioned Carolyn, Sara alerted Roybal:

> *STOP Ron Engel.*
> *Suspect wanted for murder.*
> *Last verified sighting at fair center stage at 11.*

As an afterthought, she forwarded the text to Hank.

"I told Ron to get lunch and pack up his stuff before he did his last juggling act on the center stage at two." Carolyn walked slowly to her desk to consult her computer and then looked at her watch. "He should have finished the act by now and be on his way to the Rail Runner. His bus to California leaves the Albuquerque station around seven.

Sara read Roybal's text. Suddenly she remembered the CSI van had been parked by the semi-trailer bunkhouse. *Ron saw it and split before his two o'clock act.* Sara texted the contact person responsible for FBI alerts in New Mexico to create an APB for Ron with a focus on Rail Runner Station 599 near Las Golondrinas.

"Jack, I've put out a statewide alert. Roybal can't find Ron at the fair. Carolyn must close the fair."

Carolyn gasped.

Sara called the New Mexico State Police. They had already seen the FBI alert and were examining camera views of the platform at station 599. They expected troopers would be there in another five minutes.

J. L. Greger

***

Then one text to Sara changed everything. All it said was:

HEL

It was from Hank. Sara assumed he had pushed the send button before he finished the word "help" because he was interrupted. "Jack, I'm going to Hanks' office. I think Ron's there. Alert the Santa Fe police and Carbonne."

She ran to her car without looking back. Jack had his own car in the lot.

Once in the car, its phone system facilitated communications. Jack had already alerted everyone that the agent in the FBI satellite office needed immediate—probably SWAT—backup.

Sara filled in the details. "Resident agent Hank Snow and two women—Elu and Tallulah Dosela—may be hostages of Ron Engel—a murder suspect. His most likely compatriots are Earl Scruggs and/or Vano Georgescu. They are apt to be armed."

Traffic was heavy.

"I don't have a siren and am thirty minutes from the scene. But I want to assure Hank help is on the way without alerting potential captors who might have control of the phone." She sent a text:

HELLO. Jack and I argued. Need a shoulder to cry on. Will stop by at 6.

She hoped the HELLO provided an excuse for his HEL message. She figured Hank would know Jack and she were professional partners only, but his captors wouldn't.

***

She knew others had reached the scene before she turned off I-25 onto St. Francis Drive because commentary among Santa Fe police officers at the scene had begun on the police broadband system.

As she turned off St. Francis Drive onto Sawhill Drive, she saw flashing lights in the distance. The siren blasts became louder as she approached the intersection of Rodeo Park Drive on Sawhill. She parked her car behind a police cruiser on Rodeo Park Drive about a block from the satellite FBI office.

A Santa Fe police officer greeted her. "Are you Sara Almquist?" He didn't wait for her to nod. "Our officers got here about ten minutes ago. The lights were all on, but it was quiet. One of our officers approached the door. Someone—a man—screamed, 'Go away' and turned off most of the lights."

Sara nodded. "I've been following the dialog on the police broadband. Have you seen the agent?"

"Yeah, an old man appeared at the door. He said the suspects would kill the two women and him if the suspects weren't allowed to escape. Then he went back inside."

"Heard that. Did anyone see the suspects? How many? Does one have red hair?"

"All we saw was the barrel of a sawed-off shotgun touching the old man's head as he talked. Then he was ordered inside." He led Sara to the lieutenant in charge who was crouched behind a Santa Fe police minivan across the street from the agents' office.

The lieutenant nodded to Sara. "The FBI is sending their SWAT from Albuquerque. The SWAT leader said you'd worked hostage situations before and should try to get the suspects talking." He handed her his phone. "If you hold down this button, they will hear you."

"I'm no expert at hostage negotiations, and the SWAT leader—Scott Carpenter—knows it. I'll start with a bluff."

"Is that wise?"

Sara shrugged and pushed the button. "Hi, Ron. This is Sara Almquist. We met yesterday. I know you are not a killer at heart. Portia must have provoked you. How?"

No response.

Sara let go of the black button and whispered to the lieutenant. "Have you checked the license plates of cars in the lot? The old Buick belongs to Agent Hank Snow. Did the secretary in the office leave before the captors arrived?"

The lieutenant sent two of his officers to photograph the license plates on the three cars in the lot.

Sara pushed the button on the phone "I can't help you if I don't know what you need. You obviously aren't going to ride the bus to California. Do you need a car?"

The door opened. Hank stood there with the barrel of a shotgun touching his head.

Sara shivered.

Hank spoke slowly. "My sorrel wants a car. My Megrel horse wants a helicopter."

The person holding the shotgun must have been annoyed. He slammed the butt of the gun at Hank's head. Hank ducked but not fast enough. He fell.

Sara gasped but collected her thoughts and turned to the lieutenant. "One is Ron Engel. Sorrels are red horses. Check the source of Megrel horses. If it's the old Soviet republic of Georgia, the other is Vano Georgescu." She pushed the button. "You don't want to rough up old Hank. You've got him so upset he can't think of anything but horses. Do you want a car or a helicopter?"

She noticed Hank had moved his arm. *Thank God. He's alive at least.* She remembered Tallulah had said Elu bought a love potion from Viv. Sara thought Tallulah had also mentioned Elu liked Vano more than the backup cook. She turned to the lieutenant. "Alert everyone. The young woman hostage—Elu—might be collaborating with the captors."

He groaned. "At least, the secretary is not here."

"So, looks like we have two captives, two suspects, and one undetermined captive/suspect." She pushed the button. "Can I talk to Tallulah?"

"No! We want a helicopter." The voice was too low to be Ron's voice.

The lieutenant whispered, "Megrel is a horse breed from Georgia. The SWAT leader is almost here."

"Tell Scott the suspects are Vano Georgescu with the gun and, I assume, Ron Engel." She pushed the button. "Okay, Vano." *Got to kill time until SWAT arrives.* "How big? Many helicopters only hold three people besides the pilot."

"That's big enough. The rest won't be going."

My God, he's all but admitting he plans to kill at least two captives. She noted the four police at the site wore protective gear. "You know I can't get you a helicopter unless you give me something. How about letting one of my men help Hank crawl to me?"

"I'm not stupid."

"Then release Tallulah."

She heard the whirr of a helicopter's rotor. It was hovering over the street near her parked car. The lieutenant whispered, "Seems SWAT leader and two sharpshooters are arriving in the helicopter. The rest are in cars and still on I-25. He wants you to wear this headset. So, you can follow his orders. You'll only hear his direct orders to you because he wants you to focus on the action you control."

Vano must have heard the helicopter. He kicked Hank. Hank sat up and appeared to argue with his unseen captor.

Hank, don't be a hero.

The SWAT leader's familiar voice said in Sara's ear. "Try to get Tallulah with Hank by the door. My sharpshooters will be in place in two minutes."

She pressed the button. "Vano and Ron, I've kept my promise. The helicopter is landing now. If you want to use it, bring Tallulah to be with Hank by the door."

In her ear, she heard, "One sharpshooter is positioned to blast the front door frame. He sees Hank. Radar tech indicates only one person is behind the wall—on the right—by the front door. And there's a mass of what looks like several people along the back wall of the building."

"So, they're all still alive?"

"Radar tech only notes mass, not heat."

"Vano, let Tallulah and Hank go." She knew a good agent would focus not on the release of an agent but on the release of the two women. *I'm not an agent, and I care about Hank. If he dies, his wife will die, too, within a month. Tallulah is a more valuable witness than Elu. And I don't trust Elu.* She noted Scott didn't argue with her about her demands.

A heavy bundle was almost thrown in front of Hank. The bundle had arms and legs.

Oh my God, they've killed Tallulah already.

One leg slowly stretched out. Then the other leg also straightened. *She's alive.*

Tallulah turned over awkwardly and began to crawl forward.

Vano fired a shot into the pavement about ten feet in front of Tallulah.

Tallulah shrieked, stopped moving, and grabbed her left arm.

Sara couldn't see any blood. *Bet she was sprayed by debris thrown when the shotgun pellets hit the pavement. It'll hurt but won't be fatal.* "Vano, be smart. You want to live. You won't if you kill Hank and Tallulah. Let them go. Then you can run to the helicopter."

Vano screamed, "They die unless the police leave. I know two police are with you behind the police minivan."

Good news. She whispered into her headset. "Means we can leave the fourth officer—the best with a rifle—behind the minivan. Are you ready for the rest of us to move?"

She heard a click. "Stall. Try to get Hank and Tallulah farther from the door."

She wished the SWAT leader wasn't restricting what she heard. *Probably figures I'd get confused. Might be right.* Sara pressed the button. "The

                                          J. L. Greger

first officer will leave as soon as you let Hank and Tallulah move forward six feet."

"Stupid broad." Vano's voice was an octave higher than before.

He's terrified and dangerous. "Vano, six feet isn't much. But it proves to us that you're cooperating."

"Okay."

Hank helped Tallulah. They crawled forward six feet.

Vano yelled, "Stop. On your knees."

He must have thought Tallulah and Hank didn't rise to their knees fast enough. He fired another shot. This time Sara could see pavement bits spray from the impact site. Both Hank and Tallulah rubbed their legs. Tallulah began to scream hysterically.

The lieutenant tapped Sara on the shoulder. "I'll go first." He ran in full gear from behind the police minivan down the street toward the helicopter.

Sara pressed the button. "See we're keeping our promises."

Sara heard through her earphone, "Good girl." Then, "Three, two, one, fire."

The lieutenant had almost reached the helicopter when shots rang out.

CHAPTER 12: What Happened?

As the smoke cleared, Sara could see the doorway at the front of the FBI satellite office was now a hole about twice as wide as the door had been. The body of a man had fallen through the widened aperture. He was dark-haired. *Could be Vano.*

Hank's body was covering Tallulah's as they both crouched on the sidewalk in front of the building. Both were quivering.

In her ear, Sara heard, "Someone is waving a white rag from a back window. Sharpshooters stay in position and be ready to fire until weapons are removed from captor in back. Officers behind the minivan should determine the state of captor at front door. Cover Sara as she helps the hostages."

Sara whispered, "Remember Elu might side with the captors. I think she had a crush on Vano."

A male officer ran toward the front door while a woman officer kept her rifle leveled on the body at the door. He felt the man's neck for a pulse and shook his head.

Sara ran to Hank and Tallulah. Neither had tried to stand. Both were now lying on the ground with their legs bent at the knees. Their pant legs were shredded. The legs were covered with black spots. Blood trickled from some of the spots. Tallulah's left arm had similar wounds. A large goose egg was forming on Hank's forehead.

An ambulance siren screamed in the distance.

"Hank and Tallulah, I know wounds from bullet ricochet can hurt like hell, but I don't see major wounds except the bruise on Hank's forehead. What am I missing?"

Tallulah lifted her blouse to show her waist. "Ron and Vano kicked me in the stomach."

Hank smiled weakly. "Knew you'd come." He closed his eyes.

Sara screamed, "Medic" and motioned to an EMT. "Hank was hit on the forehead by a gun butt. Both were kicked in the gut or groin."

The EMTs pushed Sara aside as they connected both Hank and Talulah to intravenous lines. Sara was walking over to the body in the doorway when she heard the SWAT leader in her ear, "Talk to me."

"Hank's head injury may be severe. He's never talkative but he said almost nothing. Both he and Tallulah may have internal injuries from being kicked. Bullet ricochet wounds on legs look painful but not serious. The dead captor is Vano Georgescu. I didn't try to take reports from these two captives because of their injuries. Do you want help interviewing Elu and Ron?"

"The young woman is hysterical. No one can get any info from her."

"What about Ron Engel?"

"Wounded but alive. You'd better go to the hospital in one of the ambulances." Sara heard a click. A minute later, she heard. "SWAT didn't wound Ron. He was wounded before we arrived. The ambulance with him is leaving now."

***

The ride to the hospital was a blur. Tallulah kept groaning while Hank remained silent as the crew worked on them in the back of the ambulance. Sara sat in the jump seat and listened to the driver complain. It seemed ambulances had also been summoned to two other sites around Santa Fe almost simultaneously.

Scott had turned his mike off to Sara, but he turned it on once just before the ambulance pulled up to the emergency room. "Three of us and Elu will join you at the hospital as soon as the rest of the crew gets out of the traffic jam on I-25 and arrives at this scene. It appears you may have been right. We're not sure if Elu was a captive or captor. She needs a psych eval."

***

A doctor in emergency took one look at Hank and had him rushed down a darkened hall for a CT scan. A male nurse grabbed Sara's arm and pulled her to the nurses' station. "Are you the FBI agent responsible for the patients from the Rodeo Park incident?"

Sara thought asking the meaning of "responsible" or correcting her status as an "agent" was waste of time. "Yes. What about the man in the first ambulance?" She had provided information on Hank and Tallulah during the ambulance ride. She had nothing to add.

The nurse bent toward a monitor. "The first man was in critical condition when he arrived from blood loss. He's in surgery now."

"What type of bullet wound?"

The male nurse looked surprised. "Knife wound, I think."

Odd. "May I speak to Tallulah, the last patient brought in, while she waits for tests? Details at the scene are unclear. She could provide info we need."

The nurse studied Sara. "The SWAT leader has radioed to give you full access to all three. Perhaps you should talk to the injured agent first. He'll be going into surgery as soon as the CT scan is completed. Surgeons will try to stop the brain bleed."

Sara gulped. "You're saying this may be our last chance to question him?"

"Yes." The nurse pulled Sara down the hall.

***

"He's not able to speak."

Sara nodded and looked down on Hank lying on the gurney. The goose egg on his forehead had grown and was darker. Otherwise, his skin was pale. "Hank, blink your eyes if you recognize my voice."

Hank blinked his eyes.

"Hank, blink your eyes if Vano knifed Ron."

Hank just lay there.

"Hank, blink your eyes if Tallulah stabbed Ron."

Hank just lay there.

Nurses started to roll Hank toward the operating room. Sara ran along. Just before they rolled him into pre-op, Sara yelled, "Hank, did Elu stab Ron?"

The male nurse from the emergency room grabbed Sara's arm to stop her. The door closed.

Sara turned to the nurse. "I blew it." Tears streamed down her face.

He pushed Sara into a chair. "Wait here." He buzzed the intercom at the door, and ran into pre-op.

Sara sat in the chair feeling defeated. *If Hank dies, we'll never know what happened.*

A minute later, the male nurse grabbed Sara's hand. "An operating nurse said the patient kept blinking his eyes, until she told him, 'Sara heard you.'"

"Thank you." Sara said a silent prayer for Hank before she stood. "Sir, I need your name and the name of the surgical nurse you spoke to. If Hank dies, you two are deathbed witnesses."

The nurse put an arm on Sara's shoulder. "Let's go back to the ER. I'll prepare the documents you need."

"I'd rather talk to Tallulah before she goes to surgery. Is she still waiting for a CT scan?"

He nodded. "The doctors noted no evidence of air in the gut area when she was x-rayed. They doubt her gut was perforated, but she has a couple of fractured ribs."

"How about her spleen?"

"Won't know until we see the CT scan." He smiled. "I can see you're used to hospital procedures. If we hurry, you can ask her a few quick questions."

They ran down the hallway. Sara was out of breath when they found Tallulah. She was the next patient scheduled to get a CT scan.

"Tallulah, we know Elu stabbed Ron. Did you see her stab Ron?"

Tallulah trembled. "He was kicking me. She tried to stop him."

"Where was Vano?"

"Not sure."

"Where was Hank?"

"On the floor."

The technician slid Tallulah from the gurney onto the ramp into the CT scanner. The male nurse pulled Sara from the room. "You're exciting her, and she has to be still during the CT scan."

"Sorry, but I think I got what I needed most. Thank you." She let the male nurse lead her back to the ER. The male nurse busied himself at the nurses' station while Sara emailed Scott, Jack, Winslow, and Carbonne.

Got perhaps a deathbed statement from Hank. Elu stabbed Ron. Non-verbal communications but two nurses are signing a statement that Hank blinked appropriately to my questions. Surgeons are trying to stop a brain bleed from when Vano struck Hank's forehead with a shotgun butt. No info on his other internal injuries.

Got info from Tallulah before her CT scan. She has cracked ribs from being kicked, but probably no gut perforations. Possible spleen damage. She claimed Elu stabbed Ron to stop him from kicking Tallulah. Previously, at the scene, Tallulah had said Ron and Vano kicked her. Shaky statement. Appears Hank had already been kicked and was on the floor when Ron kicked Tallulah.

Sorry, this is the best I could do.

She was trying to prepare a blow-by-blow account of the interviews when Scott entered the ER. He walked directly to Sara.

"First, I want to say you don't need to apologize." He sat down next to her. "Two of the SWAT team are escorting Elu directly to the psych ward where a psychiatrist is waiting. Your email provided the most complete—the only semi-coherent—account of what happened in the conference room today. It's what the psychiatrist and those agents will use to question Elu." He lifted her chin. "Are you okay?"

"Sure. Just tired."

Scott laughed. "I think we're going to have to send you for training to become a hostage negotiator, especially at hospitals."

"Was I that bad?"

"Quite the opposite. You're good at it and have medical savvy And I need a backup."

CHAPTER 13: Jack's Replay of Friday

While Sara and Winslow were examining the dorm for the men, the two other CSI members examined Viv's truck and camper. Jack ambled over to the stables and found Alonzo Wilder putting a large, blue saddle blanket on his Percheron, Betsy.

"Betsy is in the next joust." Alonzo lowered his voice. "A little excitement this morning in the stable. It's like I told your FBI friends. Vano was looking for Scruggs. He stopped by twice, but Scruggs didn't appear with the other three wranglers around ten-thirty. Scruggs staggered in around eleven-thirty."

"What did Vano want?"

"The ring he lost in the crap game last night." Alonzo looked around as he placed a saddle on Betsy's back. "Scruggs claimed he already sold it. Vano left in a huff." He tightened the cinches. "Haven't seen him since."

Consistent with what I know. The food safety inspectors held Scruggs back. Probably was about eleven thirty when he left King Art's.

Alonzo attached blue tassels to Betsy's reins. "You're looking mighty pretty Miss Betsy. And you've got a kind rider today, not that jackass Scruggs." He led Betsy toward the jousting ring.

***

Jack returned to Viv's truck and camper in the staff parking lot. The two women on the CSI team had been busy. They'd found plastic bags held by magnets on the underside of Viv's truck's fenders. He suspected the magnets were connected to Viv's side hustle when the women showed him their other discoveries.

There were at least twenty pounds of dried marijuana packed in shoe boxes in Viv's clothes closet in the camper. Secret compartments in the back seats of the truck were packed with plastic bags and vials filled with pills and powders. Jack thought one unlabeled vial of little pink pills could be oxycodone pills. Another vial of red-coated pills was labeled as "Ron's ups."

This is more than Sara and I can handle. It's time to call DEA. Why should they be the only law enforcement agency to miss the fun of this fair?

He texted Sara. Then he and Carbonne convinced the DEA that they'd make a "big score" if they took over the investigation of Viv's drug business.

Less than ten minutes after he finished those negotiations, Sara called. Ron had disappeared. As Jack ran to Carolyn Taft's office in the shed near the front gate, he wondered whether Vano had left with Ron.

***

He'd been impressed with Carolyn early this morning. She was a smart professional and pretty. *Someone he'd like to know more about personally.*

Now at two, he was disappointed by her behavior. He knew she was purposely stalling him. Sara guessed the reason before he did. Carolyn was giving Ron time to escape on the Rail Runner to Albuquerque. He feared he was letting his emotions—or hopes—cloud his judgement.

When Sara got the text of "HEL" from Hank, his first impulse was to go with Sara to the FBI satellite station. The ensuing conversations with Carbonne, the SWAT leader, and Sara convinced him to stay at the fair. No one thought Roybal could direct law enforcement activities at the fair alone.

After a thorough search of the fairgrounds for Vano, the police allowed the fair, except Viv's booth, to be reopened.

Roybal took control of the trailer kitchen of King Art's and converted it into the headquarters for all police and other investigators at the fair. Jack assigned uniformed officers to isolate and question Carolyn Taft in her office and Viv Lorenzo in the woman's dorm. Then Roybal and Jack sent officers to interview everyone who had worked with Ron or Vano during the morning. The officers were instructed to bring those who had useful info back to the "kitchen headquarters."

***

Once all the investigators were assigned tasks, Jack's main job was to integrate all the incoming information and forward useful pieces to Sara and the SWAT team.

The first piece was from Carolyn, who finally admitted she'd loaned the keys to her rental car to Ron a few minutes after eleven.

Forget getting to know her. She lied. He ordered the Santa Fe police to monitor her and figured she could be charged with obstructing justice later if necessary.

Jack's other role was to calm the frayed nerves of the other investigators. Most agreed with Roybal that the medieval fair was a "mess of festering boils." Jack sensed all the little problems had made many of them grouchy.

The first to explode was Winslow. After he finished checking the men's dorm, he began to monitor the findings of the two women on the CSI team in Viv's properties. He found no blood in the camper using his special UV light, but he found a stash of powdered, dried cannabis inside the flour and sugar canisters in the kitchen of her camper. His co-workers had missed that stash. The usually mellow Winslow lost his cool and called his women colleagues incompetent.

Jack soothed the CSI team by having beverages and donuts delivered to them from a nearby food stand. He assured Winslow and his team that DEA agents were on their way and would take over the investigation of Viv's apparent drug business.

Jack was reviewing the situation with Roybal when Winslow called again. He'd found a navy hoodie stuffed under the front seat in Viv's truck. It appeared to have streaks of blood, grease, and rust on the right sleeve. The rest of the CSI team had missed it.

Winslow is right. Those techs aren't up to snuff today.

Jack ordered uniformed officers to bring Viv and Tony Marin, her other employee besides Vano, to Viv's truck where he'd meet them.

Both Viv and Tony examined the hoodie and denied owning it.

Jack believed the two-hundred-pound Tony because the navy hoodie was too small for him. But it looked like the hoodie would fit either Vano or Viv. Jack reminded Viv that DNA analyses would prove who owned or at least who wore the hoodie. "You might as well tell me the truth and earn points for cooperating."

Viv still denied owning or knowing who owned the hoodie.

Jack had an officer escort Viv back to isolation in the women's dorm. Before he sent Tony back to the "kitchen" to wait to be interviewed, he glanced at Hank's notes on Tony from Thursday:

> *Tony Marin: Has a police record in the Carolinas. Appears to be clean now. Dislikes Viv and Vano. Would talk if given an incentive.*

Pay dirt. Jack immediately found a quiet place at the back of Viv's closed booth. "Tell me about Vano. Was he into drugs?"

"No. He's a cheapskate. Seldom eats in the food stands at the fair and keeps bread and cheese in Viv's refrigerator for lunches. The only reason he joined me and Viv at King Art's on Wednesday night was because the pork and turkey legs were half off." He scratched his head. "Guess the price drew me in, too. Boy, was that dumb. Do you know how bad this *C. diff* bug makes your gut feel? I'm glad you closed Viv's booth today. I'm still not up to snuff."

Jack snickered but stayed focused. "But Vano gambled. Was that why he was so worried about money?"

Tony made a face. "You must have heard about him losing the ring. Funny thing. I'd never seen him gamble before last night."

"Were you playing craps last night, too?"

"Yeah, I like a little action but keep to my limits. Never lose big. Another funny thing. Vano wanted to quit but Scruggs egged him on. Kept saying, 'You'll never win Elu by being cheap.' Scruggs even suggested Vano put up the ring. Don't think Vano even would have thought of it."

Jack texted snippets on Vano to Sara and SWAT as he recorded the interview. "When did you last see Vano?"

Tony scratched himself. "Why all the interest in Vano? He's just a gypsy—I guess I should say Roma—trying to get money to send back to his tribe for his sick daughter. Or at least that's what he claimed. That's what made Scruggs comments so odd. Vano wasn't interested in Elu. Whenever a silly girl came into the booth, he'd say, 'Another Elu.'"

Don't want to let on about the hostage situation. Better not ask more about Vano now. "Let's talk about Viv."

Jack quickly realized the DEA agents would drool when they heard the recording of his conversation with Tony.

Tony told how Viv had grown and processed marijuana for years. "She joined the fair circuit four years ago because it was the perfect marketing tool for the marijuana she grew in Arizona." Later Tony noted, "She seldom works in her Treasure House booth. Mainly, she wanders between the booth and the parking lot where her camper and truck are parked. That lot is the center of her drug business."

Jack suddenly had a brainstorm. "The CSI team found magnets under the bumpers of Viv's truck and Portia's truck."

Tony smiled. "Now you're catching on. Viv never sold anything directly. She left bags of merchandise after someone left cash."

"Trusting of her."

"No way. She kept a sharp eye on her merchandise and paid someone to help her."

"Who?"

Tony shrugged. "That will cost you."

"How much?"

"I'm wanted in the Carolinas for petty stuff, but it adds up. If you get my record cleared. I've got the info you want." He thought a minute. "I might also need a little cash to keep me from hustling again."

"Oh." Jack tried to sound noncommittal.

"One thousand bucks."

"I could just send you to jail."

"I just asked for a tip for my tips. Besides, I'm not dumb. I know Vano left here around noon with Ron. And Ron was high as kite and scared. You've got to be looking for them. How much damage have they done already?"

***

A pair of DEA agents arrived at the fair at four to assume control of the investigation into Viv's drug business. Jack let Winslow update them on all the data collected so far.

The DEA agents thought the most likely drug users—besides Ron—would be the jousters as they prepared to put on a good show. Thus, the DEA agents requested saliva samples from everyone participating in the joust. Alonzo and two of the jousters agreed to have their mouths swabbed. Earl Scruggs and one other jouster refused.

***

Jack was ready to quit for the day. He felt guilty because he hadn't gone with Sara to the FBI satellite office. She had saved lives. *All I did was act like a secretary today.* He thought a bit. He was performing Sara's usual role. *I guess I didn't appreciate how hard her job is.*

He thought he'd better check on the CSI crew. They were nowhere to be found. Then Jack's phone vibrated.

"Saw you were busy and knew Sara wanted the CSI team to look over the debris at the FBI satellite office. Looks like a scene from a battlefield." Winslow was obviously excited. He was talking at top speed.

Jack interrupted, "Can't this wait until tomorrow?"

"Don't think so. You won't believe what we found. Blood stains with rust and grease on the right sleeve of Tallulah's jacket. They're like the stains I found on the navy hoodie stashed in Viv's truck. I'll have tests for DNA on the hoodies run tonight."

"So, you're headed home now?"

"No, we've got to come back to the fair look for blood under the fenders of several trucks. Especially Viv's truck."

"Why?"

"Not many places would have grease, blood, and rust together. And there must be a reason for the magnets attached to the underside of truck bumpers at the fair. Wait for us to arrive."

Jack was ready to hang up. Winslow screamed, "Wait. My crew just found a wide silver band in Elu's tote."

CHAPTER 14: Unreliable Witnesses

Sara thought she smelled coffee. She looked around her bedroom. The clock said seven-thirty. Bug was not in sight. Then she remembered Sanders had told her last night he planned to catch military cargo plane leaving Joint Base Andrews around four this morning.

Sanders had clearance to fly on military planes when there was space. No one else ever seemed to want to take the early flight on Saturday from Washington to Albuquerque. Thus, he often showed up at her house around eight on Saturday morning. The flight must not have encountered headwinds today. He was early. *Not that much. It was more a matter that I was exhausted and overslept.*

She sauntered to her kitchen. Sanders was looking into her refrigerator. Bug was sitting at his feet. "Don't see much you'll like, Bug. No leftovers, just salad ingredients." He opened the door to the freezer. "Here's some sausage links. They might be good with eggs."

Sara snuck up behind him and kissed his neck. He turned and wrapped his arms around her as his tongue searched her mouth. It was great, except when the frozen sausages in one hand sent shivers down her back as he pulled her close.

He let go of her and put several sausage links in the microwave to thaw. "You were worried last night because you knew you'd have to check in on the medieval fair today. I was thinking. I've attended Civil War reenactments at Appomattox, Fredericksburg, and Bull Run. They were interesting because they provided a better view of history than most books. I wouldn't mind learning a bit about medieval history in England and Scotland while you worked at the fair."

Sara pulled a can of diet cola from the refrigerator. She'd never learned to enjoy coffee. So, her caffeine source were colas. Sanders made his own coffee when he stayed with her.

"You're over-estimating this fair. I'd say the owners' goals are to make money from selling New Age trinkets and from luring fair goers into playing silly games that are supposed to remind them of Camelot. It's weak on history, and for that matter, Arthurian legends." She popped the tab and took a swig from the can. *Gee, it tastes good.*

Sanders started to fry sausage in a pan and then cracked several eggs and scrambled them. Bug was now on alert and no longer lounging on the floor.

"Even so, Bug and I will enjoy walking around the fair. From what you told me on the phone this week, it sounds like a virtual law enforcement conference."

Sara took another swig of cola. "We also suspect the management of the fair was aware of several of these illegal activities and taking its cut."

Sanders put bits of sausage and egg in Bug's dog dish on top of the kibble. Sara toasted several slices of bread and created two place setting on the kitchen island. *It's nice to have a partner who likes to cook and cooks well.*

Sanders held the frying pan in one hand and waved a spatula in his other hand at Sara. "How much do you want?"

"You cooked a lot. I'll take about a third."

"I cooked a lot because I remembered what you said the last two mornings about food poisoning. What was it a *C. diff* and *Salmonella* infections?"

Sara smiled. Although Sanders often didn't seem to be listening as they talked each weekday morning between six and six-thirty, he usually remembered the gist of her comments. She doubted she'd done as well this week. *He was so vague about problems in Israel. Course, he knows although I've consulted in the Middle East, I've never been in Israel. Let's see if I can get him to relax and talk.*

"So do you think the Mossad and the Israeli military intelligence unit—what do they call it—are cooperating now?"

"Aman." He ate several mouthfuls. "The Mossad never cooperates with anyone. The Aman knows it and doesn't usually object. I haven't figured out why they did this week. We suspect a couple of Israeli generals wanted to annoy the prime minister. We had the Secretary make a comment about the importance of peace in the Middle East in one of his speeches this week." He chewed on his toast. "Should be enough."

Guess he doesn't want to talk about his problems today. "I'll check in with Jack and Winslow and take a shower We should be on the road in an hour. You'd better bring work along. I must check on suspects in the hospital. Guess I should give them the benefit of the doubt and called them victims, not suspects."

***

                                        J. L. Greger

"Jack and I made a deal. He'll take a crack at Art Last again and see if the lab turned up anything over night. I'll handle the patients at Christus Saint Vincent Hospital in Santa Fe before we meet at the fair around eleven." Sara merged her car onto I-25 North.

"You got the bad end of that deal." Sanders glanced at Bug on the back seat of the car. "Bug was sitting alert until you began to merge onto I-25. Now he's hunkered down."

"Yes, and he won't lift his head until I pull off on St. Francis Drive in Santa Fe. Then he'll be alert because I've never taken him to this hospital, and he's always curious about new locations." She adjusted her mirror. "I'm not sure I got the bad end of the deal. Art Last was defiant yesterday even though Jack had good photographic evidence of Art's participation in the bank robbery. I mean not many one-hundred-ninety-pound men have a large spider tattooed on the back of their right hand."

"You said the other bank robber was killed yesterday. This Art character has no reason to cooperate now."

"Jack hopes Art hasn't learned yet Vano was killed. That's why Jack wanted to do the interview early this morning before any prisoners were transferred from holding cells in Santa Fe to the ABQ detention center."

"Bet Art or his lawyer knows."

"I suspect you're right. Art is apt to risk a trial because after a ten-year stint in prison, he'll be a rich man."

Sanders checked his phone. "How many do you have to see at the hospital?"

"In theory, four. But doctors put Hank, the resident agent in Santa Fe, in a medically induced coma to allow his brain to recover from a massive bleed. So, I can't interview him, and his wife won't be at the hospital. She's not recovering well from a stoke six months ago." *If I were alone, I'd visit her today.* "Sad case."

"Would Hank have been much help? The FBI often puts their least effective agents in satellite offices."

"He's an exception. I don't know why he stayed in Santa Fe. Maybe because of family and friends there. My interviews today would be easy if I had his eyewitness account of what happened yesterday. Instead, my most reliable witness is an older woman from the Taos Pueblo, Tallulah, who appears to have worked for a drug dealer and is in fair condition after a splenectomy. Her comments yesterday were inconsistent."

"What about the other two?"

"I thought the manager of the fair, Ron Engel, was just a bunco artist trying to cheat on taxes until Winslow found Ron's shoes and clothes were covered with blood. The lab confirmed last night it was the murder victim's blood. So, he's now a major murder suspect. And he's still in critical condition from a stab wound. And that brings me to Elu. We all thought she was a naïve Native American girl until Hank through eye blinks identified her as the person who stabbed Ron."

Sanders sat silently for almost a minute. "Are you sure we'll get to the fair today?"

Sara snickered. "Oh, I forgot. Elu was hysterical last night, but I think her hysteria was an act."

"Why?'"

"Just a feeling that she hasn't not told anyone the truth from day one."

***

Sara got nothing but bad news as she checked on the two victims in intensive care. Hank was still in a medically induced coma. His daughter had called the nurses' station several times for updates. *I should call her.*

Surgeons had returned Ron to surgery because he had symptoms of continued internal bleeding. Sara was surprised to learn his cousin, Carolyn, hadn't stopped by the hospital. A secretary from the main office of Camelot Fair Enterprises in California had called for an update only once.

A nurse stopped Sara as she was leaving intensive care. "I just took a call from California. The person representing Ron's grandfather almost seemed pleased when I told him that Ron was still in critical condition."

Maybe, they hope Ron dies and can't talk about their business operation.

***

The psychiatrist on duty enthusiastically described Elu's behavior to Sara. "Elu kept rocking in a chair and chanting: 'I don't want to be alone,' until we gave her sedatives last night. This morning, she ate her breakfast calmly and answered a few questions before her memory block appeared."

"What?"

"She remembered she and Tallulah talked to a lady FBI agent—I assume that's you." He handed Sara several typed pages. "We prepared a written transcript of our recording of the interview. It's easy with artificial intelligence. You can see she listed all the Chinese food she ate yesterday No memory problem." He shook his head. "You'll also see as you read the transcript that she had no sign of memory loss or disgust at what Ron did. Then suddenly, she grabbed my hand and rubbed my wedding ring and began the chant again."

"Sounds strange."

"I agree. Together we may be able to identify what triggered her partial memory loss." The psychiatrist pointed to the last section on the printed transcript:

Question: What happened after Ron and Vano arrived?

Answer: The old agent tried to trick Vano and Ron into going into a small side room. Vano was too smart. (Giggle) He pretended to agree. Ron got behind the agent and hit him across the shoulders. The agent fell, and Ron kicked him as he lay on the floor. Vano took the agent's tie and tied his hands behind his back.

Question: Did that upset you?

Answer: No, but Tallulah cried. (Giggle)

Question: What did you do?

Answer: I picked up the agent's phone. It had fallen from his hand.

Question: Did you check the phone?

Answer: No. I gave it to Vano. He asked the agent why he had sent an incomplete message. I think it was only three letters.

Question: What did the agent do?

Answer: He kept saying, "Now boys, let's be calm. You can leave here now. It'll be hours before anyone comes looking for me or the girls."

Tallulah began to bawl like a baby. Ron went crazy and knocked her off her chair and kicked her. Vano yelled at Ron to stop and left. I ran after him. Vano pushed me away.

Question: Why did Vano push you away?

"How long did she chant?"

"After five minutes, she stopped and asked, 'Can we quit? I'm bored.'"

"Odd. Nothing indicates she was abused or shocked by the abuse Hank and Tallulah received."

The psychiatrist nodded. "She seemed to side with the captors rather than the other captives and showed no signs of fear."

"We found a silver ring that belonged to Vano in Elu's tote."

The psychiatrist sighed. "You think my ring triggered the chant. Reasonable. Others will have to study her response to the actual ring. But the chant could also be a response to Vano's rejection of her—the subject of my last question. You know she thinks he's still alive and has asked to speak to him."

Sara made a phone call and then another. "I can't get her into the psych facility at University Hospital now. What would happen if I sent to the psych unit in ABQ detention center?"

The psychiatrist closed his eyes. "She'll remain angry in either location without intense counseling."

***

"Tallulah, how are you feeling? The doctors say you're on the mend. Are you up to a few questions."

Tallulah who was sitting up in bed and picking at her breakfast of clear chicken broth and red gelatin. "This food doesn't look good. Maybe, I won't notice how bad it tastes if we talk."

Tallulah quickly reconfirmed her statements from yesterday. She reluctantly admitted Elu had giggled and hadn't attempted to stop Ron from kicking her. "I think she was nervous." When Sara asked about the stabbing, Tallulah gave a strange answer. "Elu had no reason to stab Ron, except to protect me." Then she smiled at Sara. "You saved me when you demanded to see me at the door. After Elu stabbed Ron, I was afraid of what she might do next."

"Was Vano afraid of Elu?"

Tallulah stopped sipping the broth through a straw. "Maybe. He knew Elu wanted to marry him." She ate a spoonful of gelatin. "I knew he was already married, but Elu didn't."

"Did Elu figure it out last night?"

"Don't know."

J. L. Greger

Sara looked at the pathetic breakfast. "Would you prefer another flavor of gelatin?"

Tallulah put her napkin over the tray. "Do you think I'll graduate to ice cream or pudding by noon?"

"I'll check after you answer several more question. Was Elu in love with Vano? Or was Elu just eager to escape the pueblo by getting married?"

Tallulah chuckled. "All of us old women think the same. Elu thought Vano was rich."

"Hmm. We aren't old just wise." Sara smiled at her own joke. "I know you weren't well paid for working at King Art's. How much did you earn working for Viv?"

Tallulah gasped.

"Don't deny it. We just aren't sure what all you did for Viv." Sara smiled. "But we can guess. We found blood, rust, and grease on the right sleeve of your jacket like we found on Ron's and Vano's jackets. The grease, rust, and blood were from under the fender of Viv's truck where we found magnets."

"I'm tired."

"You'll have to answer that question eventually. If you answer it completely before anyone else does, the prosecutor may give you a deal."

"I'm tired."

CHAPTER 15: New Eyes on the Fair

Sanders fingered a stained-glass angel in blue and white hanging on a stand in *Lancelot's Dreams*. "Is this a Christmas ornament re-purposed as a Camelot relic?"

Sara ignored him and picked up Bug. The poor dog was used to being respected when he walked down the hallways of hospital to see patients. In the booths at the fair, people just kicked him aside as they examined the merchandise.

"Well, what do you think?"

Sara gulped. "I think it might have been made for this fair. The ribbon hanger is blue—not red or green—and it looks freshly cut."

"Hmmf."

I warned you the fair was hokey. "I doubt you'll find anything you like in the booths, but you might find the live entertainment amusing. They've got Scottish dancing on the center stage at noon." She pointed to a large sign. "They're featuring a hammer throw in a few minutes on the athletic field."

As Sanders turned to look at the sign, the sheath of a sword struck his thigh. "That's another thing. Although all swords and daggers are supposed to be peace-tied so they can't be removed from their sheaths. I think many aren't secured properly."

Sara shrugged. "They're much better secured today than when we came on Thursday. The Santa Fe police spent a lot of time training the team at the gate to check each weapon as costumed vendors and tourists entered the fair on Thursday and Friday. The management was warned the fair would be closed if police spotted any more unsheathed weapons." *Can't resist.* "We're meeting the man in charge of that problem—Sergeant Miguel Roybal—at King Art's. He might like your advice."

"No." He followed Sara toward the back of King Arthur's Feast. "I thought this food stand was closed."

"It is." She knocked on the door of the trailer. "Roybal convinced the fair's manager, Carolyn Taft, to let us use it for meetings. I guess she didn't think it was good business for all the law enforcement people to be gathered at the front gate."

Roybal opened the door. "Welcome to the house of the dammed. This…" He gasped when he saw Sanders. "Haven't I seen your face somewhere?" He gawked at Sanders. "You gave the opening remarks for a video conference last week for law enforcement officers on the international market for stolen art and artifacts."

"Yes." Sanders held out his hand. "I'm Sara's significant other—Sanders."

Sanders obviously doesn't want to talk about why art smuggled internationally is of interest to the State Department. She saw his tight-lipped smile relax when Jack rushed forward and shook Sanders's hand.

"Welcome. I'm surprised Sara could convince you to come to this fair."

Got to give him a way to exit quickly. "He wanted to come, but I encouraged him to wander about rather than listen to our problems." She waved to the stool at the stainless-steel counter. "Jack, why don't you start. You're the closest to solving a crime."

"We're going to enjoy the hammer throw." Sanders and Bug left as Sara, Jack, and Roybal leaned forward on their stools into a huddle.

Jack cleared his throat. "The judge almost yielded to Art's lawyer, but the assistant prosecutor prevailed. Art will await trial for bank robbery in the detention center because Art is a flight risk with no residence in New Mexico."

"Good. Did the prosecutor suggest a plea deal?"

"He allowed me to tell Art that he might accept a plea for a shortened sentence if Art provided evidence against the others participating in the robbery."

"And?"

"Art sang like a bird and named Willie Shakes as the driver and Vano Georgescu as the other man in the bank. He obviously hadn't heard a rumor about Vano's death."

"Good. Your plan to talk to him early worked."

"But… he claimed Vano had the money."

"What did the assistant prosecutor do?"

"He refused to make a deal with Art and gave me a warrant to arrest Willie. Then he told Art that Vano was dead. Art still denied knowing the location of the money."

"Did you believe him?"

"No. He seemed too happy when he heard the news."

Sara laughed. "I'll tell you the only positive thing I learned this morning. Tallulah said, 'Elu thought Vano was rich.' Maybe, Elu knows—

consciously or subconsciously—where the stash from the bank robbery is hidden."

Everyone smiled.

"Don't get your hopes up. Elu's pretending to have a memory lapse. So, agents are transporting her to the ABQ detention center as we speak. She will be kept isolated in the psych unit there until the charges against her are clear. It could be murder if surgeons can't stop Ron's internal bleeding. I have two witnesses' statements indicating she stabbed Ron."

"Guess it's my turn now." Roybal put a map of Santa Fe on the table. "Two art galleries…" He pointed to their locations. "… expect someone with stolen art to stop by tomorrow."

"How did you get them to talk?"

Roybal studied his phone. "My family has been in the art trade for a long time. I have contacts." He hurried on. "I've arranged for Santa Fe undercover police to be at both locations all day tomorrow."

Sara bit her lip. "Why don't you give photos of Carolyn Taft and our other nine undetained suspects to those officers?"

"Why?"

Jack coughed and answered before Sara could. "Her current hypothesis for these crimes is: everyone who ate at King Art's on Wednesday night is guilty of multiple crimes. Thus, any of them could have been involved in art theft."

"Diablos." Roybal stroked his beard. "My thoughts exactly. They're all crooks."

Sara looked at her notes. "Okay, I want this to be a short day for me. Jack and I will talk to and then arrest Willie Shakes. Several Santa Fe PD officers should monitor Carolyn Taft and everyone who ate at King Art's on Wednesday night. They may make a nervous mistake now that two of their number are dead and five are being detained or are in the hospital."

Jack pointed at Roybal. "Do you have any officers who haven't been at the fair? Fresh eyes, like women who can flirt with the stablemen and be nosy. Tell them to not waste time on my stoolie, Alonzo Wilder."

Roybal smiled. "Done."

***

"Vano got friendly with me in Tempe." Willie scratched his head "Especially after he learned I was driving my sister from Gallup to Albuquerque early on Tuesday." Willie leaned forward and closed his eyes. "He said he and Art needed help on Tuesday between ten and one."

J. L. Greger

He certainly seems to be cooperative. "Like what?" Sara pushed a plate of homemade oatmeal cookies toward him. *Sure glad, I took time to bake on Tuesday night.* "Have a cookie."

Willie took several bites. "Vano wanted me to pick them up at the big furniture store on the north end of Cottonwood Mall in Albuquerque around ten-thirty and drive them to two locations. I warned them I had to get back to the hospital by two to return the car to my sister."

"Was there anything strange about their errand?"

"Yeah, Vano gave me two hundred dollars." He finished the cookie.

"Anything else?"

"Well, they had me drive to a bank. When we got there, they put on black knit caps and rolled them down over their faces. I asked them why. Art told me to shut up. Vano whispered, 'I'll give you an extra hundred dollars if you don't ask any more questions and wait with the motor on until we come out. Then you're driving us to this location.' He gave me his cell phone. It was programmed with fancy instructions."

He finished the cookie. "I liked playing with his phone. Portia was too cheap to install GPS in the camper, which I usually drove. She had GPS only in the truck, and I had to follow her."

He doesn't like being rushed. Got to let this interview develop naturally. "Have another cookie. Why don't you pick one with dried cranberries? I like them better with the fruit, but my friend likes them with nuts and no fruit."

"I like them with the fruit."

Now down to business. "Were they in the bank long? Did you look at a clock?"

"No, I wasn't worried about time. They were running when they came out. Art yelled at me to 'floor' the car. Vano suggested I ignore Art and drive normally. Once we were three blocks from the bank, they took off their masks. Vano took back his phone and gave me easy instructions to follow. Art seemed to be busy unpacking some bags in the back seat and putting stuff in the totes I brought along."

Sara saw the surprise on Jack's face. *Got to keep Willie calm. He'll talk more.* "What totes?"

"Part of the deal was I'd get tote bags for them. I forgot until Sunday night. Crystal had to make them fast with fabric she had on hand. One was a Christmas print. Another was blue-and-white striped. I don't remember the other two. I gave her fifty dollars from what Vano gave me in Tempe."

"Do you remember where they had you drop them off?"

"Yeah, strange. They had left Viv's truck parked in a grassy park. One with lots of crosses." Willie was quiet for a few seconds. "Guess it was a cemetery."

"What did they tell you to do with the bags in the back seat?"

"Oh, they took the totes."

"The other bags."

Willie looked at his lap and licked his lips. "You mean the canvas ones?"

Sara flashed a smile because she thought Willie knew he'd made a mistake.

"Art told me to throw them away in the dumpster at the hospital before I returned the car to my sister."

"Why didn't you do as he asked?"

"I forgot. My sister knows I'm forgetful. She searched the back seat of her car before she left for Gallup Tuesday afternoon. She put the canvas bags into a garbage bag with my clothes. You see, I'd washed my clothes for free the night before because my sister has a washer and dryer. I almost forgot them, too."

Amusing what points he emphasizes. "Did Crystal or Portia know you had the bags?"

Willie looked confused. "No, I put the garbage bag in my sleeping area in the camper right away when Crystal drove up. Portia wasn't with Crystal because she was driving the truck."

"Then what happened?"

"I forgot all about the bags. Crystal and I drove to Santa Fe and set up the booth. I asked Art before supper on Tuesday night if he wanted them back. He started screaming, 'Get rid of them.' Called me a 'fool.' I was scared. I hid them in the straw in the stables on Wednesday." He looked at Sara. "Everything in the stables is pitched each morning."

Jack rolled his eyes at Sara. "We need to talk." He grabbed a cookie. "Willie, wait here and enjoy the cookies. We'll be right back."

***

"These cookies are better than your usual ones. Too bad Willie will eat them all." He looked at his phone. "I don't buy all of Willie's story, but it suggests Crystal knew about the heist. Maybe the sister, too. I think it's time to get tough with him."

Sara studied notes on her laptop. "You can try, but I think Willie is a sad case. His sister told the agents from Gallup that Willie had two main vices. He tried too hard to please others, and he was naïve. If you question him aggressively, he may lie to please you. I wonder if we should have a psychiatrist assess whether he's mentally competent."

"Darn."

"I'll contact the resident agent in Gallup and ask them to talk to the sister again before I check on Sanders and Bug. Go ahead, do the rest of the interview without me. Remember to record everything and read Willie his rights again."

"Yes, Mother."

Sara flushed. "I'm sorry. I know you're a capable agent."

"But old habits are hard to break." He winked at her. "And you're worried Sanders will be in a bad mood. This fair is not his style. I'll process Willie. I can tell you don't think he should spend the night in the ABQ detention center."

"Seems too drastic to me and he does have family in New Mexico. But it's your choice. See if you can find out why he didn't throw out the bags until Wednesday evening even though Art yelled at him on Tuesday."

***

Sara found Sanders near the stables. The five men who worked in the stables surrounded him.

One was shouting, "They never told us."

Another cursed loudly before he said, "They let us make fools of ourselves."

She didn't think Sanders was in danger. In fact, he was smiling. She looked around. Bug was standing by Sanders' feet and waving his tail. As she listened, she realized Sanders was explaining the Scottish Highland Games to the men. They had lots of questions.

It appeared Ron had instructed them to throw carpenter's hammers at a scarecrow in their version of a hammer throw. The winner was the man who hit the scarecrow most often. Sanders explained how the hammer—a ball weighing more than twenty pounds attached to a rod in the traditional Scottish hammer throw—was whirled around the head and tossed over one shoulder. Success was measured by the distance the hammer flew. The men seemed amazed that Sanders had seen these events several times in Scotland.

Sara was fascinated by the scene. Sanders usually avoided conversations with workmen. *He's a snob.* She knew that was why he sometimes wanted her help on certain espionage cases. *I'm more folksy.* But for some reason he seemed to be enjoying talking to these men. *Maybe I can take advantage of this role reversal. These stable men might talk more to me if they saw my connection to Sanders.*

Sara walked through the circle of men and put her arm over Sanders's shoulder and looked from one hostler to the next. "Did you explain the caber toss or stone throw? With a little imagination, you could convert all these Scottish games into competitive games for kids."

Earl Scruggs spat on the ground. "Are you, his woman?"

This is a time to make friends, not score points for women's rights. "Yes. Now you can guess why I've been so skeptical about this fair. Nothing is authentic. Many of the games at Sottish Highland Games are derived from games played during the medieval period. This fair would be improved if you portrayed them correctly."

The men shuffled their feet. Earl Scruggs snorted. "Not our fault."

Sara noticed the hostler, Jack had recruited to rat on the others, appeared to fit in well with the other stable hands. *Let's see if I can get them to talk more. Maybe the local hostler will hear something important tonight.* "My colleagues in the FBI aren't trying to shut this fair down, but we want to learn about the murder of Portia Merchant. She appears to have been a good woman. Didn't she treat your horses? All we've asking is for you to answer our questions honestly?"

Sanders kissed her lightly. "She's my good woman. She wants to see justice is done"

Wow. He's really playing the crowd. Now's the time for a tough question. "Earl, we found the soles of your shoes were covered with blood. How did that happen?"

"I was the one who found Portia's..." Earl seemed to be grappling for words. "...lower body in the straw. The damn bag dripped blood when I opened it. Gross." He shook his head. "I dropped it and then stepped in the blood when I picked the bag up." Earl turned to his cohorts. "Tell her."

One stableman stepped forward and confirmed Earl's story. Then the others confirmed how the "bloody mess" had been created in the stables. Sara remembered Hank had said the scene was "amazing." *Guess he was too polite to give me the details. These guys aren't that polite.*

Sanders picked up Bug and whispered, "They've had their say. Let's get out of here."

*****

Sanders locked the doors to Sara's car as soon as he was inside. "The men in the stables are frightened and angry. Maybe angry enough to behave foolishly. They have no education and limited skills. They aren't even good enough riders and ropers to participate as extras in rodeos. Hence, they accepted Ron's rules."

"So, they know a lot?"

"Probably. They all seemed to think Ron has a bad temper. One muttered that if you had a side hustle you had to give Ron his cut. Then the apparent leader, the Red Earl, told the guy to shut up. They probably lied to protect him when you asked about the blood on his shoes."

I agree. Earl's answer didn't ring true. "Okay, you've proved you're still good at undercover work. I'll let Jack do the follow up." She emailed Jack a long message. "Where do you want to eat dinner?"

"Not here. I didn't expect the food to be great but the lack of authenticity at this so-called medieval fair is disgusting. The vendors are featuring chocolate candy, corn dogs, turkey wings and drumsticks, ears of roasted corn, and pumpkin and blueberry tarts. Do you realize chocolate, corn, tomatoes, blueberries, turkey, and pumpkins weren't available in Europe before the discovery of the Americas? And that was after the medieval era."

No need to rile him more. "How about an early dinner on the patio at a northern Italian restaurant? Osteria D'Assisi makes great veal piccata. Their pumpkin ravioli is good, too. But I always order a veal dish because Bug loves veal."

Sanders rolled his eyes. "You spoil the dog."

"Of course. Just like I want to spoil you tonight."

CHAPTER 16: Jack Hears a Confession

Sara had taught Jack there was no right way to interview a suspect. You had to tailor your natural style to the "needs" of the suspect. Jack had watched Sara be motherly, like Portia, with Willie. It had seemed to work in at least one way: Willie hadn't played his hand game. However, he thought Willie had been less than honest on several points.

Thus, Jack decided he would be sterner with Willie. He believed Willie was afraid of other men, especially big ones like Art and Earl. Although Jack wasn't overweight, like Art and Earl, he had been a football player in college. He guessed Willie thought of him as big. So, he stood by Willie during the interview and towered above him instead of sitting on a stool next to him.

The intimidation worked. Willie played his stupid hand game about the "people in the church" but he admitted several important points. Portia had been in the barn applying a mustard plaster to a horse on Wednesday night when Willie hid the canvas bank deposit bags in the hay. She had told Willie not to worry when she saw the bags. She'd "talk to Art and his partner."

Willie cried when he heard Vano was dead. He looked up at Jack. "My sister told me God punishes us when we are bad. Will I die, too, because I helped Art and Vano rob the bank?" He stopped playing his game. "It didn't seem like a big deal. I was just trying to help Vano. He was a good guy."

I'm glad I read Willie his rights as soon as I began questioning him. This admission should be enough, along with Art's statement to convict Art and Willie in court. 'Course there is the little problem of the missing two hundred thousand dollars.

Jack was surprised when Willie added, "I bought Vano's ring from the Red Earl. I wanted it because it's magical."

Wait! Sara and Winslow found the silver ring in Elu's tote. Better take this slow like Sara would. "How is the ring magical?"

"It's the key to a puzzle. Vano said, 'It will tell anyone how to be rich."

"Be serious, Willie. What did Vano mean?"

Willie blinked. "I don't know. That's why I gave the ring to Elu. She always said she wanted to be rich and free."

"When did you give Elu the ring?"

Willie rubbed his hands. "When she was crying on Friday morning. She was sad because Ron had fired everyone who worked at King Art's."

Wait. None of the five employees in King Art's or Ron or Carolyn mentioned this important detail. "Exactly what did Elu say?"

"She said Ron had laughed at her. 'No one wants a tramp like you.'"

"Did he say this in front of the other employees?"

Willie wiggled his fingers. "Don't know." He folded his hands. "I think he talked to Elu and Tallulah together. Not sure, but Elu kept muttering it wasn't fair. Tallulah could work for Viv full time now, but she had nowhere to go."

Better let Sara know before she questions Tallulah tomorrow. "You said you gave Vano's ring to Elu. Did you tell Elu the ring was Vano's?"

Willie giggled. "Didn't have to tell her. She knew the ring was Vano's. It made her happy." Willie folded his hands to form a steeple with his index fingers. "Here's the church with all the people. Open the door and see all the people." He moved his thumbs apart, twisted his hands, and wiggled his fingers.

Jack tried to ignore Willie's song and think. *Willie's story might explain Elu's motive for stabbing Ron.*

Jack placed the warrant on the counter in front of Willie. "Willie, when you do something wrong, our laws say you must be punished. You abetted a bank robbery."

"What's abetted?"

"You helped Art and Vano by driving them to and from the bank. You know that was wrong. On Monday, a judge will decide if you should go to jail."

"No! On Monday Crystal and I have to drive to Texas and set up our booth at another fair."

"That's not going to happen."

"It's half my booth now." Willie's face was red. "I need to keep the booth. My sister needs the money."

"You must talk to a lawyer. He may convince the judge to lessen your sentence. In the meantime, a psychologist—maybe two— will talk to you to decide if you understand the situation."

"Crystal will take it all."

"I don't think the judge will let Crystal take all of Portia's property. If you come to Albuquerque with me, I'll help you get a lawyer from the public defender's office."

"Where's Sara? I trust her. She's like Portia."

***

Jack read Sara's rambling email:

Sanders got the stable hands to talk a bit by teaching them how hammer throws were done in the Scottish Highland Games. They said Ron Engel took a "cut on all side hustles" and has a "bad temper." I guess I didn't assess him well at the start because he reminded me of the students at Hogwarts in the Harry Potter books.

I tried to learn how Earl got blood on the soles of his shoes. All the stablemen agreed Earl stepped in blood dripping from a bag containing Portia's lower torso that he found in the stables. The story seemed contrived. Why would anyone carry most of the bags to the garbage bins behind the stables but leave two in the stables? Earl knows a lot more than he's admitted.

I tried to make the stablemen feel guilty about Portia's death. I was hoping they'd talk more in front of Alonzo Wilder. You might prime him with questions. I'll also try to amend our warrant to include bugging the men's dorm in the semi-trailer. That's a long shot.

I'm going to ask the doctors if Ron, Hank, and Tallulah can be moved to University Hospital. Then FBI agents can monitor all of them 24/7. Their lives may be in danger if the management of the fair (not just Ron) was in on all the side hustles. I suspect Hank's wife and daughter would like him to be near to them in Santa Fe. So, the move will be a hard sell.

If I get everyone moved, you and Roybal will have to finish up interviews at the fair on Sunday. I'll take care of interviewing the patients in Albuquerque. I should have spent more time with Tallulah today.

Even though he'd worked with Sara on several cases, she still confused him. She was a scientist and tech savvy. But she couldn't get the hang of texting. *Maybe it was just as well. Long emails gave Sara a chance to explain her thinking.*

He was inclined to let Willie and Crystal run the booth as they wished for the rest of today and most of Sunday for several reasons. They'd been cooperative and didn't belong in the rough ABQ detention center. Besides, the charges against Willie for abetting the robbery were apt to be reduced because of his mental state. No agency had charged Crystal with anything, even though she could eventually be charged with abetting the robbery.

It would also be less work for Jack. He and another agent could escort Willie and Crystal with Portia's vehicles to Albuquerque late on Sunday. It would give Sara time to arrange the logistics. He emailed Sara:

I propose we let Willie and Crystal proceed as if they own the booth for the rest of today and until about 4 pm on Sunday. It will make them happy and cooperative, I hope.

Then another agent and I will notify them that the truck, camper, and all gear must go to Albuquerque and stay there until Portia's murder is solved and the will is probated. I will tell them they can stay in the camper and truck while they are parked in the FBI secure parking lot for two nights. Please get Carbonne to give permission.

Will you arrange for a psychologist to interview Crystal and Willie on Monday. You also need to get a public defender appointed for Willie. He technically may not be guilty of abetting the robbery because of mental incompetence.

No one seems to know where the cash from the bank robbery is. Willie thought (might be too strong a word) that Vano's ring was a clue.

Also, I can't figure out how Art and Vano were so lucky to hit that bank within hours of it receiving a large cash delivery. That bank usually has about $30K in the till, but it gets $200K once a month on the second Monday of the month to cover the payroll of a local business that hires mainly migrants. Any idea how Art or Vano got that info?

He reread his email. *Darn. I sound like Sara.*

***

Jack stopped by Viv's booth. The place was chaotic—the DEA agents had thrown jars of ointment and junk—probably good luck charms—from drawers and bins onto the floor. Viv's remaining employee—Tony Marin—sat on a stool in almost a catatonic state. His eyes were open, but he didn't respond when Jack greeted him.

After a minute, Tony said, "It'll take me all night to reassemble this booth. Viv's last instruction to me as they carted her off to Albuquerque yesterday was to keep the booth open and pack it up to move on to Texas on Monday." He pulled on Jack's sleeve. "The DEA agents won't talk to me. Do you think they'll let me move the booth to Texas on Monday?"

I doubt you'll have a job on Monday. "Let me check."

Jack cornered two DEA agents. "Do you think Tony helped in Viv's drug trade? Winslow on our CSI team found no evidence of drug residue on his clothes."

The woman DEA agent nodded. "Wish Winslow worked for us. He's good. We think this employee…" She glanced at Tony. "… is telling the truth. Seems to be squeaky-clean and managed the booth pretty much alone because Viv spent most of her time in the parking lot or in her camper."

"And Vano?"

"Not sure." The male DEA agent eyed Tony. "He said Vano only worked in the booth during the afternoon, never after six. We think Vano handled the drug business at night, while Viv ran it during the day."

Jack shook his head. "Are you sure? Vano was playing craps late on Thursday night."

The female agent played with her phone. "We know that. Sara gave us all the info the FBI had on Viv and her two employees." She scrolled through several pages. "Gee. She's organized. Must be nice to have such a thoughtful, organized partner."

"Sometimes."

The male DEA agent snorted. "Bet she nags."

Time to change the topic. "Why didn't you let Viv return to her property last night after you charged her on drug sales?"

"We followed the FBI's—I guess Sara's—lead and claimed she was flight risk with no residence in the state. Viv is in the ABQ detention center until she can be arraigned Monday. Then she'll be released with an ankle bracelet unless she takes a plea. But the assistant prosecutor wants us to turn up something useful before he offers a plea proposal." She swept her hand around the booth. "All we have is Viv was a drug dealer, who specialized in personnel at the fair. This booth is clean."

"So, you'll allow Tony to move the booth onto the next fair site in Texas?"

"Good question. The truck and camper are active crime sites— for prep and sale of drugs of all types. I think the prosecutor will decide this guy can move on with the fair, but he'll need a new employer come Monday."

"Why don't I tell Tony the truth?" Jack stepped closer to the DEA agents. "Then we'll watch what he does. He may be less squeaky-clean than you think."

"Good idea. Can Santa Fe police monitor him tonight?"

"They're planning to watch the trailer used as a male dorm tonight anyway. Talk to Sergeant Roybal for details."

CHAPTER 17: Side Hustles?

Sunday

"Bug was right. The veal piccata at Osteria D'Assisi last night was excellent. Even if it was a little chilly eating on the patio. How come you've never taken me there before?"

"I discovered it when they served lunch a couple of summers ago. But they don't serve lunch anymore." Sara pulled a can of diet cola from the refrigerator. "We usually don't want to drive home from Santa Fe at night. And Bug can only come along if we eat on the patio."

Sanders poured his first cup of coffee for the morning. "Logical. What's on the agenda for today?" He waited only a few seconds. "I saw on the website for the Albuquerque Museum that they had an exhibit 'Beauty in the Breakdown,' an exhibit on preserving items of historic or artistic value. It might be interesting while you are tussling with suspects and witnesses."

Sara internally sighed in relief. "Are you sure you want to see the exhibit?"

He sipped the coffee. "The techniques used by art preservationists are often similar to techniques used in crime labs. Usually, the art historians learn from the crime labs, but occasionally the process is reversed. I saw a couple of cases this week that could benefit from using new methodology to restore old photographs."

He's rambling because he doesn't want to tell me too much about a case. I bet it involves a problem in the Middle East. He's more secretive when Israel is involved. "Fine. I will try to sort suspects from witnesses at the hospital."

He choked. "You can't because everyone at that medieval fair has some sort of illegal side hustle."

"Guess so." Sara hardly heard him because she was concentrating on an email which she'd received from an analyst who had been assigned to decipher the script on Vano's ring.

The silver ring is engraved with: O manusha khelevan tut.

I think this is Romani. The problem is the Romani language is more like a group of languages often with vocabulary from local sources.

It roughly translates to "the people make you dance." I think that's an idiom which means the place is nice. Seems like a strange expression to engrave on a ring. Can you give me any guidance?

This is hopeless. Sara thought a few seconds and remembered Willie had dropped Art and Vano at a cemetery only a couple of miles from the robbed bank. She wondered if Romas ever referred to a cemetery as a "nice place." She pulled up a map on her laptop screen. The nearest cemetery to the robbed bank was Vista Verde Memorial Park.

She looked at the website for the cemetery. The cemetery was grassy. It was an active cemetery with bodies being buried there regularly. She guessed bags of loot could have been placed in a recently dug grave and the area smoothed over. *Weird.* She emailed her thoughts to Jack and the analyst.

She studied Sanders. He seemed entranced by the information on his laptop. She tiptoed over to him and wrapped her arms around his shoulders. She looked down at his screen. There were several damaged black and white photos of men's faces. Their hairstyles suggested the photos were from the fifties. *None of my business.* She kissed his neck.

"I've decided not to take Bug along because the patients I'm working with today are unconscious or I doubt like dogs. Are you sure you want to go to the museum? This isn't apt to be a Smithsonian quality exhibit."

"Yes, I'll drop you off at the hospital. When I'm done at the museum I'll drive to the hospital and wait in the food court by the gift shop for you." He glanced at his screen and closed the current shot. "You saw enough to know I have a professional interest in restoration of old photos."

Better be cautious. "You know as a big shot you don't need to do this type of legwork anymore."

He sighed. "I know, but I've seen too many in Washington who have forgotten everything but politics. I want to keep up my skills as an information specialist."

Sara smiled. *As usual, Sanders called himself an information specialist not a spy.*

***

The FBI agent waiting for Sara outside the intensive care unit looked world-weary. His sagging jawline and the bags under his eyes suggested he eaten, drunk, and/or smoked to excess in the past. She noticed his cane. *I know Carbonne is short staffed, but I didn't think he was so desperate that he'd put a man needing a cane in the field.*

"I'm Dave Roper." He looked up and down Sara. "I've heard about you." He seemed to snicker.

"Can't be that bad."

He moved his hand as if he was flicking a cigarette butt. "Nah, they say you're never lucky. And it's dangerous to be your partner."

Sara blushed. "Not true, but I've had a couple of miserable cases recently."

He nodded. "My initial assignment on this case was rough. No one wanted to be transferred from Santa Fe to Albuquerque yesterday. Hank's daughter overrode her mother's objections and approved the transfer after we told her it was your advice to transfer Hank."

"How's he doing?"

"Still in a medically induced coma, but one of the docs thought the swelling was less." He shrugged. "I couldn't follow all the medical jargon."

"How's Ron?"

"None of his family visited him in Santa Fe. However, two lawyers called to object once we informed the family that Ron was being moved."

"Didn't matter what they wanted. I had a warrant for his arrest for assault on a federal agent and for the attempted murder of Tallulah Dosela."

"Yep, shut the lawyers up fast. Since he's been here, the hospital switchboard has received several odd calls. I'm glad he was admitted under a false name, but I'll be happier when we can move him out of intensive care. There's a lot of traffic in the unit. My partner is patrolling inside the ICU while I watch Tallulah and the entry to the ICU."

"I'll talk to the doctors. I'd be happier too if Ron wasn't in the bed next to Hank. Those calls heighten my suspicions that not only Ron, but also other members of his family were benefitting from side hustles at the fair—like tax evasion, larceny, drug sales, bank robbery, art theft, and God knows what else."

"Yep, his family might try to silence him." Dave pointed to a room down the hall. "Tallulah's there. She must be feeling good. Talkative broad." He looked at his phone after it buzzed. "Oh, before I forget. A

                                              J. L. Greger

nurse called from the detention center. A doc there wants to talk to you about Elu. She disagrees with the earlier assessment on Elu."

"Can you suggest they text me? I won't get to the detention center for several hours."

"Yeah, sure."

"Good. After I say hello to Hank's daughter, I'll talk to Tallulah."

The agent scratched his head. "How did you know Hank's daughter was here?"

"Hank and his family are good people."

***

"Tallulah, it's time for you to tell me everything. No more evasions."

Tallulah mouth opened into an "O". She raised her eyebrows.

"Why didn't you admit that Ron fired you and Elu?"

"I told you we wanted to go back to Taos on Friday."

"That's not the same as admitting your job…" Sara didn't know what to say. Tallulah was cleaning King Art's on Friday. "…ended when? On Friday after the food inspectors left?"

"No, the cheapskate told us that we were through Thursday. Then he changed his mind after the food inspectors talked to him. Said he'd pay us for work on Friday and Saturday if we cooperated with the food inspectors and didn't talk."

"What didn't he want you to talk about?"

Tallulah stared back at Sara.

"Look we found stains on the right sleeve of your hoodie like those on the sleeves of Ron's and Vano's jackets. We think you all got the grease, rust, and Portia's blood on your sleeves when you reached under the bumpers of Viv's truck." Sara saw no reason to mention the lab had found no drug traces on Tallulah's hoodie. *Now comes the sales pitch.* "That's enough to charge you with drug sales. But I think you were a minor player in Viv's drug business. So, the prosecuting attorney might cut a deal with you if you tell us everything right away. You might end up with only probation."

Dave coughed. "You're a fool not to talk to Sara. No one else would bother to negotiate with you."

Tallulah began to cry. "You don't understand. Ron will get us."

"Doubt it. Besides, I can't get you out of here you until you cooperate" *and you're in decent health.* Doctors had told Sara that Tallulah should recover rapidly because they had used laparoscopic technology to remove Tallulah's spleen. However, they admitted a splenectomy was a serious surgery and their use of laparoscopy was unusual in trauma patients. "Tell me exactly what you did for Viv."

Tallulah looked at her lap. "Nothing big. I got up at four each morning and checked the fenders of Viv's truck and camper. If I found cash in bags attached by magnets to the fender of either vehicle, I took the bags to Viv. If I didn't, I still went to Viv. Usually, there was money. Viv gave me little plastic bags to attach to the fenders with the magnets." She looked at the ceiling. "Then I walked around to see no one was near Viv's booth. Mainly I kept an eye on her vehicles. If someone dropped off cash, I took the money to Viv and put more packets in place."

"What was in the packets?"

Tallulah shook her head. "I'm no fool. I never examined the packets. I figured Viv might be checking on me." She pouted a bit. "The packets with money were thick with twenties and fifties."

"What did Viv pay you?"

"She gave me a twenty every morning at the end of my shift at eight. Then I began work at King Art's at nine."

"That's all?"

"When we left Tempe, she gave an extra hundred. I expected the bonus when we left Santa Fe, too."

"You took a big risk for only about two hundred dollars a week."

Tallulah looked down.

"Who did you see at Viv's trucks?"

"Ron often. Vano but he didn't use drugs. He worked shifts like I did, but from seven at night until four in the morning. The guys from the stables. Most of the other vendors at least once."

"What else did you do for Viv?"

"Nothing."

"What about Elu?"

"Viv didn't like Elu."

"How else did you and Elu earn money?"

"We worked in King Art's from nine until closing, usually around eight."

"Nothing else from Ron? Or Willie? Or Portia?"

Tallulah gazed back at Sara without the slightest movement of her eyes.

Dave tapped his cane on the floor repeatedly. "Look Tallulah, if you don't give Sara everything you know, you're going to lose the best deal you'll ever get. If it were up to me, I'd move you to the detention center today and have you facing a federal judge on drug charges tomorrow."

Tallulah bit her lip. "Ron knew I saw a lot in the early mornings. He paid me twenty dollars if I saw or heard anything useful."

"What does useful mean?"

"Depended on Ron's mood. I stopped by the shed where he worked around eight-thirty every morning. I told him who had left or picked up packets at Viv's truck and if anyone had stopped by Portia's and the other vendors' trucks early in the morning."

Why would Ron care? How could he use this info. "Was Ron blackmailing the vendors?"

Tallulah took a sip of water. "How would I know why Ron was jerk? He just is."

"Give me an example."

"After he learned Vano and Elu spent time together one night in Tempe, he threatened to contact Vano's wife. Vano yelled a lot at Elu for talking too much and was less friendly with her here in Santa Fe."

"Did Elu know you tattled on her?"

"No." Tallulah brought her fist down on the overbed table "I didn't tell Ron about Elu and Vano. I knew Elu would do anything to escape the pueblo. I wouldn't try to stop her." She lowered her head. "But I did tell Ron about Willie's sick sister, Portia's visitor in Tempe early one morning, and Earl's constant coughing at night."

Wait Tempe is near Scottsdale—the site of a recent art theft. "Do you remember when you saw Portia's visitor in Tempe? Can you describe him."

"Maybe. It was around five. It was the second… No, it was the third day of the fair in Tempe—Saturday. The guy was a cowboy."

Roybal needs to talk to her about the art theft. "What does cowboy mean?"

"Cowboy hat and boots, deep tan, thin, and bowed legs."

"How tall?"

"He took off his hat to enter the camper."

Dave snorted when his phone vibrated. His hand shook when he read the text. "We got to go. Problem in intensive care."

CHAPTER 18: Emergency in the Hospital

Dave grabbed Sara's arm as soon as the door to Tallulah's room closed. "We're going to surgery. I didn't want Tallulah to know her friend Elu was the problem. She slashed her wrist. The detention center is sending her here for surgery."

"How can that be? The detention center was supposed to have her isolated and to have kept her under a psych watch."

"Stop squawking and run. We can catch her before they take her into surgery."

"No, you've got to get extra security here to protect Tallulah and those in the ICU. I'll go alone to surgery. You can join me once this area is well secured. Better have extra hospital security guards sent to surgery, too."

***

The nurse at the entrance to pre-op sighed, "You again. They said an FBI agent would be meeting the suicide patient from the detention center. The ambulance should reach the hospital in two minutes."

"Ask the docs to consider if the injury could have been done by others."

The nurse's eyes widened. "You mean non-suicidal?" She gulped. "I was about to say I hoped this time you'd bring less excitement to surgery. The shoot-out in post op last time you were here was traumatic for all of us."

"Sorry, but the detention center appears to have goofed. This patient was under a suicide watch."

The nurse motioned to a closed door behind her. "You can confront the staff from the detention center in that room."

The elevator doors opened, and a gurney, pushed by EMTs, rushed forward. Two men in black tactical uniforms worn by guards in the detention center and two hospital guards ran beside the gurney. The nurse greeted the EMTs. Sara pulled the guards into the side room.

***

Sara tried to control her voice, but it wasn't easy. "How did Elu who was supposed to be in an isolated cell under a suicide watch get a knife—or something sharp—to cut her wrists?"

One detention officer pulled his phone from his pocket and studied it.

The other said, "That's what my boss was yelling as we left in the ambulance."

The officer with the phone grunted. "They found a shiv on the floor a few feet from the victim's cell. It had been wiped clean." He stared at Sara. "Suggests it wasn't a suicide attempt. The warden at the detention center has staff reviewing output from the cameras focused on the hallway by the cell. We'll have the shiv processed by the Albuquerque Police Department (APD) crime lab."

"Thanks." *Get control of yourself.* "I know this situation isn't your fault. But this woman is an important witness for several cases, including a murder."

"My boss said FBI agents would probably create a new hole for us." He winked at Sara. "But he said if we were lucky, we'd meet the woman scientist who the boss of the local FBI sends when the mess is deep. Must be you."

"The name's Sara. Did the victim say anything in the ambulance?"

"I recorded everything. I expect your FBI lab will want to study it. I thought she said something like, 'Talludange.'"

"Say it again."

"Tall u dange"

Could it be Tallulah is in danger? Sara called Dave at the ICU.

There was no response.

Sara pulled the nurse who was still admitting patients to surgery into the side room with the guards and announced, "This is an emergency. Lock down the ICU and the hallways leading to it. Send armed security there. The agents on duty at the ICU aren't answering me."

The nurse's face turned white as she pushed several buttons. "I'm locking us down, too. Is this a Silver Alert?"

Sara had to think for a second. A Silver Alert was the code for an armed shooter in a hospital. "Yes, probably." She turned to the hospital security guards. "You've got to isolate Surgery and its waiting rooms and keep the crowd in the waiting rooms calm and in place." She motioned to the detention center guards. "You can help isolate us by stopping anyone from using the nearby elevators, except incoming APD police and FBI agents."

All, but Sara, ran from the room.

Darn. It's Sunday. Sara used an emergency radio channel. "EMERGENCY! FBI agents under attack. Back up is needed in ICU at University Hospital now. Agent Dave Roper and other agent in ICU not responding to my call. I have summoned hospital security to ICU and Surgery where I'm located."

As Sara waited for orders, she heard doors slamming shut and toots from the alarm system. *Glad the toots are softer than the deafening blasts from the fire alarms.*

She sighed internally when Carbonne interrupted the operator on the emergency channel. "What's up?"

"Elu Dosela—the suspect transferred from the ABQ detention center—didn't attempt suicide. She was attacked and thinks Tallulah Dosela in the ICU is in danger. Dave Roper is supposed to be with Tallulah, and he didn't respond to my calls. I initiated a Silver Alert for the whole hospital and directed hospital security to the ICU. Hospital security and detention center guards are isolating us in Surgery because I thought attackers might want to finish the job on Elu."

"Good. Stay in Surgery. APD is on scene and is blocking off all entrances to the second floor of the Critical Care Tower. Our SWAT is on its way. Stay on the line."

The nurse touched her shoulder. "The docs think the victim will survive but can't answer questions."

She heard Carbonne cursing as he gave orders to others for over a minute. She also heard Scott Carpenter, the SWAT leader, announce SWAT would go directly to the ICU with only two of its members coming to Surgery.

Sara leaned toward the nurse. "APD is blocking all hallways to Surgery and ICU. The FBI SWAT will take over shortly." She saw the nurse's paleness. "Tell the staff here, they aren't in danger. But get ready for potential patients from the ICU. I'm arranging for you to hear the SWAT leader announcements through a headset."

The nurse gulped and found a headset in a drawer.

Experienced nurse. Guess she'd have to be to be the supervisor in surgery. Wish we knew what's going on in the ICU. All she and I can do is keep surgery functional.

She forced herself to walk slowly through the surgery waiting rooms. The hospital security staff had calmed the crowd. The noise level was high, but everyone was seated. The security guards had already communicated with APD and the detention center guards at the elevators. They were all convinced no one had entered the Surgery area or its waiting rooms in the last five minutes. However, the detention center guards reported when they first arrived, two men in scrubs had complained when they were not allowed to exit the elevator.

***

Sara heard Scott order different members of the SWAT team to check the hallways around the ICU. The background noise as he spoke was loud. *There must be a crowd around the ICU.*

She heard one voice in her earphone announce, "Two suspects—claiming to be docs—found in a back side room by the ICU. No one in hallway behind ICU."

A second voice said, "Side Hall A clear."

A third voice yelled, "Side Hall B clear."

Another voice said, "Man in scrubs injured at front entrance to ICU. Another man in scrubs is kneeling in front of Agent Dave Roper."

A fifth voice could barely be heard because Tallulah was screaming so loud. Sara thought he said, "Woman patient unhurt but frightened. Need medic."

She heard Scott announce, "SWAT will take control of all four men in scrubs. Surgery should send medics for injured man. He was tripped by an agent and hit his head when he fell. Condition looks serious. Docs in ICU indicate no one inside was injured because agents prevented the entry of the unknown men in scrubs. These men are..." He emphasized the next word. "...NOT believed to be hospital staff."

After more noisy background sounds, Scott said, "Dr. Almquist report to ICU as soon as agents have checked surgery for intruders. When the agents complete their search, this Silver Code alert is over."

Sara responded, "Scott, better check with detention guards at the elevators by surgery. They reported stopping two men in surgical scrubs trying to enter the second floor before you arrived."

Scott cursed. "Silver code maintained."

After more background noise, Scott said, "Sara, bring the detention center guards to ICU immediately to identify suspects."

***

Sara had never seen the waiting room by the front of the ICU so crowded. Two men in scrubs were talking to SWAT members. Sara recognized one of the men as a pediatrician whom she and Bug had often seen in the pediatric ICU. He stood immediately. "She can vouch for me. Or at least her dog Bug could."

Sara turned to the detention center guards. "Were these the men you stopped?"

Fair Dreams 107

One detention center guard shrugged. "Everyone looks the same in those green scrubs with their hair covered."

The other guard said, "Have them say, 'You can't stop me.'"

Both physicians said the sentence.

The guard said, "Yep, those are the arrogant boys we stopped."

Scott had listened to the conversation. "Doctors, we've got your names and fingerprints. You can go. I'm sorry for the inconvenience but we had to be careful."

Sara whispered to the detention guards. "Good work guys. You did what had to be done." She turned to the physicians and smiled. "I'm sure this was unpleasant, but we had a security problem."

The pediatrician said, "Where's Bug?"

"I left him at home today. But thanks for asking." She winked. "Do you need some of his kisses?"

The other physician put his hand on Sara's shoulders. "I thought it was a great idea when the University Hospital stopped keeping police suspects with psych problems in the hospital and moved them to a special unit in the detention center. But they're short-staffed at the detention center. This isn't the first time the detention center sent us a seriously injured psych patient. I'm going to ask the hospital director and chief of medicine to convene a meeting with APD, the FBI, and the detention center in the next week to reconsider how injured suspects are handled."

Another useless meeting. She removed his hand from her shoulder. "What a good idea."

***

Scott motioned to her to follow him toward Tallulah's room. "Thanks for smoothing their ruffled feathers. They were belligerent with APD and my crew."

"No wonder. You'd be annoyed if someone stopped you from moving around the FBI building." *Time to change the subject.* "Is Hank okay? How about Tallulah and Ron? Elu thought someone would try to kill Tallulah."

"The ICU staff never missed a beat. All the patients are fine. I had my doubts when the old alcoholic Dave Roper was reinstated as an agent, but he performed well today. He locked down the ICU with his partner inside before you sent your first message. Seems as soon as they arrived, he and his partner had arranged a message to be used with the ICU if they needed to lock down the ICU in an emergency. Let him tell the story." Scott knocked on the door to Tallulah's room. "It's Scott."

Dave stepped into the hall and slapped Sara on the back. "Thanks for getting the calvary in fast. Figured you would when I didn't reply to your call."

Sara smiled.

"I didn't like the looks of the two men in scrubs as soon as they entered the hall. All the other staff had walked quickly to the ICU. So, I said to them, 'Hi, docs.' They stopped and said, 'Hello.' That's when I was almost sure that they weren't docs. Docs never acknowledge police in the hospital. So, I texted my partner to lock down the ICU. I then dropped my glass of ice water in front of them." He glanced at Sara. "Figured it'd make the floor slippery and give my partner and the crew in the ICU time to act. The two men didn't react. Now I knew they were up to no good. A real doc would have cussed at me. These two didn't."

Sara laughed. "So, you were absolutely sure they weren't doctors."

"Yep, and I asked them if they were looking for Hank Snow? One ignored me and started to press a code into keypad at the door of the ICU. I knew the door wouldn't open because by then my partner and the ICU staff had decommissioned it. I didn't want the two men to flee. I was counting on you to get a generalized lockdown going. So, I said, 'They're having trouble with the door today. You must wait a minute before you re-enter the code.'" He smiled. "Then I heard all the doors along the hall click and a tooting sound."

"Did they run?"

"One started to. Seems he didn't notice my cane. He fell. I took my cane and hit the other one on head as he was tapping on the keypad."

Sara blinked. "I was told the man was unconscious and in serious condition. A cane wouldn't do that type of damage."

Dave handed his cane to Sara. "My cane would. It has a steel shank. One good whack was enough."

Scott rolled his eyes. "Dave is old school. He didn't want to draw a gun because he thought bullets might ricochet against the terrazzo floor and lower walls."

"Yep." Dave leaned on his cane. "While both were on the floor. I got out my gun. Forced the one to throw his gun aside. Took the gun from the unconscious one. Then I just waited."

Sara turned to Scott. "This must have been one of SWAT's easiest assignments. Dave had your two suspects under control."

"I wouldn't say that. The real docs were a handful. Tallulah was hysterical." Half under his breath, he added, "These two appear to be from a local gang. But I have no idea who hired them."

Sara whispered back, "I'd guess Carolyn Taft—young, good-looking California blonde. Have Jack find her at the fair." She thought for a second. "Could be Viv. She's at the detention center."

"Anyone else Jack should check on at the fair?"

"Everyone at the supper at King Art's on Tuesday night." She sighed. "Of course, three of them—Ron, Tallulah, and Elu—are patients here."

CHAPTER 19: Carbonne Forms a New Team

Ostensibly the man was nursing a cup of coffee as he sat in a booth in the food court of University Hospital not far from the gift shop. He was seated so he could watch the people milling around the nearby elevators. Carbonne could tell by the way the man cocked his head that he was intent on observing the anxious crowd.

"Sanders." Carbonne slid into the booth across the table from the man. "Sara's okay."

"Good. I recognized the Silver Alert. Did SWAT catch the shooters?"

"They think so."

"I figured they were after the suspects Sara was interviewing."

No need to ask how he guessed the truth. "Yes."

"I was at the fair with her yesterday. What a shady bunch. More than she and Jack can handle, even with the support of DEA and Santa Fe police. You got to give her more support on this case."

Not like Sanders to give me direct orders anymore. Carbonne remembered the old days when he reported to Sanders in Cuba at the US Interest Section in the Swiss Embassy. During those critical years, the US didn't even have an embassy in Cuba. *The quieter Sander's voice, the more serious the situation.*

"I talked to the men in the stables at the fair. Desperate men. Poor, no skills. They know more than they said, but they're not smart enough to have run this complex network of crimes." Sanders sipped his coffee. "I thought about calling friends in Homeland Security, but the only crime no one mentioned was trafficking of people from Latin America. I think this is a totally home-grown operation."

"Want to join me on the floor?" *Don't want to admit that I've never heard Sara so discouraged.* "Sara suggested I move one native American woman to a safe house as soon as possible. But she's convinced Hank and the top murder suspect—Ron—are too ill to be moved."

Sanders stood. "Ron was probably the hit squad's main target. Lots of people at the fair hated him. How do we avoid the public elevators?"

"Follow me."

***

"Please direct us to Sara Almquist."

The head nurse in pre-op looked up and down Carbonne and Sanders. "Nice. The bosses finally came around. We wouldn't have this problem if APD wasn't so cheap and ran that detention center reasonably."

"We're not with APD." Carbonne flashed his FBI identification. "We're upset too."

The nurse sighed as she studied his ID. "Sara said not to admit anyone but the SWAT leader and the SAC from the FBI." She stared at Carbonne. "I guess that's you. Can you vouch for your colleague?" She peered at Sanders. "Did we interrupt your golf game?"

Sanders coughed. Carbonne nodded.

She knocked on a nearby door. A member of the SWAT team opened the door. "Mr. Carbonne, I didn't expect you."

Carbonne assumed the young woman on the gurney with the bandaged arm was Elu and the older woman in the wheelchair was Tallulah. He was surprised to see Sara was sitting quietly as Dave Roper with his back to the door waved his cane. *I've warned Roper about that cane.*

"You two fool broads not only almost got yourselves killed but everyone around you as well. I'm tired of listening to Sara plead with you. Tell us everything or I swear the FBI will put you both back in the detection center. You won't last twenty-four hours."

Sara blanched. "Ladies, I'm afraid he's right. I'd like to put you in an FBI safe house, but I can't until you cooperate fully. Tallulah, the info you gave this morning isn't enough for someone to want you dead. And Elu the psychologist at the detention center has determined you are not suffering from memory loss. So, stop pretending." She pointed to Elu. "We'll start with you. Tallulah, feel free to add comments."

They are a good cop/bad cop team. Carbonne cleared his throat.

Sara looked around. She must have seen Sanders, too. Tear welled up in her eyes. "Dave why don't you start the interview? I need to talk to this man." She grabbed Sanders's hand.

***

Sara was smiling when she returned to the interview room without Sanders. She slipped Carbonne a note.

Food is coming.

J. L. Greger

Carbonne leaned over and whispered, "Dave is doing well. Tallulah identified Bodet Harper as the cowboy she saw at Portia's camper in Tempe. She also admitted later that day in Tempe she heard Ron screaming at Vano."

"Ladies," Dave looked back and forth between Elu and Tallulah. "What did Vano say about his talk with Ron?"

Both women stared at him. He picked up his phone. "I don't think the detention center guards have left the hospital yet. They might as well load you up."

Tallulah spoke, "Vano didn't say much at first, but he finally said Ron forced him to work with Art on…" She seemed to count on her fingers. "…Tuesday morning, I think."

"Anything else?"

Tallulah's brows almost knit together. "Vano didn't want to do it. Elu knows more. They talked a lot that night. She didn't come to our camper until after midnight."

Elu didn't move, except her lower lip jutted out a bit more. *She's pouting.*

Dave smirked. "Why don't I just hand you a gun to shoot yourself? You'll be dead before midnight if you don't talk. You know Vano is dead. Nothing you say can hurt him now."

Elu screamed and began to wail.

Carbonne gasped. *Guess Sara hadn't told Elu.*

"I'm sorry Elu." Sara touched Elu's hand. "The psychiatrist in Santa Fe didn't think you should be told until you regained your memory. The psychologist at the detention center notified me this morning you were not suffering from memory loss, but I didn't have a chance to talk to you before you were attacked."

Tallulah leaned over and whispered in Elu's ear. Elu nodded. She wiped her eyes. "I guess I should help myself and Tallulah now." She answered questions for fifteen minutes.

At the end, several points were clear. Ron knew a bank in Albuquerque with no special police protection was receiving a big shipment of cash on Tuesday morning to pay migrant workers. Vano had no choice but to help Art in the robbery because Ron threatened to call his wife and tell her about Elu. Vano had insisted that he and Elu have a loud argument which everyone heard on the last night of the fair in Tempe because he wanted to convince Ron he was through with Elu.

"He was trying to protect me from Ron. So, we couldn't spend time together when we reached Santa Fe." Elu wiped tears from her eyes. "But he told me he would send his ring to me when we could be together again. All I wanted was to be free and pretty, like Crystal when she's wearing the pink fairy outfit."

There was a knock on the door. The head nurse in pre-op said to Sara, "Your friend had enough meals delivered to feed the staff in pre-op and post-op. Thank you." She blinked. "Oh, he said he was going to get his stuff and return with Bug in two hours."

***

Carbonne felt sorry for Elu as she spoke of her dreams with Vano. Both had wanted to escape their past and start a new life. Vano wanted to become a rancher and escape the fair. Elu wanted to leave the pueblo with a man. At the FBI satellite office, she thought at first her dreams would come true. Then reality had set in. Ron would never let Vano escape his clutches.

"I was hopeful when Vano went to the front of the building to negotiate with police the first time." She smiled. "He was so smart. But Ron went crazy and started kicking Tallulah and Hank. Vano didn't even yell at Ron when he returned to the conference room. He just yanked Hank's arm and pulled him out of the room." She bit her lip. "Suddenly, I knew what I had to do if I wanted to survive when I saw the knife on the counter." She gulped. "I did it."

Tallulah said, "Can't you say she was crazy with grief? Or the truth, Ron would have killed both of us if she hadn't acted."

Carbonne wasn't surprised to see Sara smiling as she typed rapidly on her laptop. He was surprised when Dave said, "Works for me. Provided you get some help on anger management."

***

Sara arranged for Elu and Tallulah to be returned to post-op to determine whether they could be released to a safe house. When she returned, she closed the door before she spoke. "Dave, how did you break Elu down so fast?"

"Easy. I recognized Elu as a spoiled princess. Just like one of my ex-wives."

Sara sat down. "How did you get so much from Tallulah?

"Remember, I had a lot of time with Tallulah while guarding the ICU."

"So? I begged her to talk, and she talked to you just out of boredom?"

He tapped his cane on the floor several times. "I reminded Tallulah of her father. To make a long story short. Elu was the baby in family of five children. Her brothers were star athletes. One older sister

J. L. Greger

excelled in school. The other became Miss Taos County. As Tallulah put it, 'Elu was just average.' To compensate, especially after Elu's mother died, her father called Elu 'his princess' and catered to her whims." He laughed. "Guess Tallulah felt guilty. She admitted to catering to Elu's whims, too, even though her father—Elu's grandfather—kept saying, 'Spare the rod and spoil the child,' whenever he saw Elu."

"Amazing."

Dave laughed. "I should admit you softened Tallulah up. She said several times, 'Sara's a good woman like Portia, but I'm not sure she can protect us.'"

Enough. Carbonne stood. "You've convinced me. You make a good team." *And no one else but Jack is willing to partner with either of you. Sara because she worries too much about details. Dave because he is oblivious to protocol and details.*

CHAPTER 20: Jack's Perspective on Sunday

Jack looked at the clock on the FBI car's dash. It was already nine. He had no excuse for his late start, except he was exhausted, hated the medieval fair, and missed Sara's company. If she were with him, he'd be eating homemade cookies now. She'd also would be summarizing the tedious reports from the analysts.

He pushed a button and listened to an analyst's summary of the results of the sound recordings from the exterior of the men's dorm. Sara had been unable to get a warrant to "bug" the inside of the dorm. However, devices to assist the Santa Fe police monitoring the dorm's exterior were legal. Generally, the dorm was quiet except one man appeared to have a severe cough that only stopped after the exterior door slammed around four. The analyst noted the exterior door slammed again twenty, thirty, and fifty later, but the coughing didn't resume.

Not much. Sara had learned from Tallulah that Earl Scruggs had a severe cough and often stopped by the fender of Viv's truck. The analyst hypothesized two men had left and returned to the trailer.

Not necessarily true. Earl could have left twice. *Too bad Tallulah was in the hospital and not patrolling the area for Viv.*

***

Alonzo and two of the stablemen were helping children onto the backs of three large horses used in the jousts. Betsy was the biggest and a dappled gray, the other two horses were brown. *Wonder why they aren't using the black horse Earl rides in the joust.* As the men led the horses around the jousting field, he knew the answer. The black horse was too nervous to be used for children's rides.

Jack checked with the man managing the line of children and parents waiting for "horsy" rides. Alonzo would be busy until eleven.

Jack sauntered over to King Art's. The Santa Fe police had kept it stocked with coffee and donuts since they had turned the defunct food stand into their headquarters at the fair. One of the officers patrolling the fair last night reported he'd spotted Earl around four at Viv's truck.

Wait! Viv, Vano, and Tallulah weren't at the fair anymore. Moreover, the DEA officers thought they'd confiscated all of Viv's drugs.

He should have thought of this earlier. Who was operating Viv's drug business? Was it Tony? He asked the officer, "Did you see any of the other men living in the semi-trailer between four and five?"

The officer consulted with another officer. Both had seen an "individual in a black hoodie walking through the fair. Thin and about five-eight in height. But not near Viv's vehicles or the semi-trailer in the staff parking lot."

Jack's phone vibrated. He read Sara's email:

> *Elu slashed her wrists. Detention center negligent. Will update you after she arrives at University Hospital.*

His phone vibrated again. Roybal was talkative and nervous. He had stationed plain clothes officers at the two art galleries that expected a delivery of "lost" art. "The FBI agents in Gallup told me no one had entered Bodet Harper's trailer in the last forty hours. I hope Bodet hasn't figured out our scheme and escaped."

Jack knew he shouldn't be honest but couldn't help himself. "Wouldn't surprise me. Nothing else in this investigation has gone as planned."

His phone vibrated again. Another email from Sara.

> *Elu didn't slash her wrist. It was a murder attempt. Occurred around 9:30. She's still alive.*
>
> *I put hospital in lockdown because two outsiders tried to attack the ICU.*
>
> *We want to learn who gave the order for the attacks. You should determine the location of Carolyn Taft and the usual suspects.*

Sara's rattled. She hadn't taken time to write lots of details and instructions. He reviewed the data. The orders could have been given any time after Elu was sent to the detention center yesterday. Both Art and Viv were already in the detention center then. Since men and women were segregated there, Viv was the most logical contact person. *Might as well be thorough.* He filed a request with the detention center for recordings of all calls to Art and Viv in the last forty-eight hours.

He checked Sara's many warrant requests. Somehow, she'd forgotten to request the phone records for the last week of all those who ate supper at King Art's on Wednesday night. He assigned an analyst to implement the warrants as soon as they were granted.

***

Carolyn Taft looked calmer today than when he'd first seen her on Friday. Her hair was now in a perfect updo rather than a ponytail. She again wore a denim pant suit, but today her top was pink, not blue.

She flashed Jack her perfect smile when he arrived at her desk. "How can I help you?" She winked. "I can't imagine you've found more problems here now that Ron is gone."

Unfeeling comment to make about your cousin. "Gone but not forgotten. Besides he's going to survive." Jack studied her face. She showed no emotion. "Do you plan to visit him at University Hospital before the fair leaves Santa Fe tomorrow or Tuesday?"

She fluttered her eyelashes. "Why? What would I say? Thanks for almost destroying this fair troupe."

She's bitter enough to have ordered the attack on Ron but why would she care about Elu? "I'd like to know about the troupe's banking arrangement. Where did Ron get the payroll? I understand several employees expect to get cash payments tonight or tomorrow morning."

"What?" Carolyn's eyes widened. "I plan to distribute checks tomorrow morning. No cash." She shrugged. "However, I expect several of our employees will cash their checks before they leave town."

"What about checks for those hospitalized, in jail, or dead?"

Carolyn turned to her computer. None of our employees died. I believe the man killed was Viv's employee. Those being detained are a problem for me." She traced her index finger along a column on her laptop screen. "I believe that's Art Last, Elu Dosela, Tallulah Dosela, and Ron." She unlocked a drawer in a file cabinet and pulled out a file. "We calculated the hours they worked and wrote checks. Can you deliver them?" She handed the checks to Jack and relocked the file.

She gives new meaning to the term, ice princess. She never asked about the health or charges against the four employees, including her cousin. *Maybe she knows and doesn't need to ask.* "What will happen to the remaining clerk and assistant cook from King Art's?"

"What's King Art's?"

"That's what many of the staff and law enforcement officers call King Arthur's Feast." He thought a second. "And what about Viv's remaining employee?"

"Viv's employee is her problem. And I've decided we don't want Viv to rejoin the fair after you release her. Lawyers at our headquarters

J. L. Greger

put a clause in all contracts this year that allows us to ditch any vendor with legal problems. Do you need to see the contracts?" She studied her computer screen. "We arranged for the two remaining employees in King Arthur's Feast to drive the rig to Texas. They are working in another booth today. Our central office has located a new head cook and two new servers who will join King Arthur's Feast in Lubbock."

"Aren't you curious about your employees?"

"Past employees. The show must go on. Are we through?"

"Not quite. Aren't you afraid that Ron's activities reflect badly on Camelot Fair Enterprises?"

"Sure. Our lawyer said to distance myself from Ron. If you have questions, contact him. I believe you have his number." She flashed another perfect smile.

A popsicle wouldn't melt in her mouth. His phone vibrated. He chuckled as he read his messages and hoped Carolyn was melting a bit. "Did you know Viv while in detention received a call from Santa Fe around ten last night? It bounced off the tower near the fair."

"Why do I care?"

"We just found the phone making the call in the semi-trailer used as a men's dorm. That means one of the employees moving on with the fair made that call."

"So? I'm busy." She pulled a page from the pile on her desk and studied it.

"Did you know someone tried to kill Elu Dosela this morning in the detention center?"

"No."

"Are you sure? Did you know two men were arrested in University Hospital as they tried to enter the ICU. That's the unit where your cousin was being treated."

Her lips trembled. "I told my grandfather I couldn't clean up all of Ron's messes. He and the lawyer kept saying, 'Relax. How much more trouble can Ron cause now?' But I watched Ron turn from an annoying brat to a grifter with a drug problem during the last three years. I knew they were wrong."

After thirty minutes, Jack had learned several pieces of information. Carolyn had passed the California bar exam less than two months earlier. She feared this assignment in Santa Fe would tarnish her reputation as a lawyer and she'd be stuck working for her grandfather for the rest of her career. She hated carnivals and fairs. She'd gotten a call around four-twenty this morning from an unidentified male. He had said,

"You've still got two drug dealers on your payroll. They're part of the King Art's crew or their friends."

Carolyn sniffed, "He hung up before I could ask any questions."

"Can you describe the voice?"

"Raspy. Nothing special." She appeared to think a second. "Not a tenor, nor a bass. Average."

"So, what did you do?"

"Cried. I guessed it had to be one of the employees who ate at King Arthur's Feast on Wednesday night." She sighed, "Dirty crew. I learned my first day here that the rest of the vendors avoided them. At least their numbers are decreasing because two are dead and five are in jail or the hospital. That left a male clerk and backup cook from King Arthur's Feast, Portia's two flakes—Crystal and Willie, four men from the stables, and Viv's remaining employee. Seven of those nine were housed in the men's dorm. I put on my hoodie and sweatpants and raced over to watch the dorm."

Smart, thorough assessment. "And what did you see?"

"One man returned to the dorm as I was walking toward it. Another man returned at about ten-to-five. The first man was big. Over six-feet, heavy. The second man appeared to have come from another vehicle in the parking lot. He was under six-feet, thin, and wearing a hoodie."

"That's disappointing." *No need to admit your list is the same as ours.* "Several of the men on your list could meet that description."

"I know."

"What did you do next?"

"Walked around the booths for thirty minutes. I saw two others walking around." She shook her head. "I think everyone working for this fair has a plain navy or black fleece hoodie."

No kidding. Her comments are consistent with those of police officers circulating around the fair. He had a brainstorm. *Crystal would also fit the criteria of about five-eight and thin.* No one in law enforcement had bothered to talk to her over the weekend. *That's my fault because I haven't gotten my nerve up to tell her she can't move on with the camper and truck tomorrow.*

Jack looked at his notes. "Could you recognize the voice of your caller?"

Carolyn bit her lip. "Maybe." She winked at Jack. "I also have a key to the dorm trailer and the authority to search it."

"Really?"

"Yes, we added a clause to the statement that all prospective employees signed this year. Management has the right to search booths and housing of all employees or employees of vendors for contraband."

Why didn't she tell me this sooner? Better keep up a friendly dialog. "You could do that in California?"

"California isn't as liberal as you think. It's true we can't force those who are employees to sign a search consent form." She smiled. "But we can make signing the consent form a condition of employment."

"Can we search the camper used by the women?"

She wrinkled her nose. "It's just me and two women I brought from California with me."

Jack stared at her.

"All right because it will prove to you that I'm not part of this mess."

"Let's go to the stables first. You can listen to the voices."

***

As they approached the stables, Jack heard, "Damn. It's the black FBI agent again with the boss."

Carolyn whispered. "Not him. He's a bass and too tall and thin."

Jack passed the man and spoke to Alonzo Wilder. "Betsy looked like she enjoyed giving rides to children."

Alonzo patted Betsy's rear. "Of course, wouldn't you rather have a fifty-pounds on your back instead of over two-hundred pounds? Men, even with our fake armor, are heavy." He lowered his voice. "The crew is nervous today. Jumpy."

"Did they say anything about Elu?"

"Yeah, someone heard she was attacked."

Jack replied at a louder pitch than usual. "Hadn't thought of it that way. I expect galloping toward another horse is frightening."

Alonzo laughed. "You haven't watched our jousts. We don't gallop or even trot. No one wants to get hurt."

Carolyn whispered, "No, he's a tenor but his size is right for second man."

Jack pulled aside two other stablemen and asked, "Did you hear rumors about Elu?"

Each man denied it. Carolyn noted the voices weren't raspy enough and the men were too tall and thin to be the men she'd seen this morning.

Jack noticed that Earl Scruggs seemed to be avoiding him. He yelled, "Earl. I want to talk to you." He grabbed Carolyn's hand and pulled her forward.

After two steps, "That's the tall, heavy man I saw enter the dorm." She planted her feet and refused to go further toward Earl.

Jack took several more steps toward Earl. "Did you hear about Elu?"

Earl sniffed. "Yeah, seems you police types can't protect us." He glared at Jack. "Did you even try?"

"Don't go there. One FBI agent—Hank—is in critical condition. Sara could have been killed this morning protecting Elu, Tallulah, and Ron. We're annoyed with the detention center, too." *How do I get him to say several of the words in the phone message.* "Why were King Art's and Viv's booths the center of problems?"

Earl snorted. "Easy. Viv was a drug dealer. Ron was into anything illegal. Art was his slave. But you already know that."

"Why was Art willing to do Ron's bidding?"

"Willing. That's a laugh. Art had no choice."

"Why?"

"Don't know." He walked closer to Jack and whispered, "Art liked coke. So did Emmet." More loudly, "Why don't you talk to Crystal?" He walked rapidly away.

Why didn't he admit that earlier?

Carolyn sidled up to Jack and whispered, "That's the voice on the phone."

CHAPTER 21: Jack Digs Deeper

The foul odor of sweat and urine drifted from the semi-trailer when Jack opened the door to the dorm. "I guess you don't clean it."

"We do. Once a week on Monday mornings." Carolyn studied Jack. "What are we looking for? I only have the authority to search for drugs and firearms."

"That's good enough. The Santa Fe police should be here any minute with a drug-sniffing dog." He scanned a long email from the analyst for anything useful.

Carolyn pointed to two German Shepherds with two uniformed Santa Fe police officers approaching. "I don't see how the dog will smell drugs in this trailer with all the other odors."

"I'm told they can. The analysts reminded me a CSI team checked out this dorm on Friday. So, any drugs we find were acquired in the last two days."

"The CSI team might have missed something."

"Doubt it. It was Winslow and Sara. The original Picky and Pickier team." He greeted the officers and the dogs: Sam and Annie.

During the next ten minutes Sam and Annie nosed their way from one bunk to the next. They only pawed at bedding or a duffle bag twice. Annie thought Earl's duffle worthy of a bark. Jack found a variety of cough medicines, including prescription ones containing hydrocortisone and less than an ounce of marijuana in a bag from a state-licensed dispensary in Earl's duffle.

Both dogs found Emmet's berth interesting. Their barks became louder as Jack pulled out a vial of white powder. Annie also thought Emmet's sheets were worthy of barks.

Her handler smiled. "Annie has the better nose and has been trained to detect coke metabolites in the urine. Bet that's what she smelled on the sheets."

This may not be Emmet's first arrest for possession since Earl knew of Emmet's liking of coke. I can buy some time for discovery if I let Santa Fe police arrest him for possession.

He turned to Carolyn. "I don't think Emmet Ant will be going to Lubbock." He turned to the two officers. "Can your colleagues arrest the user of this berth—Emmet Ant—for possessing cocaine? This lady can tell you where to find him. The FBI may relieve the Santa Fe police of their responsibilities if he ties into the bank robbery and murder. See if the state court can arraign him on Monday."

The younger dog handler grinned. "No need to explain. Sergeant Roybal has entertained most of the Santa Fe police force this week with tales of this fair."

The senior officer growled. "There are only two good things about this fair. They leave tomorrow. And the mayor promised his staff would check the credentials of future applicants for events more carefully."

Carolyn turned white. "Officers, as the current manager of this fair, I want to stress we regret the activities of some of our employees. We will work with you to prosecute our errant employees and guarantee that next year our staff will be vetted more carefully."

She whispered to Jack as she left the trailer. "And you wonder why I have no pity for my cousin."

***

The dogs never barked as they inspected the camper used by the women. Jack noted Carolyn seemed relaxed during the search. *She may be into the graft of this fair, but she's not into drugs.*

As he headed toward Portia's booth, she announced, "I've got things to do before we pack up tomorrow. With luck, you won't have to inform me of any more problems among my vendors." She walked away.

Odd. She wasn't she curious about the other man she saw leave and enter the men's dorm or the other drug dealer. He texted for a Santa Fe officer to follow her and lurk around her office.

He quickly led the officers and dogs to Portia's booth. Willie was swamped with customers. A line of five women waited to pay for their merchandise. Crystal was nowhere in sight.

Willie swallowed hard. "Crystal disappeared less than five minutes ago. Must have needed a bathroom break. I can't leave. Here's the keys."

Darn. Jack rushed the canine corps to Portia's truck in the parking lot. The dogs whimpered a bit but found nothing, while Jack noted Crystal' s pink wings were on the passenger seat in the truck cabin. *Proves nothing, except she's not dressed as a fairy now.*

J. L. Greger

The dog teams inspected the camper. They didn't even whimper. Jack noted that Willie had a red hoodie and blue jacket but no black hoodie in his tiny bedroom. *Again, proves nothing.*

Viv's sole remaining employee—the "squeaky clean" one—was busy in the booth but was cooperative. He tossed the keys to Viv's truck and camper at Jack and said, "I've nothing to hide."

The dogs whined a bit in Viv's camper, especially in area where Winslow had found drugs on Friday, but the officers found no vials or packets of drugs. Jack assumed residue could be on the floor or counters. He checked his notes. Winslow had confiscated all Vano's and Viv's clothing on Friday. The large black fleece jacket on the built-in seat near the microwave must be owned by the squeaky-clean clerk. *Again, proves nothing.*

His phone vibrated. An analyst had sent a text:

Crystal received a text from Carolyn less than two minutes ago.
All it said was: Meet at usual spot in 11:15.

He texted all police and agents at the fair:

EMERGENCY
Stop Carolyn Taft and Crystal Star.

Police at gate: check Carolyn's office.
I know they're not in Portia's or Viv's booths/campers/trucks.

He rushed to the joust with the canine corps running behind. *If anyone knows their meeting spot, it's Earl Scruggs.*

Earl was standing by his large black steed when Jack ran up. "Jehoshaphat, just stay calm. One more joust and we're out of here."

Jack knocked on Earl's armored sleeve. "Where would Crystal talk to someone in private?"

Earl snorted. "About time you asked?" He pointed to the stables. "They're empty now because we're ready to joust."

Jack ran to the stables. He saw two individuals about equal height—five-eight to five-ten—standing near the door to the blacksmith's shop. Both wore black hoodies.

If they see me, they'll run. They might not run if they saw the officers with the dogs. Carolyn would assume they're just searching for drugs. He motioned for the officers to enter the stable. "Don't get close until I yell." He ran to the blacksmith's shop.

The blacksmith was at work with ten people, mainly children, watching him shape a horseshoe. He ignored Jack and continued his spiel.

Jack circled behind the crowd toward the door to the stable. He almost stumbled as he avoided a woman holding a screaming tot. He opened the door to the stables. *Want to yell, but the kids could be trampled if either of the individuals in black hoodies raced into the blacksmith's shop.* He stepped into the stable and closed the door to the blacksmith's shop behind him. He was less than ten feet from the two individuals in black hoodies. "Lower your hoods."

The officers and dogs moved closer.

Suddenly one hooded individual charged toward Jack. He remembered his days of playing college football and faked a move to the left. The person ran to his right. Jack swung to his right and grabbed for the individual's legs. *The person was a woman.*

"Stop struggling. Why did you run?" He pulled the hoodie from her head. It was Carolyn. "Do I need to cuff you?"

"No." Carolyn shoved Jack away. "I don't want you to claim I resisted arrest. You had no right to tap my phone. I'll sue."

He ignored Carolyn's tirade and glanced over to a wall where two growling dogs and two officers surrounded the other hooded figure. "Crystal, don't be a fool. We just want to ask you questions."

The other hooded figure started to run. When both dogs raced forward, she screamed and dropped her hood. An officer clamped handcuffs onto Crystal wrists.

Jack helped Carolyn stand. "Before you make any more threats, you need to learn the facts. I had a warrant to monitor Crystal's phone calls. An FBI analyst notified me when Crystal received a text."

Carolyn seemed to shrink as he spoke.

He guided her toward the other officers. "Do you want to tell me what was so urgent? Why did you want to talk to Crystal? Or do I have to take you to the Santa Fe police headquarters?"

"No comment." She strode to Crystal and put an arm over Crystal's shoulder. "You can't keep your secret any longer."

CHAPTER 22: Sara Takes Control

Sara could hear men's voices as she approached Carbonne's office. Instead of knocking, she stood at the door and listened. It was obvious that Sanders had pulled rank on Carbonne or at least reminded Carbonne that he had trained him.

Carbonne said, "I know Sara shouldn't have been assigned to this case. It doesn't require much scientific expertise, but Jack was investigating the bank robbery and had to respond to Hank's call from Santa Fe. Sara is Jack's partner. Then things snowballed. And…."

"Many on your staff resent them. But Dave Roper was good with Sara today. He was a natural for being the bad cop with Sara's good cop. You know she and Jack are almost too alike in temperament."

"Yes. I noticed Scott Carpenter, the SWAT leader, works well with Sara, too. He even wants her to get training in hostage negotiation. He thinks she could be his backup in hospitals because of her understanding of medicine. I was thinking maybe I should break tradition and make Sara, Jack, and Dave a three-person team. God knows Dave never met a short cut he didn't take. It will drive Sara and Jack crazy. But he adds the surly toughness to the team that Sara and Jack lack."

Although neither man would admit it, they are each other's best friend. And neither has any other close male friends because their lives revolve around secrets. She heard scratching on the door. *Bug knows I'm here.* Sara knocked, opened the door, and caught Bug as he leapt toward her. As Bug led her into the room., she said, "I'm glad you agree on what's best for me."

Both men reddened.

Glad to see they're embarrassed. "I should be angry, but you're right." *Hate to be defensive but I will be.* "I could add that no other team could have addressed all the technical problems Jack and I faced at the fair. We were managing until Hank was almost killed." She smiled. "I've been thinking and have come up with a plan to maximize our effectiveness. It will take cooperation from both of you."

Both men snorted.

She turned to Sanders. "It means you might as well go back to Washington as planned this afternoon. But be prepared to party this coming weekend because Carbonne…" She winked at Carbonne. "…is giving me a week of paid leave starting this Thursday. Bug and I will fly out to Washington or somewhere interesting then."

"You can't tie everything up that fast on this case."

"Watch me. You've got to get Dave with a more cautious agent—so we're not all sued—to tear into Art at the detention center this afternoon. I'm expecting a call from Roybal in the next hour. I think he's going to catch a major suspect in the art robbery case. Both he and Jack will need backup. You might as well send two more agents off to Santa Fe now. I can text them their destination in thirty minutes."

"What about you and Jack?"

"Jack must get the truth from Carolyn and Crystal. Carolyn claims Crystal has a big secret. Jack also needs to get Earl Scruggs to talk. I think once Jack knows Carolyn's and Crystal's secret he'll get useful info from Earl."

"What do the two agents, I'm sending to Santa Fe, need to do?"

"Haul back those arrested by Jack and Roybal for federal crimes to the Albuquerque detention center. These suspects need to be held until their arraignment hearing tomorrow because all are transients."

"And what will you do?"

"You should ask what I've already done." She picked up Bug and cuddled him. "I settled Tallulah in the safe house and casually noted that the money from the heist was marked with a fluorescent dye and couldn't be spent."

Sanders looked surprised. "You lied."

Carbonne winked at Sara. "Your girl has gotten to be quite proficient at misleading suspects." He stared at Sara. "What did Tallulah say?"

"She admitted Vano explained the code in his ring to Elu."

"And?"

"Elu is a problem. She can't survive in the detention center. I didn't want to put her in the safe house because she can be violent." Sara frowned. "So, I put her in the University Hospital adult psych unit for observation." Sara made a face. "Kinda logical. I have two opposing professional opinions on her mental state."

Carbonne shook his head. "Did she talk?"

"She sulked until I let her talk to Tallulah by phone. After ten minutes on the phone, Elu looked at me and said, 'The police killed Vano? How do I know you won't kill me after I answer your questions?' I replied, 'Because I need you to be alive to testify in court.'"

Sanders choked.

Carbonne said, "And?"

"It made sense to her. She admitted the two women who beat her in the detention center kept asking, 'What's the code in Vano's ring?' She claimed she didn't know them."

"So, you got nothing?"

"Elu gave me an easy way for identify them, but Dave will have to do that grunt work."

She stood and pulled Sanders to his feet. "We have to discuss where we're spending next weekend before Bug and I work with the analysts."

***

Sarah, Sanders, and Bug walked around the outside of the building before Sanders departed for Washington. The walk was productive. They negotiated where they'd spend the following weekend and ways to make it special. His final question before he left for Kirtland Air Force Base was, "How could Elu be sure the two women who attacked her could be identified?"

"She bit them so hard on their knuckles, she drew blood. They're bound to have teeth marks or at least cuts on their hands. They also had spider tattoos on their arms near their elbows."

Sanders gave Sara slow, deep kiss. "Stay away from Elu. I don't want you to learn her biting techniques."

***

The young analyst who had been tracking phone records jumped to attention when Sara and Bug entered her alcove. "You know, tracking the calls of the fifteen people who ate at King Arthur's Feast on Wednesday night is a lot of work. Several of them had multiple phones. Most used their phones frequently, especially Ron Engel." She tapped her screen. "I think I found what Jack has been praying for. Ron—or at least a person using one of his phones—called a woman living in Albuquerque a week ago Thursday while he was still in Tempe."

"So?"

"She's the assistant manager of the bank that was robbed. The conversation lasted almost an hour. Here's what's odd. The conversation was on a phone that you and Winslow found in the men's dorm under someone else's bed—I think Emmet Ant's. The only other time that phone was used in the last two weeks was for two short calls to Albuquerque yesterday. I've not had a chance to research them yet."

"How do you know the woman worked at the Wells Fargo Bank that was robbed last Tuesday?" The analyst leaned back and rolled her eyes. "That's what took so long. And I'm still not finished. I've determined the bio of everyone who was called or who called the suspects and victims listed in Jack's warrant."

I've been properly chastised. "I'm sorry I didn't recognize how thorough you've been. I know cases are solved by the type of excellent detective work you've done. Thank you."

The analyst smiled. "I'd like to go with an agent to question the assistant bank manager tomorrow. I think I can get more info from her because I know more about her than anyone at this point."

"Good idea." Sara emailed Carbonne with the request. "Carbonne will get back to you with details yet today."

As Sara fussed with Bug's lead, she thought nostalgically about her cases with Carbonne. Generally, he had done most of the leg work, and she had time to think about the cases and collect data. "You made a good point. I usually analyze the backgrounds of suspects to understand their motivations. But I've run around like a chicken with its head cut off during the last three days and haven't had time to think. For example, I'd like to understand the relationship between Vano and Elu. She claimed she and Vano were making plans. Everyone else was sure Vano had no interest in Elu. I guess we don't know enough about Vano."

The woman nodded. "I was hoping you'd let me delve into Vano's background. I'm curious why Ron chose him to do the bank robbery with Art."

This is a smart analyst. "Agreed. We need to know their motivations."

***

The other analyst working on the case scowled when Sara and Bug appeared at her alcove. "I sent you a message thirty minutes ago. Why were you so slow to respond? Do you think I enjoy working on Sunday?" She lowered her voice. "I only do it because I get paid overtime rates when I come in on a weekend."

"Sorry."

The woman pulled her obviously dyed red hair behind her ear. "I know why Elu gave you the code for the ring. She couldn't use it anyway. Are you sure all Vano told her was 'the first three letters' were the key?"

"Yes." *As sure as I can be about anything Elu said.* "That's why I asked for your help. You've broken codes before for us. We were told the money taken in the bank heist was last seen at a cemetery near the robbed bank. That's Vista Verde Memorial Park. Another analyst thought the phrase engraved on the ring was an idiom, which means this is a nice place."

"I read the other analyst's comments and thought about Elu's supposed clue." The woman pointed to her computer screen. "The phrase might refer to names on gravestones. So, I made a list of names beginning with at least three-letter sequences from the phrase." The phrase on Vano's ring was displayed with a list of names underneath:

> *O manusha khelevan tut.*
> **Omar**, **Oma**ha
> **Mann**, **Man**fred, **Man**sfield
> **Usher**
> **Shakes**, **Shake**speare
> **Helen**, **Hel**man
> **Levant**
> **Usher**
> **Ant**, **Ant**hony
> **Tuttle**, **Tut**chner

"This list in incomplete. Hundreds of names start with three consecutive letters in the phrase."

"Okay."

The analyst pulled up another screen with the names of plots in the cemetery. "The funeral home managing the park gave me the names and dates when bodies or ashes were interred in each plot. I agreed with your suggestion that it would be easier to hide four tote bags in a recently dug grave, where the sod wasn't well packed. So, I looked for those plots where someone was interred in the last two weeks. The names of only four of those interred recently contain at least three consecutive letters from the code." She pointed to the names on the screen:

Manfred Owens	Burial: March 30
Helen Lane	Burial: April 2
William **Levant**	Burial: April 4
Eileen **Tut**chner	Burial: April 7

"If nothing is found at these sites, the code could yield dozens of other names. It's not a good code. I'm surprised the Romas used it." The analyst studied Bug. "It must be nice to be allowed to bring your dog to work. None of the rest of us can."

"Bug is useful when I have to interview children or patients in the hospital." *Best to ignore the chip on her shoulder.* "The next step is to get a warrant to dig around these graves. Unfortunately, families get touchy when the bodies of their loved ones are disturbed. But it's logical, and we won't open caskets or even the vaults around the caskets. A judge should approve it. While I write the request, please send these names to Dave Roper and Jack. They're hopefully interviewing Art and Willie, respectively, in the next hour."

"Why bother?"

"I doubt Vano hid the cash in four tote bags alone. Either Art and/or Willie must have helped. Although neither have admitted helping to hide the cash."

"No, I mean why give the other robbers hints?"

"When Art sees these data, he'll know he'll know we'll find the cash before he leaves prison in ten years. What you call hints may help us focus Willie's thoughts." Sara thought a second. "Photos of area around each grave might help Willie remember where he dropped off Vano and Art in the cemetery after the robbery. Send a map of the cemetery or photos of the gravesites to Jack, too."

The woman flipped her red hair behind her ears again. "Doesn't seem worth the effort."

Sara knew which analyst she'd request the next time she needed help. Her phone pinged. *Good it's one of the calls I've been waiting for.*

CHAPTER 23: Jack Discovers a Secret

Jack couldn't believe his ears. "We've been investigating Portia's murder for four days. How did you forget to mention that detail until now?" He pushed Crystal onto a bale of hay and put his foot on the bale next to her. He motioned for the Santa Fe police officers and dogs to guide Carolyn to sit on another bale of hay.

Crystal mouth formed a large "O." "Well, you never asked. And besides, it was a secret. No one knew."

Jack coughed. "It seems Carolyn knew the identity of your father. I suspect Ron did, too."

Crystal's eyebrows arched as her eyes widened. "But I never knew. All Portia ever said about my father was 'his itchy feet and palms made him exciting to her when she was in her twenties.'" She fluttered her eyelids.

This girl has perfected her ingenue routine. "Come on. You must have known who created the trust which paid for your schooling." *Wait. She said she never knew. That's past tense.* "When did you learn your father's identity?"

"I… I… I didn't say…" She looked at Carolyn as if begging for help. "Carolyn told me this morning. She says I'm her aunt." Crystal sniffled and buried her head in her hands. "It's all so confusing."

Jack managed not to snicker as he turned to Carolyn. "Would you like to explain?"

The two Santa Fe officers were less polite. They didn't try to hide their chortles.

Carolyn cleared her throat. "It's simple. My grandpa was the son of circus performers who escaped Germany in the late 1930s. In his youth, he was a high-wire walker. His wife made him quit and focus on circus management after his son and daughter were born. His daughter is my mom. His son, who died in a trapeze accident, was Ron's father. After his wife's death, Grandpa disappeared for about ten years. I don't remember him when I was a young child. When I asked questions as a teenager, after he returned, Mom made it clear she didn't want to talk about 'Grandpa's wild days.' Besides, Mom was too busy. After Grandpa disappeared, she and Dad took over the carnival business. Mom hated circuses. They quickly sold off the animal acts and converted the circus into several traveling fair caravans."

"You still haven't explained how Crystal entered your world."

Carolyn glared at him. "It's obvious. Grandpa had a fling with Portia during his wild days. Crystal is his child with Portia. He only came back to California after Portia threw him out. When he came back, he and Mom negotiated a truce. They split the company. Grandpa ran Camelot Fair Enterprises. Mom and Dad ran California Fair Enterprises. But Grandpa owned it all."

"What do you mean they negotiated a truce?"

"He wasn't happy with what Mom and Dad had done to his company, but they had increased its profitability. So, he accepted the changes. At least, that's what Mom thought. Two years ago, Mom requested an audit of Camelot Fair Enterprises. She got a real shock. Not only had Grandpa given a large settlement to a woman named Portia Merchant when she divorced him about twelve years ago, but he also created an endowment to pay for the education of a girl named Hannah Merchant. Then about three years ago he bought a camper, a portable booth, and a truck for Portia Merchant. In the meantime, my aunt had struggled raising Ron alone with modest financial aid from my grandpa. My aunt and Ron were furious."

Crystal had sat quietly during Carolyn's speech. "Now, I understand why Ron almost spit every time he saw me. When I asked Portia, why he was so hateful, she'd just laughed."

Jack turned to Carolyn. "Did you plan to tell Crystal the truth?"

"Not until the end of this fair circuit."

"What made you change your mind?"

"Mom called me last night. Grandpa added a new clause to his will last week. If any of his children, in-laws, or grandchildren are convicted of any major crime, they are excluded from inheriting anything from him."

"Why did he change his will?"

Carolyn shook his head. "He's dying and wanted one more chance to make his family miserable. He set Ron up to fail when he appointed him to manage this caravan. Ron knew it and told Grandpa this fair was a 'poisoned chalice.'"

That sounds too sophisticated for Ron. "Why didn't Ron want this management job? He was out of work, wasn't he?"

J. L. Greger

Tears welled up in Carolyn's eyes. "I understand how Ron felt. Grandpa thought he'd done a big favor for my mom and dad in allowing them to run his business when he took off twenty years ago. It ruined their lives. My parents and I never took another vacation together after they left their jobs as teachers and took over the management of the fair caravans. The only time I saw my mom smile at work was when she sold the last of the tigers to a zoo. We—my parents, aunt, me, and Ron—all hate the fair business and call the medieval fair a poisoned chalice. But Ron was the only one who had the guts to tell Grandpa what he thought."

Crystal stood and walked over to Carolyn. "I don't understand. I think living on the road is freedom. Every week in an adventure in a new location."

Carolyn snorted. "You wouldn't if you were the one scheduling the events and meeting payrolls."

Crystal patted Carolyn's arm. "And I meet so many wonderful people. I can't wait to meet my father."

Carolyn pushed Crystal's hand away. "Get real. This fair is a den of social misfits who turn to crime in desperation. Portia was smart enough to walk away from your father—my grandfather—before he ruined her life. Coming back to this life got her killed."

Interesting discussion but it's not answering my questions. Jack swept his hand between Carolyn and Crystal. "Nothing is going to improve until you two stop playing games. Two FBI agents will be arriving soon to help me get your statements. If we don't get straight answers, you two won't be moving on to Texas."

Crystal whined, "That's not fair."

Jack pointed at Crystal. "Let's start the questions now. Who sold Emmet Ant coke after Viv and Tallulah were arrested and Vano was killed?"

Crystal waved her hand. "That's easy. I spotted Emmet hand a wad of cash to two locals at the gate yesterday morning. Of course, I don't know what he got in return."

Jack pointed at Carolyn. "Is there any chance your grandpa wanted Portia dead? You said she threw him out twelve years ago."

Carolyn flushed. "Anything is possible with Grandpa, but he called Portia 'his only true love.'" She paused. "Mom cites it as proof he's senile. I think it was just another way he found to make Mom miserable. He's always had a mean streak. And I remember he and my grandmother—his first wife—fought constantly when I was a young child."

Jack turned back to Crystal. "Did Bodet Harper have a reason to want Portia dead?"

Crystal gave him a wide-eyed stare. "This fair could be mine someday."

She's zoning out again "Only if you tell me everything you know." He thought a second. "Ron described this medieval fair as a poisoned chalice. It appears to have destroyed him, Portia, and Vano."

Crystal bit her lip. "A poisoned chalice is so medieval and romantic."

Carolyn groaned. "She'll grow out of that fantasy."

Jack emailed Sara:

> *Not sure Crystal has a firm grasp on reality. She needs a psych eval more than Willie.*

CHAPTER 24: Guilt Is a Relative Concept

"We spotted Bodet Harper—gray hair and sparse beard. We put a boot on his van as soon as he rolled three boxes—we assume filled with art—into a gallery. Then I realized I needed CSI team to claim the art. Can you…"

Sara sighed. She should have foreseen the problem. Roybal was a beginner. *Again, it's because I haven't taken time to think.* "It will take more than an hour to get a CSI team to you."

***

Carbonne snorted. "I hope Sergeant Roybal never meets our lab chief. She called him one of the 'stray dogs' that Sara attracts and said she couldn't spare any staff today but Winslow. He's willing if you are his backup. I figured you needed to be there anyway."

"Great."

"Winslow will have the van at the front door in five minutes. I warned him you'd have Bug with you."

***

As Winslow drove, Sara spoke to the assistant federal prosecutor and wrote the request for a warrant to dig around four graves at Vista Verde Memorial Park. She hadn't finished the project before she remembered she'd forgotten to have agents search Portia's property near Tucson. That would require a warrant, too.

She turned to Winslow who was driving. "I hate this case. Working with transients makes everything more complicated. Most of these men and women don't belong in detention—at least not one as dangerous as the one in Albuquerque. And the fact the fair is moving weekly increases the time pressure on us."

Winslow coughed. "I think you created the time pressure on yourself."

"Not really. If the fair doesn't move onto Texas on Tuesday, all the employees will lose their jobs. By the looks of many, they're already destitute."

Winslow didn't take his eyes off the road. "When I was a kid, I thought running away with the circus would be a way to escape the Zuni pueblo. As I gathered evidence at this medieval fair, I saw how the vendors lived on the road. Guess I didn't miss much that was fun. Didn't you dream of running away to the circus as a kid?"

Sara closed her laptop. "No. I wanted to escape the farm and small town where I was raised. But I never thought of being a circus performer or movie star."

"Why not?"

"I knew I wasn't pretty or athletic. I figured my escape route was through a college education by the time I was in sixth grade."

Winslow blinked. "I've seen photos of you in about seventh grade. You were a knockout if you forget about the dated clothes, and that you were awfully thin."

Sara laughed. "Thanks. But for a young girl, what matters is that others tell you and treat you as if you're pretty. Everyone acknowledged I was smart after we were given national tests in fifth grade, but they sighed when my appearance was mentioned. My father called me 'his zinnia.' He said, 'Zinnias aren't as pretty as roses, but they last longer.'"

"If I wasn't driving on I-25, I'd pull off and give you a hug."

Sara laughed. "It's not a problem anymore. I'm happy being me. But I can't understand why anyone with common sense would want to work for a circus or traveling fair if they had other opportunities." She paused. "I think it's why I've not done a good job of interviewing our victims and suspects. And Jack is too much like me to have any insights into their psyches either. It's why I've encouraged him to focus on Carolyn Taft."

Winslow snickered. "I figured you were just doing matchmaking again. Carolyn—if she's not a crook—is Jack's type of woman. Smart, slightly reserved, elegant."

***

Sara, leading Bug, entered a gallery on Canyon Road in Santa Fe. Roybal must have alerted the clerk to Sara's appearance, because she said, "Señora, the owner is expecting you in the room at the rear of the shop."

She gasped when she pushed open the door. An oil pastel by R. C. Gorman of a Native American woman with her sheep was on an easel. She nodded to Roybal and pointed to the drawing. "Is it real?"

"I think it was stolen from a home in Scottsdale." He waved his arm over a couple of Gorman prints on the counter. "He..." Roybal pointed to a deeply tanned, gray-headed man with a scraggly beard. "... claims he got these at a garage sale this winter, but I think they were stolen, too. I'm waiting for verification. Experts have already determined two of the prints the agents found in his trailer were stolen." He looked around the room. "Where's your CSI team?"

"I'm here." Winslow placed his case of supplies on an empty space on the counter. "I'm going to collect fingerprints and DNA from the frames and the back of the artwork. I assume you don't want me to touch the fronts."

Roybal nodded and focused on Sara. "Bodet declined to take a DNA test, but he accepted a glass of water from the shop owner. The glass he used is on the counter. He also refused to answer most of my questions."

Sara gave a broad smile. "Bodet, I'm not interested in your sale of art. I'm from the FBI and want to learn more about your wife and stepdaughter."

Bodet's eyebrows almost met as he squinted at Sara. Then a smile spread across his face. "How did Hannah—I guess I should say Crystal—get into trouble this time? Portia has been too patient with the girl."

Roybal pushed two chairs toward Sara.

"We should sit down first." Sara took her time settling Bug and opening her laptop. "When did you last see your wife?"

"Maybe two months ago."

Sara mouth straightened. "Lying to the FBI is a crime. We have sworn statement from someone. Try again."

Bodet pulled at his collar. "It's no crime to visit your wife."

"True but lying to me is."

"Let's see. I might have stopped in to see her when she was in Tempe last weekend."

"Did you leave some artwork with her then?"

"Portia never could keep her mouth shut. Yes."

"Were they a gift to her? Or was she transporting them for you?"

"I thought you said you weren't interested in my art business?"

"I'm not, but I am interested in who killed Portia."

Sara watched as Bodet seemed to melt onto his chair. His shoulders slumped and he uttered a low moan.

"What happened? Did Crystal have another temper tantrum? Or did Weird Willie finally lose it entirely?" He paused. "Wouldn't have pegged him as the violent type. He seemed so fond of Portia."

"I'm sorry for your loss." *Might as well follow up on his comment.* "Can you tell me about Crystal's temper tantrums?"

"Darn girl is a dreamer. Well, that's good. But when Portia asked her to do anything useful around the ranch, she'd get defiant." He hummed a bit. "That's why I encouraged Portia to keep Crystal in that fancy school—Green Pastures. She had the money from her first husband anyway."

"So, did Portia have more time for you when Crystal wasn't around?"

"You got the wrong idea. Portia and I had our problems, besides Crystal."

"What type of problems?"

"Portia and I didn't appreciate each other's work."

"She didn't like cubism in Western art?"

Bodet slapped his knee and chuckled. "Sergeant Roybal told me you were a doctor. I didn't expect you to appreciate art."

"Or did she dislike having stolen art stored on her property."

Bodet stopped chuckling. "Portia was a bit prim and proper. I only asked her to store and sell art I got at garage sales and in Goodwill-type shops."

"That's not entirely true. One of the signed prints we found in her truck was stolen property."

Bodet scratched his beard. "A sorting mistake on my part." He changed the topic. "I believe you wanted to know about our differences. Well, she could have made real money with her tinctures and poultices, but she refused to go with the times and include a little weed in her products. I finally gave up and moved out."

"Did you fight over your differences?"

"You couldn't fight with Portia. When she disagreed with you, she told you what she thought and then left you alone. Drove Crystal crazy."

"How about you?"

"It's why we never divorced. Portia was easy to be around."

Don't think he killed her. "Did you ever tell anyone that Portia had some of your valuable art finds?"

"Wait, you think I set her up to be killed." He turned pale. "Oh God, I swear I never told anyone. And Portia wouldn't have let on to others in the fair. She said they were a rough, greedy crowd. Portia only joined the fair three years ago because she thought it might be an opportunity for Willie and then Crystal to find an alternate lifestyle that suited them better than the farm and the dairy. I bet that silly Crystal got her mother killed by talking too much. Darn girl."

He's more apt to make a mistake now that he's getting emotional. She probed what he knew about members of the fair troupe but learned nothing new. Finally, she asked, "What did Crystal do when she was angry at Portia?"

"Screamed, 'I hate you,' or 'Set me free.'" He stopped. "Or the best one, 'My REAL dad would let me quit school.' Portia never told Crystal her father's name or that he had kicked Portia repeatedly when she was pregnant. Guess Portia didn't want Crystal to know her father tried to kill her several times when she was an infant."

"Did Crystal and Portia argue?"

"Like I said already, no one could argue with Portia. She wouldn't respond or she'd brew you some chamomile tea or bake cookies for you. That's why Willie stayed around." He stared at Sara. "I've talked a lot. It's time for you to tell me how Portia died. Bet it was an accident."

"Doubt it. Someone cut her body into pieces after they killed her."

Bodet put his hand over his mouth. "I'm going to be sick. Where's…"

The owner pointed to a closed door. Bodet ran to it and threw it open. He wretched for several minutes before he reappeared. "Get the bastard or bitch who did it."

"Help us by telling Sergeant Roybal the truth—even if it's ugly." Better add an incentive. "The FBI sometimes negotiates better terms for helpful suspects."

***

Roybal asked a Santa Fe police officer to take Sara to the medieval fair. As he walked Sara and Bug to the waiting car, he said, "Do you think Bodet is being honest when he said, the Gorman oil pastel and a couple of the signed prints were the only art he knew was stolen?"

"No, but I doubt he fenced much stolen art over the years. It was too easy finding valuable pieces at garage sales and thrift shops. And I also think he was being truthful when he said Portia refused to market stolen art."

Roybal looked at his feet, and his voice was softer. "Will the FBI take this case away from me. It's my big chance."

"The last thing I want is more paperwork. I expect the FBI will let the state court systems in Arizona and New Mexico prosecute Bodet, unless he's needed as a witness against Crystal in a murder trial. I hope that won't be necessary."

"Thanks for saving my ass. I wasn't prepared for this assignment."

Agreed. You weren't, but no need to be petty. "Thanks aren't necessary, but I do expect your and the Santa Fe PD's continued help. That may mean detaining suspects who aren't bad enough to be sent to the ABQ detention center."

CHAPTER 25: Confessions

Jack's face took on an ashy cast as Sara told him about what she learned from Bodet. "You mean in a temper tantrum, he thinks Crystal could have abetted Portia's murder. After my interviews this morning, I'd concluded the best suspect was Ron." He shook his head.

Sara leaned forward. "I'm concerned that Grandpa Engel in California is the ultimate murderer. He inflamed Ron because he wanted revenge on Portia."

"I doubt you can prove it. He must be over eighty and can claim senility. Besides, Carolyn claims he has metastatic cancer and is not expected to survive long."

"Okay, but perhaps I can use him to scare Crystal. I'd like someone to provoke her enough to display her real self."

"That's easy. She's going to blow when I tell her she and Willie can't move Portia's property on with the rest of the fair. It must stay in the state until Portia's estate is probated. Willie knows, but I doubt he told her."

"Why didn't you tell her?"

"No need to create a firestorm earlier than necessary."

Coward. May be just as well. "I watched Dave. He can break her, especially if she's agitated when we arrive in Albuquerque." Sara looked at her watch. "Guess we'd be better off focusing on those who will be moving on tomorrow. Tallulah told me at the start that Emmet Ant was a rat, presumably for Ron. The lab found Emmet's and Ron's fingerprints on the burner phone found in the men's dorm. An analyst confirmed it was the phone used to call Viv in detention and to call an unidentifiable burner phone also in Albuquerque."

"I'll grill him, but first I think we should both talk to the stablemen. They know more than they've said. And Alonzo says they're eager to talk to you about the games played in the Middle Ages."

"I guess I can bluff a bit. Round up Earl and his three coworkers. We'll sit in the kitchen of Portia's camper. I'll call Carolyn to come, too."

"Why?"

"We've got to make them feel guilty for not helping Portia, while instilling them with hope for a better future. Carolyn is the route to their future."

Jack choked. "Good luck."

***

Sara slowly looked from one man to the next as the stablemen huddled around the dinette table in Portia's camper. They stank from sweat and working in the stable. She had placed Styrofoam cups, a jug of iced tea, and cookies on the table. The men eagerly grabbed the cookies.

"Guys, I was raised on a pig farm in the Midwest. I know how hard it is to escape a poor farm background. I also know the management of this fair has been abusive, but you can make your future better." *Now for the bluff.* "The FBI can't let you move on with the rest of the fair until Jack and I have all the evidence to solve the bank robbery and Portia's murder. We don't think you're guilty of murder or bank robbery. However, if you hide details from us, you are abetting a crime after the fact. That by itself is a crime and not the way to build your future."

The four men breathed more heavily and shuffled their feet.

"Once we have the info, I've arranged for Carolyn Taft—the new manager of the fair—to listen to your ideas on how to improve the guest experience at the fair."

Earl shook his head. "We can't trust her. She's related to Ron."

"She is Ron's cousin, but she's angrier at Ron than you and just as scared about the future of the fair. So, here's what I need. Details about what happened on Wednesday night. We know Portia put poultices on a couple of your horses. When did she leave? What did she talk about? Who else was in the stables? No detail is too small."

The men mumbled among themselves. Most of what they said was not new to Sara or Jack. Except, two stablemen noted Portia asked a couple of strange questions. "Did Ron ever force you to do something illegal? Did you ever get the feeling someone was looking in your camper or dorm at night?" Despite multiple questions from Sara and Jack, the men couldn't—or at least didn't—provide more details.

When Sara asked if anyone followed Portia when she left the stables, the men shuffled their feet. They finally admitted Crystal stopped by the stables twice. Each time she stood by the entrance and said, "Hurry up. Ron needs to see you." They snickered because Crystal was wearing her "silly pink fairy" outfit and didn't want to get it "dirty" by entering the stables.

Finally, Earl said, "As Portia was leaving, she spotted Willie. Poor guy was trying to hide something in the hay. She read him the riot act and led him out of the stables."

"Did you check the hay for the items he hid?"

"Not then. We figured it was girlie magazines that she wouldn't allow him to bring into her camper." Earl gobbled another cookie. "I guess we should have. The next morning, we found the bags from the bank and called the police."

One of the other men stopped drinking his tea. "We should have known something was strange right away on Thursday morning. Emmet was in the blacksmith's shop when we arrived at the stables. I'd never seen Emmet up that early."

Earl coughed. "The strangest part was Ron. He locked the door to our trailer and wouldn't open it." He stopped. "Actually, it wasn't locked. My key worked. There was something braced against the door so I couldn't open it. He told me to call the police about the bank bags. He was busy."

"Do you know who else was in the men's dorm with Ron?"

The men shrugged. Earl said, "The four of us are usually the first ones out in the morning."

Another man added, "Vano and the assistant cook at King Art's Feast usually get up as we finish dressing. Doubt they were inside when Earl tried to get in."

"What about Emmet Ant and Art Last?"

The men shrugged. One said, "I just told you Emmet was in the blacksmith shop Thursday morning. So, it had to be Art with Ron."

"What happened when you found the body parts?"

All the men began to talk all at once. Earl said, "One of us walked over and got the police already on the grounds. One of us saw Emmet running to our dorm."

Sara stared at Earl. "It seems strange that the murderers took the time to put bags with most of the body parts in boxes before they threw them in to the garbage but left two bags in the stable. You know what I think?" She smiled at Earl. "I think one or more of you got nosy and went through the garbage and pulled out two bags. That person or persons figured dumping the bags in the stables was a way to get even with Ron. That means you saw Ron caring the bags to the garbage."

Earl stared back at Sara. "You'll never prove it. I've already told you how I got Portia's blood on my shoes." He looked around the table.

The other three men nodded.

 J. L. Greger

After thirty minutes, Sara gave up on questioning the men as a group. Jack brought in Carolyn Taft.

Carolyn admitted she was appalled by the poor quality of the food and some acts in the center court, but she noted the horse rides had gotten rave reviews.

Sara was amazed how seriously the men had taken Sanders's comments. They were prepared to run competitions for throwing the shot put and lifting stones for children and adults. They wanted Carolyn to buy real Scottish hammers for their hammer throw demonstrations.

Carolyn must have been surprised, too. "Why didn't you suggest these ideas to Ron?"

"He wouldn't listen to us. He thought Vano had better ideas. He promised Vano that his wife could join the group as a gypsy dancer and a tarot card reader in June once his son was out of school for the summer."

Sara choked. *That's the most interesting piece of info I got today. I've been asking the wrong questions.* "Did Ron take advice from Portia or Viv?"

Earl groaned. "He wanted Viv to expand her business. But neither of them thought she could get a license to be a registered dispenser of weed."

Another stableman said, "You should have seen Portia's face when he suggested she hire several girls to be fairies and have them give massages in a trailer outfitted like the men's dorm."

Carolyn coughed. "A medieval fair should be family friendly. We will not be implementing those ideas."

Time to ask an incriminating question. "Earl, I noticed you have a nasty cough and frequently get up at night."

"Damn. Tallulah must have told you. She's always lurking around."

The three other men snickered in agreement.

"Who paid Tallulah to watch you?"

Earl shrugged. "We knew Viv paid Tallulah to watch drug sales from her truck's bumpers. But I always thought she tattled to Art or Ron, too."

Let's check his honesty. I know what he had in his kit at his bunk in the men's dorm. "Earl, what medicine do you take to stop the coughing?"

"I take anti-something for my allergies and a variety of cough medicines. But there's no drinkable water in the men's dorm. Portia always put a jug of clean water in the refrigerator on the outside of her camper. So, I get up most mornings before sunrise to get some water from the refrigerator to take my pills. Besides, I'm stiff when I get up. Guess I was kicked by too many horses. Walking around loosens me up."

Sara thought of two questions. She started with, "So, Portia must have had people stopping by her trailer all the time. Who did you see at her camper most mornings?"

One of the guys said, "All of us."

"How about Viv or Crystal?"

"Viv had a refrigerator in her camper, but she didn't allow her crew in it at night. Crystal had a key to Portia's camper but often got her water at the outside refrigerator."

"How about Elu and Tallulah?"

"Yeah, they used Portia's refrigerator, too."

Means the hooded figures are apt to be Crystal, Elu, Tallulah, or the men in the dorm. I'm back where I started.

Sara thought it was time to focus the discussion on Portia, Willie, and Crystal. The men seemed to agree Willie was a "gentle soul," quiet, loyal to Portia, and naïve. They described Crystal as a "kook" and a "spoiled brat." All used the same phrase: "salt of the earth," to describe Portia.

Sara smiled. She'd often been described as "salt of the earth" by colleagues. *I wish I could have met Portia. But why did she join this fair?*

***

While Jack interviewed Emmet Ant at Portia's dinette table, Sara sat in Portia's bedroom compartment and checked with the analysts. They confirmed most of the stablemen's comments on Vano. He had an apparently healthy wife and ten-year-old son. Everything he'd told Elu was a lie *or* Elu had trouble distinguishing between her fantasies and reality.

The analysts had collected a mass of details about Carolyn Taft, her parents, and her grandfather. Everything they'd uncovered was consistent with Carolyn's comments.

The manager of the Better Business Bureau in Henderson, Nevada, seventy miles from Nipton, praised the Tafts for turning California Fair Enterprises into the best carnival business in the California. He rated Camelot Fair Enterprises as a grade B business. *Interesting B is the lowest grade in their rankings.*

Several teachers in the Snowline Unified School District, which served students in Nipton, reported Ron Engel was a "clever" young man with a "minor police record, who was likely to deteriorate into a hardened criminal" because he had so much "pent up rage against his grandfather."

The descriptions of the grandfather, Herbert Engel, were consistently negative: "abusive to family and employees," "bully," and "a shady carnie." The only inconsistent point about Herbert Engel was whether he was "senile" or had "always been wacky."

Sara noted Jack was making little progress with Emmet Ant and asked the analyst, "Did you have a chance to learn anything about Emmet Ant? He's facing state charges for drug possession. We thought he'd be cooperative, but he's not."

The pitch of young analyst's voice went up a half octave. "I'm glad you asked. He was a classmate of Ron's in high school and was arrested with Ron twice for disorderly conduct while being under the influence of drugs."

"Odd, they haven't seemed that close. Neither mentioned the other in interviews. It also means this will be his third arrest for drug use. So, he should be cooperative."

"Hmm. I might have the reason. Did you know old texts are seldom lost if you have the right software?"

"And the FBI has the software?"

"Yes. Emmet texted Camelot Fair Enterprise's headquarters in Nipton, California daily and left short messages, like 'Adderall today,' 'Viv ran out of Adderall. Ron substituted Speed,' and finally on Friday 'Bought Ecstasy.' I checked the blood analyses done on Ron after he was stabbed. There was Ecstasy in his blood."

"So, Emmet was reporting Ron's drug use to someone in Camelot Fair Enterprises. Any idea who got the texts?"

"No, the texts went to a burner phone. No evidence the user of the burner phone ever responded to anyone."

***

Sarah emailed Jack and then strode to the dinette table. "Emmet, you really are a rat. Several have told us you spied for Ron, but I've just learned you were also spying on Ron."

She leaned closer to his face. "Who paid you to report on Ron's drug use?"

Emmet lost his smug grin. "What are you talking about?"

"We have your phone records." She sat down next to him. "You might as well admit who you texted daily in the Nipton area."

"It's not illegal."

"Mmm. I don't know. How do I know you weren't procuring drugs for Ron? That could get you a year in jail."

Emmet shook slightly. "It's not worth covering for Ron. Damn fool. I was reporting to his grandfather."

"How did you know what Ron used?"

Emmet snorted. "Ron visited Viv's truck like clockwork. It was easy."

"Why? Weren't you Ron's best friend in high school?"

Emmet snorted again. "No one could be Ron's friend. He chewed us up and spit us out. I would have never been arrested if he hadn't made a scene." He shook his head. "Both times."

"Then why did you take a job with this troupe?"

"Paid well."

"Doesn't a clerk at a food stand get paid a minimum wage?"

"Yeah."

"Then why?"

"Ron's grandfather puts a hundred dollars in my account every time I send him a report. I sent reports at least five times a week."

"Why did Ron's grandfather hire you to spy on Ron?"

"The old man isn't as crazy as everyone thinks." He looked at the table. "When he hired me, he talked—more like muttered—a lot. Said he was like Ron before he met a good woman."

"Do you know who the woman was?"

"Yeah, he had an old picture of Portia on his phone."

Checks with what Carolyn said. She straightened. "What about your own drug use? The courts aren't kind to someone facing a third arrest. We might be able to help if you cooperate. Someone saw you on Saturday buying something from locals. We'd like to know more."

CHAPTER 26: Follow the Money

Carbonne sounded almost joyful. "Agents found the money. It was around the vault for William Levant. It was in four handmade totes. One with a Christmas print, one with blue stripes, two with a gray print."

"So, Ron and Elu gave us accurate information. Any usable prints or DNA?" Sara put her phone on speaker mode so Winslow who was driving them back to Albuquerque could hear.

"The lab did a quick check of prints on the paper wrappers around a few stacks of bills. Only Art's prints were found. The lab chief said Winslow would check the rest of the money and would have to use slower techniques to lift prints from the fabric totes."

"Well, Art's prints or DNA on the fabric would tend to substantiate Willie's story that Art transferred the cash from the security bags to the totes while Willie was driving the get-away car. But I don't think Crystal's prints or DNA—which I assume will be found—would be useful because she made the bags presumably without knowing their intended use." She turned to Winslow. "We'll want these data eventually, but they shouldn't be your highest priority."

She heard Carbonne's "Damn."

Sara focused on Carbonne, "I'm sorry I didn't say the obvious. Thanks for sending agents to retrieve the money. I was afraid friends of the robbers or others at the fair would retrieve it first."

"Agreed."

She didn't wait for Carbonne to say more. "Do you think Dave would be willing to bring Art to the FBI building.? Together Dave and I may be able to convince Art to tell us more about his collaborators. We've got him for the bank robbery and desecration of a corpse. We'll bluff and say the prosecutor will charge him with Portia's murder unless he cooperates."

Sara could hear background voices as Carbonne appeared to talk to others. The voice of the assistant prosecutor boomed, "I like your thinking. Is Ron Engel the most likely murderer?"

"Yes, but Jack and I got comments this morning suggesting Crystal Star—aka Hannah Merchant—and even Emmet Ant abetted the murder. Unless we can get something from Art, we don't have enough to hold Crystal or Emmet Ant."

The assistant prosecutor's voice was softer now. "I'll arrange for Art and his lawyer to be here in an hour. I thought you felt Crystal wouldn't leave New Mexico without Portia's property. So, I assumed we were in no rush to charge her."

"Yes, but that was before her stepfather, Bodet Harper, told me about her fights with her mother. I'm afraid the sequencing the inquiries in this case has been unfortunate. Agents in Arizona are supposed to check-out Portia's home in Tucson area tomorrow."

The assistant prosecutor chuckled. "No kidding. However, my boss was thrilled the cash from the bank robbery was retrieved in less than a week. He'll be helpful."

***

Two days in the detention center had changed Art Last. He had lost his swagger when he entered the conference room in the FBI building. Sara turned to Dave Roper who was with her in the observation room. "Had he lost some of his bravado when you saw him earlier this afternoon?"

"No, he was arrogant as hell and smirked as he whispered to his lawyer when I started talking to him. Then you called and I got to tell him we'd found the cash. He turned quiet, but he didn't start shaking until I bluffed and said we planned to charge him with Portia's murder. When I mentioned he might get a deal if he named his cohorts, he and his lawyer seemed eager to talk."

Sara turned to the assistant prosecutor. "I'll hear what you say in my earphone but may not be able to react quickly. Please be patient."

***

Sara and Dave entered the conference room. Sara outlined the facts and added a few embellishments. One of the embellishments was: "We'll be talking to Ron Engel tomorrow. I suspect he'll deny all knowledge of the robbery and murder but will talk about you." Sara figured she hadn't lied exactly. *She could talk to Ron, but he couldn't answer unless his medical condition improved.*

Art whispered to his lawyer. The lawyer nodded. "What can you offer us?"

Honesty will impress them, I hope. "I can't make a plea deal, but I think I can influence the prosecutor if you answer my questions honestly." She heard the young assistant prosecutor sigh through her earpiece of her headphone. "Let's start with an easy question. How did you decide which bank to rob?"

Art's shoulders seemed to relax. "Ron told me of his plan about ten days ago. Before we left Tempe."

"Did he tell you, Vano, and Willie together?"

"No. Ron spoke to each of us separately. My jobs were to pick up the guns in Tempe a week ago Saturday and to be in charge in the bank. Vano was assigned to plan a way to hide the stash." He paused. "Vano and Willie didn't even know which bank we would rob."

"That doesn't make sense. Vano selected the cemetery because it was near the bank."

Art stiffened. "At least that's what Ron told me. I'm sure Willie didn't know. Vano had to tell him where to drive."

"Okay. It's your word against Ron's. Do you have any proof Ron planned the robbery?"

Art whispered to his lawyer. His lawyer drew a crumpled sheet of paper encased in a plastic sheath from his brief case and handed it to Sara. "Your experts will recognize the handwriting as Ron's. I expect his DNA is on it."

"Ron and your lab crew weren't as smart as they thought. I asked Ron to write out the address of the bank for me back in Tempe. I told him I needed to check out the location ahead of time. He let me read it and then insisted I chew it and swallow it. I faked it." He snorted. "Even horses can fake swallowing a pill. I flattened and dried it out and stashed it in the kitchen in my recipe file. No one ever searched the file."

Sara frowned. *It wasn't like Winslow to not search something as obvious as a recipe file. The note was probably gone already on Thursday when Winslow first searched the kitchen.* "Are you sure one of your colleagues didn't remove the note?" She paused. "Like Emmet?"

Art snorted. "You're dumber than I thought if you think that. Why would Emmet give it to my lawyer when he could force Ron or his family to pay big for it?"

Good point. "We know you didn't sleep at the fair on Tuesday night, and you left the fair to do laundry either Wednesday night or Thursday morning. You could have given the message to someone then."

Art groaned and had a hushed conversation with his lawyer before he spoke. "He says you don't need to know where I stayed those two nights, but he received the note from my friend."

Sara decided not to argue the point, even though the assistant prosecutor was muttering the detail was needed. "Let's go onto the next topic. The women in the detention center who beat Elu had spider tattoos—like yours—on their arms. Elu claimed they wanted to know the code of the ring. They thought it would help their friends find the cash from the robbery. Did you send them?"

"Is that a trick question?" He frowned. "Elu was confused. I know where Vano and I buried the money in the cemetery. I didn't need any code. Stupid broad."

"Well, then it looks like your friends still at the fair were trying to steal the money."

"Yeah Emmet."

"How about Willie?"

Art chuckled. "The half-wit wouldn't even think to steal the money."

Now for the hard questions. "What happened on Wednesday night? We know Portia left the stables with Willie after treating a couple of the horses. We know Ron sent Crystal to the stables to get Portia."

The lawyer cleared his throat. "Tell her what you told me."

"Around midnight, Emmet Ant woke me and said, 'Ron wants to see you in the kitchen.'" Art hunched over the table more. "I figured Ron wanted to talk about the robbery." He wiped his eyes. "Damn, did I get a surprise. Portia was lying on the floor. Ron refused to answer my questions. All he said was, 'We got to get rid of the body. You're a butcher. Do your thing.' I just stared at him." Art wiped his eyes.

Sara touched his hand. "Okay, I understand that you were shocked. Did Emmet Ant enter the kitchen trailer?"

Sara heard the prosecutor say on her earphone. "Good."

"Not sure. I don't think so." He leaned back. "No, he ran away after I unlocked the kitchen door."

"Did he mention your meeting in the kitchen with Ron later?"

Art's eyebrows merged into a unibrow. "No. He seemed more jumpy than usual on Thursday and Friday. But everyone was on edge after the police arrived."

"Do you know how Portia died? Where did you see bruises or stab marks? Crystal and Ron must have said something."

"Portia was covered with blood. Came from the neck. Ron made me lift her onto the stainless-steel counter after Crystal removed a kitchen knife from her back. Ron pointed at another knife on the counter. It was bloody too. That's when he told me to do my thing and butcher her."

"Were these knives from King Art's kitchen?"

"Yeah, I recognized them. We get whole briskets and racks of beef and pork delivered the day before a fair begins. I use the knives to cut the meat into pieces which will fit in our pans for roasting."

"Did you argue with Ron?"

Art reddened. "You don't argue with a man who has already killed someone."

"What did you do?"

"I… I… I'd never cut up a human before. I started like we would in a meat processing plant." He glanced at Sara. "I quit that job because it was so bad. This was worse."

"What did you do with all the blood?"

For the first time, Art smiled. "That was easy. The stainless-steel counter and fancy flooring were designed to be hosed off after we cut up meat. Crystal hosed the area as I worked."

"Did Crystal help in any other ways?"

Art coughed. "She used the meat cleaver like a pro on Portia's hands. Then she and Ron packed the bags. That girl is tough… and crazy. I was almost glad when I was arrested. It got me away from Ron and Crystal."

This is the most disgusting murder I've investigated. Guess I must keep going. "The body parts were double bagged when they were found. Did the kitchen have a big supply of heavy-duty large bags?"

Art's brows knit into a unibrow again. "We buy cheap black garbage bags normally for the kitchen. Those were… gray. Come to think of it, they were heavier than what I get for the kitchen." He shook his head. "I don't know where they came from. Crystal held the bags open so I could put pieces inside. Then she put the bag inside another bag, and Ron carted the bags away."

"You said earlier Ron bagged and carted bags away. What's correct?"

Art's lawyer put his hand on Art's shoulder. "You're doing fine. She knows this is tough for you."

Art nodded. "Mainly Crystal packed the bags." He paused. "Ron avoided touching the body. He was busy carting stuff away." He shook his head. "I didn't know where he took the bags until the police questioned me."

"Dave, do you have more questions for Art?"

Dave studied Art. "No, I'll wait until you're through with your easy questions."

Sara turned back to Art. "Maybe you can explain some odd comments made by others. What were you doing in the men's dorm when Portia's body was found? Who was with you?"

"Ron and I were cleaning up."

"No, I think by then you had left the fair and done your laundry."

Art hunched forward. "Let me think. It was around two when we finished in the kitchen. Crystal had the crazy idea we needed an excuse for being in the kitchen. She insisted I prepare a brisket and a rack of pork ribs for roasting. Then I peeled off my jacket and went to the men's dorm for clean clothes."

"Weren't Crystal's and Ron's clothes bloody, too?"

He stared at Sara. "I guess. Not as bad as mine. Anyway, when I got back to the kitchen, they were gone."

"What do you mean?"

"There was pile of dark jackets, a half-empty bottle of bleach, and a container of laundry soap on the counter. He paused. "There was also a bottle of something Crystal had used to remove blood from her clothes."

Holes all over his comments. He didn't notice blood on Crystal but knew she was cleaning the blood from her clothing with an unknown substance.

"What did you do?"

"Took the car keys on the counter and went off and did laundry at a friend's house."

I thought Ron didn't have a car. He borrowed Carolyn's keys on Friday. "Whose car?"

"Don't know. A rental. It was parked by the kitchen trailer."

"Let's get back to my earlier question. Earl tried to enter the dorm after the stablemen found the bank bags. He said he couldn't enter but the door wasn't locked."

"We wedged the door shut and ignored him because Ron and I were stashing our washed clothes. Then we saw bloody footprints on the floor and used the liquid Crystal left on the counter."

"Was it hydrogen peroxide?"

Art rolled his eyes. "How would I know? It fizzed a bit and formed a white foam when it hit blood."

Probably hydrogen peroxide. "What did you and Ron talk about?"

"He was silent until the end. Then he said, 'If you tell anyone, Crystal and I will say you stabbed Portia and forced us to help you in the cleanup. Everyone will believe us because Portia was murdered with your knives in your kitchen. And there are two of us.'" Art sighed. "I figured he was right."

Sara went to the observation room to confer with the assistant prosecutor while Dave questioned Art for the next hour. Dave slapped the cane against the legs of the table whenever he doubted Art's answers. The technique was effective in making Art nervous and eventually elicited an important detail.

Art remembered stepping in some hot ashes near the back door of the kitchen around five—shortly after he returned from doing laundry. Evidently, he hadn't wanted to enter the dorm until the others had left for work. Thus, Art had worked in the kitchen prepping a barbecue sauce for at least ten minutes before Ron claimed two dark hoodies that Art had laundered and the car keys. Art thought the ashes were gone when he left the kitchen thirty minutes later.

CHAPTER 27: Jack Learns What Matters

"What do you mean you won't allow me to take my property to Texas?" Crystal stood with her arms akimbo and glared at Jack.

Jack was glad that another agent was present as he explained Portia's property didn't belong to Crystal or Willie until Portia's will was probated, and it would take a while because she was murdered. Moreover, Willie had admitted to abetting a robbery and couldn't leave the state.

"Fine. I'll hitch a ride and help run Viv's booth."

"No, Viv's booth can't move on either because of the drug trafficking charges against her."

Crystal stamped her foot. "Okay, I'll work in King Art's. Emmet says they need new servers."

"No, I'm afraid you've got a lot of questions to answer before you move on. I'm taking you to the FBI building in Albuquerque. You and Willie can stay in Portia's camper and truck for at least tonight while they're impounded there."

"I won't go." She began to walk away.

"I can detain you for questions concerning your involvement in the murder of your mother, Portia Merchant. I have a material witness warrant."

"What's that?"

Don't want to name Art and Bodet or admit Ron is still unable to speak. "A judge is convinced on the basis of what we learned from others that you may have participated in hiding Portia's murder."

Her eyes widened. "They're lying. I'll get even with them."

As Jack recited her legal rights, Crystal turned slowly. She sprinted toward the gate.

The other agent ran faster.

***

Roybal and four Santa Fe police officers showed up at seven. "Sara thought you needed help transporting the confiscated vehicles and suspects to Albuquerque. The Mayor of Santa Fe felt we owed the FBI for your help during this investigation."

Jack wiped a tear from his right eye. Sara and Roybal had turned this impossible mess into an unpleasant, but doable, assignment.

Jack suggested two Santa Fe officers immediately leave with Viv's two vehicles. Viv's sole remaining employee—Tony Marin—had already closed Viv's booth and loaded her truck and camper. Tony had found employment with another vendor and was ready to move on to Texas on Tuesday. He had also supplied his contact information to Jack without being asked.

His final comment to Jack was: "I already knew in Tempe I had made a mistake in signing up to work for Viv, but I was desperate for work. Maybe, I can do you a favor. I forgot a detail until I heard you ask Crystal about a bonfire behind the kitchen on Thursday morning." He'd swallowed hard. "For what it's worth, I saw flames behind the kitchen when I went for a walk around five on Thursday morning. I hadn't thought about it until I heard Crystal screaming there was no fire."

Bet he'll have to testify at Portia's murder trial. Crystal will never take a plea. But that's a long way off.

Now Jack had to get Crystal and Willie to Albuquerque. The two FBI agents on site felt they couldn't handle two arguing suspects—Crystal and Willie—in their car without hand cuffing them. No one thought it was a good idea.

So, one agent departed with Crystal in the back seat of an FBI car. Jack emailed Sara to find housing for Crystal that was not near the housing of other suspects.

He asked two of the Santa Fe officers to drive Portia's truck and camper back to Albuquerque after Willie completed dismantling Portia's booth. The scene was sad.

Willie blew a kiss at the departing vehicles. "I thought I finally was going to be able to take care of my sister." There were tears in his eyes as he said, "I don't think I can survive in the detention center."

Neither do Sara and I. Jack knew Sara wanted to get a plea deal for Willie and get his punishment reduced to only probation. *And she usually gets what she wants.* "You won't be in the detention center tonight. Sara has already arranged for a psychologist and a lawyer to talk to you tomorrow. They'll help you decide what to do."

Jack turned to Roybal. "How would you like drive one of your Santa Fe police cars to Albuquerque so you can bring your fellow officers back to Santa Fe?"

"Thought you weren't going to invite me to the party." Roybal snickered.

Jack turned to the remaining FBI. "We can leave as soon as I finish discussions with two witnesses. Please watch Willie."

***

"You again. I thought I answered all your questions."

Jack looked around the almost empty men's trailer, glanced at Emmet Ant, and turned on his recorder. "We gained new information. I'd like to check it with your memories. You said you took a short walk around five and then went back to bed on Thursday morning."

"I told you I saw people in hoodies but don't remember any details."

"Think hard. Did you notice anything unusual about the kitchen trailer for King Art's?"

"Like what?"

"Lights on, aromas, noises?"

"No." Emmet's voice took on a whining tone. "I know, I should call you if I remember anything. You left that message already."

Jack stood. "Art had a lot to say. I'm trying to confirm his story."

"Art was all right by me. I don't want to hurt him." Emmet paused. "He came back to the dorm around two and pulled out his tote. That's what woke me. I took a walk after he left. Saw him go to the kitchen. Its lights were still on."

"I thought you said you took a walk around five."

"I did. I didn't mention the earlier one because I didn't want to snitch on Art. Your question about aromas made me think. There was the smell of smoke coming from the kitchen. I figured Art burned the meat. He sometimes cooked at night." He rubbed his head. "Don't see how that would happen in an oven set on low."

"Did it smell like burned meat?"

"No."

That ties in with What Sara learned from Art. "Thank you for your help. Don't forget your arraignment for drug possession first thing tomorrow morning at the Santa Fe courthouse."

***

Jack knocked on the door to the women's camper. "Carolyn, it's Jack Drum."

He could feel the camper sway with movement before Carolyn opened the door. Her blonde hair fell loosely to her shoulders. There were no traces of makeup on her eyelids or lips. She looked the best he'd ever seen her.

J. L. Greger

"The last of the FBI agents and Santa Fe police will be leaving soon. I wanted to check to be sure you hadn't spotted anything unexpected as you closed the fair tonight." He handed her his card. "Please inform…"

Carolyn touched his arm. "Jack, thank you. I know you could have closed the fair and hauled many of us off to Albuquerque to be questioned. I also know I'll probably end up testifying in court here if Ron survives." She bit her lip. "If I were practical, I'd hope he didn't. It would be better for the company and easier for my family." She smiled slightly as she looked at Jack. "But I do hope he survives because I'd like to see you again."

Jack wanted to put his arms around her. Instead, he coughed. "I wish we could have met in a different way. Camelot Fair Enterprises hasn't brought out the best in anyone. Art had a lot to say today. I'm afraid your family will be getting more bad news." He swallowed hard. "The good news is you are apt to have to return to Albuquerque to appear in court." He turned away quickly before he did something foolish, like kiss her.

***

Willie's face crinkled into a smile when Jack slid into the back seat with him.

It's pathetic. I feel like I'm slaughtering an innocent lamb. Jack turned on a light and began to ask Willie questions as the other FBI agent drove the car from the fairgrounds. After listening to Willie's first answer, Jack knew why Sara had warned him not to "lead Willie." Willie had said as he answered the first question, "Is that what Sara wanted me to say? She reminds me of Portia."

So, Jack didn't use his usual interview style and asked an open-ended question. "Do you remember when you and Portia left the stables on Wednesday night?"

Willie nodded. "Crystal told me to go away because she wanted to talk to Portia." He smiled. "Portia said she needed to talk to me first. It made me feel important."

It took Willie at least five minutes to tell Jack what he already knew. After Portia had spotted the bank delivery bags in the hay, she had told Willie to not worry. She'd talk to Ron and Vano. Then she left Willie in the camper.

Jack noted Willie's comments were consistent with his earlier admissions, except he hadn't mentioned Crystal the last time. As Willie looked at him with the dilated pupils of a pathetic dog, Jack asked another open-ended question. "What did you do?"

"I waited a couple of minutes and went to King Art's."

"Why?"

"That's where Crystal said Ron was waiting."

"Did you see anyone go into the kitchen?"

"No, but the lights were on. There was a music playing."

New info. The music would have hidden any other noises.

Willie listed two songs that he heard and then indicated he was tired and went to bed in Portia's camper as usual. He indicated he awoke later when someone opened the door to the camper. He didn't know the time. All he remembered was Crystal was rummaging in the closet under the sink in the camper's tiny kitchen. "She told me to go back to bed." Willie shrugged. "I did."

"Did you see, smell, or hear anything else?"

"Not until my alarm rang at five. I took a shower and went out. I always leave the camper before Portia gets up. Thursday was like every other day. Lots of people from other booths get up early. Most don't want to talk. I went by King Art's. Crystal was scooping up some gray stuff by the back door. I asked her what she was doing. She was still grouchy with me and told me to go away."

Willie continued to enumerate what he saw and heard that morning. None of it seemed important to Jack, except it reinforced his notion that Willie was naïve.

Gray stuff could be ashes. "Why didn't you tell me earlier that you saw Crystal cleaning up by the kitchen?"

Willie stared at Jack. "Because Crystal told me not to snitch on her." Willie must have thought Jack didn't understand and added, "Portia always said families stick together. Portia, Crystal, and me are family. I don't want to get Crystal in trouble." He looked down. "I didn't, did I?"

CHAPTER 28: Carbonne Cuts a Deal

Monday

"Two of my agents busted their asses to search Portia Merchant's house this morning. The two resident agents in Tucson are on sick leave, and these two agents based in Phoenix had to drive to Tucson. Now they can't reach the agents requesting the search: Jack Drum and Sara Almquist. It's ten-thirty. Where are they?"

Carbonne sighed. He had to maintain a good working relationship with other SACs, especially the one in Phoenix. "Sara and Jack were handling unwilling witnesses and suspects until midnight last night. A suspect finally regained consciousness this morning. They're at the hospital getting his statement. Sorry they didn't get back to you yet, but we're short-handed, especially since our resident agent in Santa Fe is still in a coma because of his injuries on this case."

"Heard about that. We're all rooting for Hank. He may be the agent with the longest service in the Southwest. Sara told my agents about the medieval fair in Santa Fe. It sounded like an accident waiting to happen. We're thankful it didn't blow up in Tempe. I called because my agents were worried about Jack and Sara's safety after they uncovered the data on Portia Merchant, Hannah Merchant aka Crystal Star, Bodet Harper, and Willie Shakes at the Merchant homestead. It looked to them like a messed-up family with several having severe personality disorders."

"I didn't follow the case closely until yesterday when it cycled out of control. However, I doubt either Sara or Jack will be surprised by what your agents found. One agent on the case called the fair 'a loony convention.'"

"Doesn't sound like Sara or Jack."

"No, Dave Roper made the comment."

"So, he finally beat the bottle. Are you sure about him?"

Carbonne didn't want to answer the question. "Sara felt this fair was the 'unfortunate combination of people with no options because of poverty, stereotyping, and personality disorders'." He coughed. "In other words, she agreed with Dave."

"She should read my agents' report carefully as soon as she checks in. Seems Crystal and Bodet have attempted to kill each other more than once. And Willie isn't as gentle as he may seem at first."

***

The man in charge of the evidence room sailed past Carbonne's secretary and plunked down at the table in Carbonne's office "I try to be patient with agents. But Jack went too far. I want Willie Shakes out of that camper immediately. We never allow anyone to live in a vehicle in the impoundment lot. Do you know what he's done?"

No, but I'm going to. Carbonne forced himself not to smile or laugh. "Please tell me."

"He is hawking trinkets from the medieval fair to everyone trying to use the back entrances to the building." The man squirmed in his seat. "Sad. He's calling it his 'going out of business sale.' And is telling everyone about his dying sister and dead friend. And…"

"I get the picture. I think it would be best if Jack Drum solves this problem when he returns from the hospital."

The man laughed. "You don't want to argue with Willie. That's why he's selling so much. No one does. Ergo, they can't get into the building without buying something." The man stood. "At least, Sara did something useful. She put Crystal in protective custody in a safe house last night."

Which was a gutless action on her part.

***

The next person to ignore Carbonne's secretary and barge into his office was Dave Roper. He lowered himself carefully onto a chair at Carbonne's small conference table. "I just finished interviewing Crystal Star. I interviewed Art yesterday and thought his story was logical." He shook his cane at Carbonne. "The only thing consistent between Crystal's story and Art's story is they both agree Portia is dead."

Carbonne had reams of paperwork to do. He didn't want to hear the details of this case. "Sara should be back soon from the hospital soon with another rendition of the story from another prime suspect."

"That's what I wanted to talk to you about. All the prime suspects in this case belong in prison for as long as possible. They'd all do it again. Sara and Jack will worry about justice. Why bother? The three prime suspects are all killers at heart. We can nail each of them with one major crime. Ron for attempting to murder Tallulah. Art for armed robbery. Crystal for abetting Portia's murder. And all for abuse of a corpse. Why

J. L. Greger

waste time deciding which one cut Portia's throat? We all know the assistant prosecutor doesn't have the guts to try anyone for murder one."

Carbonne ignored the last comment. "The case against Crystal isn't clear, yet."

"True, and she's the meanest one. Art and Ron will name her as the instigator of Portia's murder."

"So, you've talked to Sara about Ron's statement?"

"No. You missed the point. Crystal is psychotic and in an ideal world belongs in a mental institution permanently. But she's smart and pretty enough to get released by a hopeful psychologist. Prison is where she belongs in the real world."

"We aren't judges or executioners. You know our job is to seek justice"

Dave pounded his cane on the floor. "I was afraid you'd hold the line. Crystal will be hard... very hard to convict. She's perfected her little girl act and can outsmart any jury or judge. Why do you think Sara put her in the safe house? She knows Crystal is guilty but couldn't build a case and knew Crystal would flee if she didn't restrain her." He stood. "Well, I've given you my best advice. Now Sara, Jack, and I are in the middle of a hopeless battle."

As Dave walked to the door, Carbonne said, "Would you like to talk to a psychologist about work exhaustion?"

"Nope. Nothing wrong with me, except I'm a realist."

"So are Sara and Jack. I have confidence in the three of you." *And I'd like a drink now.* He emailed Sara and Jack.

Read report from Arizona FBI. The SAC says it's a bombshell.

Willie must be out of the lot by four today.

You've got to come up with charges against Crystal or release her today.

Don't let Roper encourage you to make deals too quickly.

He knew he should offer to listen to their theories but didn't have the guts to do it. He hoped that the next person who called or entered his office wasn't involved in one of the cases related to the medieval fair.

***

Carbonne knew it was bad news when the assistant special agent in charge (ASAC) of the Albuquerque district of the DEA started his call with, "Do I have a deal for you." The gist of the ASAC's message was simple. The DEA wanted to unload the case against Viv Lorenzo onto the FBI.

"I'm happy to let you get credit for prosecuting Viv Lorenzo for drug trafficking." As he listened to the ASAC, Carbonne read a summary on Viv Lorenzo that Sara had cc'd him on Sunday around noon:

> *There is no obvious reason why Viv received a call from the phone found in the men's dorm. The fingerprints on the phone were those of Emmet Ant and Ron Engel. When the phone was used on Friday night around ten to call Viv, Ron was in the hospital and unconscious. Thus, the most* likely *caller was Emmet Ant.*
>
> *The analysts just got the recording of the call from the detention center. The caller was a male and identified himself as Ron Engel. He said, "Do you know the ring code? I misplaced it. See if Elu knows the area code." Viv said, "Okay." Nothing more.*
>
> *Analysts have found Viv Lorenzo has a long history of non-violent crimes: prostitution, drug possession, and shop lifting. Her ex-husband is in prison for repeated arrests for major drug trafficking.*
>
> *There is no evidence that Viv is a member of any gang or has spent more than six months in jail. However, she should be checked for spider tattoos. The women who beat Elu had spider tattoos.*
>
> *Emmet Ant also has a history: repeated drug possession and shoplifting. However, Emmet was held in a Maricopa (Arizona) County jail with Viv's ex last year.*

Good old Sara, she always comes through with useful details when needed. He noted the email had been sent to a DEA agent as well as Jack and Dave. He bluffed anyway. "I'm sending you the info we have on Viv."

His hopes of ditching the case against Viv faded when the ASAC admitted he already had an email from Sara Almquist. "We acted on it and found one small spider tattoo on Viv's arm. When DEA agents questioned her this morning, she admitted that Emmet Ant had called her and asked her about a telephone area code for a friend. We knew it wasn't

                    J. L. Greger

true. She finally admitted the code was an engraving on a ring. It sounds to me as if you have more charges against her than we do."

Carbonne wasn't willing to give up. "What are you charging her for?"

"Possession and repeated sales of small quantities of controlled substances. A judge will give five to six years."

Then the real negotiations began. DEA agents would offer Viv Lorenzo a plea deal of five years in a low security prison for drug sales and would not charge her with soliciting for a violent crime (i.e. arranging for women to attack Elu while in detention) or conspiracy to commit a crime (i.e. helping Emmet obtain the hidden money from the bank robbery and grave robbery) if she agreed to testify in court against Emmet Ant.

Of course, the DEA offer didn't preclude the Santa Fe police or FBI from arresting Viv for the non-drug related crimes. Moreover, if Viv accepted the plea deal, she would be incarcerated. Carbonne and the ASAC agreed that Viv would "disappear" if she was allowed to leave her arraignment today on the DEA charges without a signed plea deal.

Carbonne thought of his warning to Sara and Jack not to settle for quick deals. *Jack is polite enough not to mention it.* He smiled. *Sara won't complain much because he'd given her the gift of time. Now there was no need to rush to have the non-drug charges against Viv clarified immediately.*

CHAPTER 29: Partial Truth?

Ron looked terrible. He was pale, his eyelids drooped, and his face was puffy. Doctors reported that the infection resulting from the leakage from his partially severed large intestine was now under control. However, nurses reported he had to be sedated last night because he kept screaming "No." Even so, a doctor assured Sara that Ron could understand her questions. He was in serious but not critical condition.

Sara decided this was not the time for honesty. It was time to be motherly. "Ron, you gave us quite a scare. Are you feeling better today?"

Ron didn't respond.

Sara looked at his tray. It was the typical array offered on a liquid diet: soup, water, a popsicle. "Would you like a sip of chicken broth or just water?"

Ron turned his head away from Sara.

"The nurses say you'll be allowed sherbet later today."

Ron moaned. "Doesn't matter. I'll die in prison. Go away."

Time to act like a strict mother. "It doesn't work that way. You must listen as Jack reads you your rights and must answer a few basic questions."

He pressed his call button "You sound like my f****** mother." When the nurse appeared, he said, "I want to sit up."

The nurse pursed her lips. "We've explained the buttons to you several times." She lectured him on the function of each button on his hand control and left after he was in a sitting position.

Ron pointed to his tray. "Broth."

Sara held the cup as Ron positioned the straw in his mouth. He sucked, yelled "Yuk," and spit the broth toward Sara.

Sara smiled because she knew it would annoy Ron. "Life is what you make it whether in prison or in a resort. If you fight with everyone, you will make your life hell." She nodded to Jack who read Ron his rights.

As soon as Jack finished, Sara said, "Do you want to talk first about what happened on Friday when you were stabbed? Or would you rather talk first about what happened Wednesday night when Portia was killed?"

"What a choice." Ron held up his middle finger. "I want to be sure that bitch Elu pays. She stabbed me 'cause the chicken Vano didn't tell her he was married." He spat out a series of expletives. "Hope they both rot in prison."

I could admit Vano was dead. A scare might be good for Ron. Or maybe, he'll be more honest if he thinks Vano can testify against him. "Why are you angry with Vano? Did he refuse to tell you where he and Art hid the money from the bank robbery? We know you were the smart one who planned the robbery."

Ron's eyes widened, but he said nothing.

"You took a big risk when you cozied up to the assistant bank manager. She remembered your slender build and red hair. And she was thrilled when you called last week."

"You're lying. The stupid cow couldn't describe me."

Jack coughed. "You should never toy with an ugly woman. They remember when a man gives them attention. She was really upset when you didn't meet her for lunch last Tuesday and explained how you tricked her into talking about the bank."

"Guess so. It only laid her once a year ago." His eyelids and the corners of his mouth sagged again. "Maybe I told Art and Vano about a sweet situation at a bank, but I didn't participate. It was Art and Vano who stole the money. Have you arrested them?"

He's admitted to conspiring to commit a robbery. "Yes. But you expected they'd share the take, didn't you?"

"Nothing wrong with gratitude."

Not as much as I wanted, but he hasn't asked for a lawyer either. "What I don't understand is why Portia picked an argument with you, not Art and Vano, on Wednesday night?"

"Crazy broad. Came screaming at me 'cause Weird Willie was crying."

Got to get him talking about Crystal. "Oh, I thought she was arguing with Crystal, and you were trying to help Crystal."

Jack coughed.

"Jack, are your allergies acting up? That's too bad because Ron is going to tell us why Crystal was arguing with Portia." She flashed a broad smile at Ron and offered him a sip of water.

Ron waved his hand. "Portia was bossy. Always prying into everything Crystal did."

"Was there a reason why Portia didn't trust Crystal?"

Ron uttered a string of curses. "Mothers think they have the right to control their kids." He rubbed his eyes. "Crystal said it was worse when Bodet was around."

Jack had been studying his phone. He stopped. "Did Crystal say when Bodet moved in with Portia?"

Sara thought this aside was unnecessary, but trusted Jack had spotted something in one of his messages. *Wonder what?*

Ron blinked. "Who cares? I think Bodet moved in eleven to twelve years ago—not long after Portia's second husband left." He blinked again. "Crystal said he was fun."

Jack leaned forward. "Did Crystal ever tell you the name of Portia's second husband?"

Sara was pleased Jack was exploring that puzzle. She'd been unable to find any records of Portia marrying anyone besides Herbert Engel and Bodet Harper.

"Does it matter?"

"Guess not. Did Crystal ever mention her dad—I think he's your grandfather? Crystal would have been around five or six when he left Arizona."

"No." He closed his eyes and rubbed his forehead. After thirty seconds, he muttered, "Why?"

Jack asked several more questions but couldn't get Ron to explain the muttered "Why."

Sara hoped Ron would be more forthcoming if she changed topic. "Let's get back to last Wednesday night. We know Crystal went to the stables and told Portia you wanted to talk to her. What happened when Portia came to King Art's?"

"Nothing unusual. Willie was whining. Portia and Crystal were arguing."

First time anyone mentioned Willie was in the kitchen. Sara leaned toward Ron. "We know Portia was killed sometime between then and midnight. What did you see?"

Ron flashed the grin of a Cheshire cat.

I'll wipe the smirk off his face. "We've talked to everyone else. This may be your last chance to tell your side of the story. Don't throw away this opportunity."

Ron yawned. "So, it's my word against Crystal's?"

Maybe this will force him to be honest. "We also have statements from Art, Willie, and Emmet."

"Willie and Emmet weren't in the kitchen."

That confirms Willie's and Emmet's comments but contradicts his comment that Willie was whining. "They might have heard more than you think."

"Nah. Like I'm sure Crystal told you, Art stabbed Portia with one of his kitchen knives when she accused him of making Willie help in the robbery." Ron grinned again.

"But Art didn't recruit Willie."

Ron backtracked a bit. "I forgot. Vano did."

Another mistake. "Perhaps, but you recruited Vano to help Art rob the bank. And Vano did as you told him." *Now for a little bluff.* "Vano must have been scared you'd tell his wife about Elu."

Ron closed his eyes. "Are you trying to confuse me?"

"No, I'm trying to learn the truth. Did you see Art stab Portia? He claims Emmet woke him up around midnight and sent him to the kitchen. Portia was already dead."

"He's lying."

"Doubt it. Emmet admitted going with Art to the kitchen around then."

Ron's lips quivered. "You're confusing me."

"The truth isn't confusing."

After a long pause, "I… I was trying to protect Crystal. She stabbed Portia. I just watched."

"That's all? Didn't you help clean up the mess?"

"I never touched Portia, but her blood was everywhere. Art and Crystal did all the dirty work."

At least we have agreement on the work distribution at the end. And all three can be charged with abuse of a corpse and abetting murder.

CHAPTER 30: Is the Past Important?

Jack took Sara's arm and guided her out of the ICU. "Dave has been busy this morning. After he talked to Crystal, he transferred her to the psych unit. I'll drive us to the Behavioral Health Crisis Unit while you scan the report from the agents in Tucson and his comments."

"Wow. Yesterday I tried to get her into that unit, but the FBI psychologist didn't think she needed in-house care. Dave is amazing."

"You didn't have the report from Tucson."

As Jack drove, Sara read the initial report from the two FBI agents who searched Portia's homestead near Tucson.

> *We searched the home of Anne Portia Merchant Engel Harper with a search warrant. The warrant also allowed us to investigate the property of her daughter Hannah Merchant aka Crystal Star.*
>
> *Before we entered the property, we determined the sixty-acre property had been purchased by Herbert Engel within weeks of his marriage to Anne Portia Merchant twenty years ago. The deed to the property was changed to indicate the property was owned solely by Portia Merchant Engel shortly before their divorce twelve years ago. At the time, Herbert Engel created a trust of $250,000 for Hannah Merchant. Portia Merchant Engel is the trustee until Hannah is twenty-one. Then all remaining funds revert to Hannah Merchant. The trust stipulated funds could be used only for the education and medical needs of Hannah Merchant.*
>
> *The homestead consists of a home (about 2,000 sq. ft.) where Portia and Hannah Merchant lived, a home (about 2,000 sq. ft.) where John Shakes and his son Willie live, a barn for sheep, and a dairy facility (about 2,500 sq. ft. with cold room and equipment) for processing milk into cheeses, and a workshop (about 1,500 sq. ft.) with a shop and office.*

John Shakes appears to run the dairy and care for the homestead when Portia Merchant is away.

John said his son Willie was a "disappointment" and didn't seem to know anything about his daughter who had left home about ten years ago and has never written or called him.

Sara noted the agents thoroughly assessed the property. Their documents indicated the dairy met state health standards, sold its artisan cheeses throughout southern Arizona, and employed several teens part-time. A large herb garden separated Portia's home from the workshop. It included a workroom for making herbal products and storage facilities. The front of the workshop was a modern business office and sales room. John claimed a woman from town "handled the bills and managed the store."

Sara read the next section of their report with more interest

The house was neat, except for Crystal's bedroom. Crystal's room was cluttered with junk on fairies and multiple sets of wings made from coat hangers and fabric.

A pink notebook and letters in a lavender portfolio were found under the mattress in Crystal's room. Two letters were from Ron. He offered her sympathy for being forced to go to school. Two others were from a boy, evidently from school, who mentioned how much fun they'd had together. All were dated in the last year.

Sara skimmed the letters. *Nothing incriminating.* Crystal probably hid them because Portia disapproved of Crystal's friends.

Finally, Sara reached the part of the report on Portia's documents and correspondence. The agents found copies of two marriage certificates and one divorce decree in a wall safe in her bedroom. They found only one note from Herbert Engel dated in February of the current year. All it said was:

They found several letters from Bodet to Portia. They reaffirmed
Bodet's statements to the Santa Fe police. He was fond of Portia but
disagreed with her on how Crystal (sometimes called Hannah) should be
handled. In essence, Bodet thought she was dangerous. Portia thought
she was a "difficult" teenager who did well in school.

The agents highlighted comments from a letter sent by the head
mistress of Green Pastures School to Portia the previous year in
December:

                                                                    J. L. Greger

Sara looked up from her laptop.

Jack had parked the car and was staring at her. "You know, it's possible that Ron told the truth at the end." Jack studied his phone. "Dave had no problem convincing a psychiatrist at University Hospital this morning to admit Crystal for a ten-day observation period after he showed her this report."

"I bet Herbert Engel and Bodet Harper know something about the traumatic incidents."

"Bodet can only give second-hand info. The important initiating incidents probably occurred before Bodet married Portia."

"Yes, but Bodet has nothing to hide. Herbert's divorce settlement with Portia seems unusually generous, and he retained no visitation rights with Crystal. He had something to hide."

"Are you suggesting Herbert Engel molested his own daughter?"

"Maybe. Or he could have been physically and emotionally violent with Portia, and Crystal witnessed the violence. I bet Carolyn knows more than she admitted. It's likely Herbert Engel displayed similar violence with Carolyn or her mother, too." She paused. "Of course, the limited info we got from the agents in Arizona suggests Willie's father, John, is not an ideal parent either." She sighed. "It's clear Crystal has serious chronic mental problems. Risperidone is given to those suspected of schizophrenia or bipolar disorders."

Jack looked at his watch. "Dave has reserved a conference room for us inside. We'd better hurry."

***

Dave was tapping his cane on the floor when Sara and Jack entered the conference room. "I've got a name for this case—revenge of the mean girls."

Jack stared at him. "What are you talking about? Everyone agrees that Portia was a kind woman."

Dave tapped harder. "And everyone agrees that both Elu and Crystal were brats or worse."

Sara sat down at the table and pulled a diet cola from her tote. "You're drawing sweeping conclusions from limited evidence." She savored her cola. "But you may be right. Let's start with the simpler young woman—Elu."

Jack glared at Sara. "We don't know if Elu is retarded."

"I didn't say that, but she's not as bright as Crystal. Her motives also seem more obvious. So, she's a simpler case."

Jack nodded. "Sorry. I guess this case is making me nervous."

Sara winked at Jack. "Don't give up on Carolyn, yet."

Dave coughed. "She's saying meanness isn't hereditary. Besides Carolyn is only Crystal's niece."

Jack busied himself in the notes on his phone.

She pointed to Dave. "No wise cracks. Let's get down to business. You said you had talked to the psychologist who spoke with Elu."

Dave leaned his cane against the table and pulled his phone. "Talk about a mean task master." He didn't pause. "The psychologist says Elu has seen a lot of violence in her short life. She claimed she witnessed two murders of relatives due to drunken brawls. He thought it might explain her behavior."

"Not surprising. Violence due to alcoholism is common on many of the pueblos."

Dave studied his phone. "But the psychologist found no evidence of parental abuse." He looked up. "Tallulah probably explained the situation right. Elu is just a spoiled princess. But like a typical psychologist, the doc said it was too early to give a definite answer. Sounded to me like he will judge her mentally competent to stand trial for deadly assault of Ron but not for attempted murder. Then again, he might surprise us and say she was mentally unstable because her lover had just rejected her."

Sara stopped typing on her laptop and pointed to Dave. "You'd better check the facts with Tallulah and Taos Pueblo public safety officers."

Dave frowned. "I'm afraid. Elu will walk with only a short stay in a psych hospital. Too bad because she's got a nasty temper."

Sara sighed. "The public defender's office has arranged for a lawyer to speak to her this afternoon. I'd better warn the assistant prosecutor that his chance of winning this case is small."

Dave tapped his cane on the floor. "It shouldn't be. There's no question she tried to kill Ron Engel."

"Yes, but a jury will not find Ron a sympathetic victim. And Tallulah will be a convincing witness. And this assistant prosecutor is…"

"Afraid of his own shadow. We can't depend on him to win even simple cases in court. Can we push this case to the state courts?"

Sara nodded. "That might be best. She can be found guilty of an attempted murder but mentally incompetent in this state. In federal courts she'd be found innocent if she convinces a jury of her mental incompetence. So, in the state system, she'll get psychological help but won't be out in less than two years."

"Can you arrange it?"

Sara shrugged. "Our assistant prosecutor will agree to anything that saves him work. Officials in Santa Fe seem cooperative."

Jack rolled his eyes. "So, you're ignoring Carbonne's advice to not take short cuts."

Dave pounded his cane. "Now on to the real mean girl."

Sara checked a file. "I already emailed the FBI psychologist and asked him to give Crystal, Art, and Ron tests for intelligence and functional assertiveness."

Dave shook his head. "Don't need a test to know she outsmarted the two men."

"We don't know that. Since Portia's murder trial is likely to become a case of conflicting claims, I think we need to determine the dominant personality among the three—and hence the instigator of the murder." She sighed. "Besides, it may be a waste of time to build a case against Willie because he's mentally incompetent."

Jack looked back and forth between Sara and Dave. "The idea is for us to determine who did it. Not to plot court strategies."

Sara ignored Jack's comment. "I don't think we'll ever know whether Crystal or Ron killed Portia unless we can agitate them enough that they make mistakes and blurt out something."

"Agreed." Dave tapped his cane on the floor. "I think Jack should take the lead as the good cop. Crystal likes young men and dislikes motherly types. You shouldn't talk until I've riled. her Then be syrupy sweet. That will annoy the heck out of her."

***

The interview with Crystal was short. She demanded a lawyer as she walked into the conference room.

CHAPTER 31: Jack and the Roma

Jack whistled as he entered Sara's office. "The medical examiner's office called. Vano's family is eager to claim his body for burial. I'm hoping I can get evidence from them to prove Ron convinced Vano to participate in the bank robbery."

"I thought the family lived in California."

"They—at least five family members—are in Albuquerque now. Vano's brother called the ME's office Saturday and again yesterday. His sobbing wife appeared in the office today and asked to see the body."

Sara stopped scanning her laptop. "Are we sure the body won't be needed if the family tries to sue Santa Fe police or the FBI for Vano's death in the shootout to end the hostage situation?"

He sat down. "It's been judged to be a clean kill necessary to save the lives of Tallulah and Hank." He paused. "Lawsuits are always possible but Vano—if he were alive—would be charged with deadly assault on a law enforcement officer besides bank robbery. I'm hoping Vano's family might want revenge on Ron for ultimately causing Vano's death."

"Do you want my help?"

"Yes and no. Yes, I need help because I've got to interview all five family members. However, I'd rather not involve you because you were at the scene."

"Oh, I guess…" Her shoulders sagged.

Jack chuckled and put a hand on her shoulder. "The main reason I don't want you to do an interview is I want you as backup checking the files of the interviewees and looking for their weak points. None of the other agents can do that as well as you do." He handed her a page with names of Vano's family members. "The ME's secretary made them sign in and give their address and phone number when they requested to see the body." He started to leave and then stopped to pet Bug. "If you get a chance, see if there's anything we should know about the assistant bank manager at the bank that was robbed."

Sara nodded. "The good analyst was going to tag along with an agent today when he interviewed the assistant bank manager. I'm eager to hear what she has to say."

Jack snorted. "I know the real reason you're so interested in her. She reminds you of yourself when you were starting out at the FBI. If she's as good as you think, maybe we can force Ron to cop a plea for the bank robbery. Then, we'll have time to develop murder charges against him."

"Yes, and thanks to Roybal, we have the Santa Fe Police chief and Santa Fe County district attorney on board. They're willing to charge Ron in the state court system of attempting to murder Tallulah and Hank during the hostage situation last Friday."

"Are you saying my efforts today with Vano's family are unnecessary?"

Sara's eyebrows arched. "Quite the contrary. I want to get plea deals or convict Ron and Crystal of as many crimes as possible because I'm convinced that they are unfixable." She bowed her head. "I hate being negative, but all the data, which the analysts and I are finding, are consistent."

Sara checked her laptop. "The analysts noted there were several visitors to the grave of William Levant in the last two days. I'll send you the feed. They might include Vano's family."

***

Vano's wife was gorgeous with long, black hair and black eyes rimmed with long black eyelashes. She walked like a queen with perfect posture as she entered the conference room at the ME's office.

Doesn't prove Vano wouldn't divorce her, but Elu had stiff competition for Vano's affections. Jack offered his condolences and offered her a beverage. "We want your help in guaranteeing the man who convinced Vano to make poor choices—like bank robbery and kidnapping—is punished."

Jack thought he saw a fleeting smile on the woman's lips.

"Did Vano send you any letters, emails, or texts in which he mentioned Ron Engel or Art Last or for that matter Willie Shakes?"

The woman blinked.

"Perhaps he casually mentioned their names on the phone."

She took a sip of coffee. "Vano was not a talkative man. Although he often complained that his boss, Viv. She was cheap."

"Did he mention finding ways to earn more?"

She studied him. "He arranged for my son and me to join the caravan in June after school was out. He said Ron would pay me to read tarot cards and tell fortunes at the fair." She sipped more coffee.

She's cautious. "We already saw the contract. Didn't Ron also hire you to entertain on the center stage?"

She stiffened and her eyes narrowed. "He arranged for me to dance and sing traditional Roma songs while my son and Vano played the guitar and castanets."

She's annoyed. "We suspect Ron offered Vano other ways to earn money. You don't need to be hesitant to mention them because we can't pursue charges against Vano…" *It's tactless to add because he's dead.*

She lowered her eyelids and studied her hands.

The silver rings on most of her fingers reminded Jack of Vano's ring. "We found one of Vano's rings. It had an interesting inscription." He displayed the message on his phone: *O manusha khelevan tut.* "It roughly translates to 'the people here make you dance,' but we think it's a way of saying the location is nice."

She pulled her hands from the table.

Jack continued. "We assumed the phrase was the code he used for hiding things in a cemetery." He leaned forward. "And we found the money from the bank robbery buried next to the vault that held William Levant's casket at Vista Verde Memorial Park."

She didn't move a muscle.

"We've had the grave under surveillance and saw two men near it on Sunday afternoon and again that evening." He showed her pictures on his phone. "Don't you think the men look a lot like your brother-in-law and brother? They were carrying shovels the second time."

"They didn't do anything wrong."

"Disturbing a grave is illegal." He flashed more pictures. "But they did place the sod back in place when they didn't find anything. We might ignore this vandalism if you cooperate. Why did they dig around this grave?"

"I don't know."

"It's illegal to lie to an FBI agent. It's your choice whether we prosecute you and them. The sentence can be as long as ten years for disturbing a grave and five years for lying to agents." He studied her face. "Can your mother-in-law run your family's roofing business without your men and you for several years? Or will your son end up in the state's protective services?"

Her hand shook slightly.

"How did they know to look for this grave? What did Vano tell you or write you?"

Her hands stopped shaking. "He texted me last Tuesday night."

"That's all? Show me the text."

She hesitated but finally removed a phone from her purse, played with it, and then handed it to Jack. The text was:

He glanced at it. "I'd like our lab to check your phone's contents. You might as well tell me the whole story."

***

Jack found Dave and another agent smiling broadly. They had hit a brick wall when they attempted to question the other three adults in the Georgescu family. As soon as they played the recording of Vano's wife, the men became talkative. Even Vano's mother spoke when she heard Jack's comment on Vano's son.

The net result was by noon, Jack had signed statements from the four adults in the Georgescu family, and the FBI lab had pulled all data from their phones. Jack emailed Sara:

> *Thanks for the hints on the Georgescu family and the bank manager.*
>
> *Vano texted his wife at least two useful messages proving Ron's involvement in the robbery.*
>
> *The assistant prosecutor thinks these texts, the detailed statement from the assistant bank manager, and Art's testimony will be enough to convict Ron of participating in the bank robbery.*
>
> *Now we've got to assess his involvement in Portia's murder. When do you want to confront Ron?*

Jack was not surprised by Sara's response:

> *We don't want to make any mistakes by rushing. Before we confront Ron, I'd like to interview Elu and Tallulah one more time with Dave. Bring a photo of Vano's wife. It will crush Elu's spirit and make her talk.*
>
> *The psychologist and principal at Green Pastures School won't speak to me and show me school records until a judge issues a warrant. That should occur yet today.*

                                   J. L. Greger

He handed his phone to Dave. "Sara is in no hurry to talk to Ron because she's got a lead. The last paragraph says it all."

Dave thumped his cane. "You're saying Carbonne was right. He told me to 'cool it' when I doubted Sara's toughness."

"You've got to remember. Sara and Carbonne are almost family. He knows Sara is tougher than any of us if she thinks it's necessary." Jack gulped. "That applies to you, too. If you need a cane, she'll tell Carbonne you're not physically up to being an agent."

"No worry. She's already seen through my act and told me, 'not to trip on it.'"

CHAPTER 32: The Price of Tattling

Sara sat back in a recliner in the safe house and watched Dave show off as he seated Tallulah at a small table and sat in the chair across the table from her.

Dave pretended to look puzzled as he leaned forward. "Tallulah, your answers don't jive with what others have told us. At least six people have told us you knew everything going on at the fair in the early morning hours."

Tallulah shrugged. "I told you Viv paid me to watch her truck."

"Yeah, I know, but most say you also worked for Ron or someone else, too. Seems you were watching a lot more than drug sales around Viv's truck. But that's the problem." He sped up pace and tapped his cane as he spoke. "You never admitted seeing anything on Thursday morning after Portia was killed."

Sara thought Dave had met his match. Tallulah had perfected the art of keeping her face motionless.

"Nothing to see."

"I doubt that. Someone carrying big bags or boxes made several trips to the garbage bins behind the stables. Weren't you curious about the lights being on in the kitchen at King Art's?"

"No."

"How about the fire behind the kitchen? Who started the fire? What was burned?"

"I just saw people in hoodies by the truck and around the booths."

He leaned forward. "You know Viv is being charged in the federal court system for drug sales. She has named you as an accomplice. It will stick because several are willing to say you worked for Viv." He shook his head. "Seems a shame. You'll get five years in prison because you aren't willing to tell me everything you know. And your sacrifice won't help Elu. She'll be charged with attempting to murder Ron. No one is buying she was protecting you, especially after what she told the psychiatrist."

Tallulah's ruddy skin paled. "I forgot. I heard noises in the kitchen when I first went out on Thursday morning. A person in a black hoodie left the kitchen, put a large bag in a box, and carried the box to the dumpsters behind the stables. I thought it was funny because Art usually just discards garbage in the dumpster by the back of the kitchen and he never uses boxes." She rubbed her nose. "I figured some meat went bad and he didn't want the stench by the kitchen. It wouldn't be good for business. The person made several trips."

"Who was the person?"

Tallulah shrugged. "Too small to be Art."

"How do you know that?"

"Art stomped out later with a bag of clothes or at least something light. The other bags looked heavy."

"How do you know it was Art?"

"I could see his face."

"How soon afterward did someone start the fire?"

"Right away. The fire smelled bad."

Dave's winning the battle. Sara leaned back and enjoyed the exchange. "Explain."

"Not wood, paper, or meat. Funny. When the person stirred the fire, it formed clumps."

Tallulah leaned back. "That's it. The person kept the fire small and added one item at a time."

Sara decided it was time for her to play the bad cop. "I think you could see what was burning. Maybe fleece jackets or hoodies? They might melt and maybe become clumps? Or was it shoes?"

Tallulah gave her stoic look again.

"I think you saw the face of the person." Sara leaned forward. "You don't want to name the person because you spied for him or her. It's time to be honest, or we won't cut you a deal. In fact, if you withhold info, we will charge you with abetting Portia's murder."

Dave rose and put his hand on Tallulah's shoulder. "It's time for you to get yourself out of this mess. Don't worry about Elu. She'd going to get the psychological help she needs."

Tallulah pulled away from Dave. "Elu isn't crazy, just spoiled."

Dave sat down. "I'm afraid the psychologist thinks she's so narcissistic that she'll attack anyone who threatens her. Her lawyer is ready to plead her guilty but mentally ill for the charge of attempted murder of Ron in the state court system. The Santa Fe district attorney will accept the plea."

Tallulah studied Dave and then Sara. "What does that mean?"

Sara winced. "It's hard to say. Elu will be evaluated further for maybe six months. Then she'll spend two to eight years in a low-security state prison for women. She can get vocational training there. An early release will be possible if she responds well to treatment and training."

"That's too much. Ron is a bad man. He would have killed Hank and me. Will he get off easy on an insanity plea? Elu saved my life."

Sara sighed. "We know Ron is bad. Every detail you give us is important as we build a series of charges against him. We plan to charge him with bank robbery in the federal court system. Santa Fe police will charge him with attempted murder of you and Hank in the state court system."

"That's all?"

"There are legal limits to what we can do about Portia's murder until we have all the facts."

"Sara, stop being so polite." Hank pounded his cane and stared at Tallulah. "We know Crystal is also a bad person. We can charge both Crystal and Ron with mutilation of Portia's body. But we can't prove who killed Portia. We need to get both in prison and you know it. Talk."

Tallulah seemed to mumble to herself. "All I did was watch crazy people be mean to each other. Can I help it everyone was willing to pay for what I saw?"

Sara sighed internally. "Go on."

"I already told you. Viv paid me to watch drug purchases from her truck." She looked at her lap. "I guess I didn't mention Ron hired me three years ago to watch Art. Ron was convinced someone was selling meat purchased for King Art's on the side. I soon learned butchers at two of our sites delivered less meat than Art ordered. When I told Ron, I expected he'd be angry. He wasn't. He just said he'd talk to Art, but he continued to pay me a hundred dollars for reports on the staff at each site."

That might explain why Art did as Ron ordered. Ron could have charged Art with embezzlement. "What else did you report to Ron?"

Tallulah shrugged. "Later that year, I told him about Viv selling drugs. He gave me a bonus, and shortly afterward, Viv hired me, too." She frowned. "What I did wasn't illegal. I was acting like a store security officer. I was protecting the boss's merchandise."

"Hmm." Sara did mental calculations. *Tallulah probably earned an extra two hundred dollars each week from Viv and Ron. Thus, she earned about six thousand each fair season beyond her pay which according to the fair's records was five hundred dollars a week.* "Did anyone else pay you for watching others?"

"No." Tallulah bit her lip.

                                                    J. L. Greger

Doubt her answer. "Did you ask Carolyn if she wanted your security services?"

Tallulah sucked in her breath. "How did you know? Carolyn became angry when I asked her last Friday morning. She started screaming that she wouldn't be blackmailed. That's one reason Elu and I were so eager to leave."

"Did you also ask Ron for the money he owed you when you saw him at the FBI office in Santa Fe?"

Tallulah shoulders shifted forward and began to sob. "That's when he started to kick me. Said I ratted him out to Carolyn."

Might also be one reason Ron was so eager to leave on Friday. Carolyn had proof he was skimming from the company. "Who else paid you?"

Tallulah sniffed. "Portia paid me fifty dollars a week to watch Crystal. She was afraid Crystal would have sex with the men who worked the stables." Tallulah giggled. "She didn't need to worry. Crystal was too proud of her pink outfit to get it dirty in the stables. They didn't like her either, but Ron did. Crystal and Ron spent a lot of time together." She frowned. "I think they were more like a brother and sister."

Dave stood. "No wonder you look more rested now. There's no one to spy on in the safe house."

"Sit down Dave." Sara tapped the table. "I think Tallulah got money from someone else." She grabbed Tallulah's hand. "Who else paid you to watch others?" She thought a second. "Or maybe to not tell others about what you saw?"

"You sound like Portia. She accused me of taking money from Crystal so I wouldn't report on Crystal's activities."

"Was it true?"

"No, I told Portia the truth. Crystal wasn't interested in any of the men working at the fair. But I took the five hundred dollars Crystal offered me for not telling her mother about her friendship with Ron."

Sara stroked Tallulah hands. They were chapped. Her knuckles were large and misshapen by arthritis. *She needs money.* "Is that why you aren't admitting what you saw on Thursday morning?"

"I didn't do anything wrong. I saw Crystal tending the fire. First, she took off her own hoodie and burned it. Then she went inside the kitchen. When she returned, she had on clean clothes and threw her soiled jeans onto the fire. After a while, her T-shirt. Finally, her slippers. She stood there shaking and singing an old song 'Daddy, Don't You Walk So Fast' as she tended the fire." Tallulah blinked as she looked at Sara. "Do you remember it? Sad song about a little girl begging her daddy not to leave her and her mother. Ron came out of the kitchen and threw his T-shirt in the fire. I moved away when Ron spied me, but I don't think Crystal saw me."

"Is that everything? If anything shows up, we'll charge you with lying to us. That felony can cost you five years."

Tallulah's jaw dropped.

"Do you think Ron wanted to kill you because you told Carolyn he hired you to spy on others or because he saw you watching Crystal at the fire?"

Tallulah put her head on the table. "I don't know." She was quiet for thirty seconds. "Oh dear, I saw Crystal and Ron cleaning up after the murder."

Dave was breathing deeply. "Think. What did Ron say on Friday as he kicked you?"

"Nothing clearly." She paused. "I'll shut your mouth."

***

Dave twirled his cane. "Even if Crystal and Ron continue to point the finger at each other, we've got them. Art and Tallulah's comments are enough to convict them of first-degree murder."

Sara shook her head. "The assistant prosecutor doesn't have the guts to pursue a murder one charge."

"But the viciousness of the cleanup should get them long sentences."

"A jury will be kind to Crystal. Think about how Tallulah described her tending the fire."

"How kind will the assistant prosecutor be to Tallulah?"

"Don't know. She basically was blackmailing everyone, but I don't think either the district attorney for Santa Fe County or the federal prosecutor will press charges against her if she continues to cooperate."

"Like I've said all along, I want to get the loonies put away because they're dangerous. Tallulah is harmless and has already paid a high price for her greed. See if you can get our useless assistant prosecutor to not press charges against her."

J. L. Greger

CHAPTER 33: Not the First Time

Jack whistled as he walked into Sara's office and petted Bug. "Thanks for emailing me about Art's larceny. It got me thinking. I don't think Ron was the type to sit on info a long time before he acted."

"Agreed."

"Made me think the bank robbery in Albuquerque was too smooth. It wasn't Ron's or Art's first. So, the analysts and I looked for bank robberies within a hundred miles of the medieval fair during the last three years. We found nothing. Then we looked for other robberies."

"Great idea."

Jack smiled. "There were five robberies in Pennsylvania from roadside vendors within a fifty-mile radius of the fair three years ago. Last year there were six robberies from stores doing most of their business in cash, not credit cards, in Oklahoma, Texas and Michigan that fit the same location pattern."

"What types of stores deal mostly in cash nowadays?"

"Groceries, fast food stores, nail shops, beauty salons. Also, none of those businesses had functioning surveillance cameras. Anyway, all the stores reported they were robbed by two men wearing black ski masks. One over six feet and big. One around five-nine and thin. And another individual drove them away quickly."

"It might be enough to get Art to talk."

"It will be because one vendor reported he saw a spider tattoo on the hand of the large robber."

"Besides Art, someone should talk to Vano's wife. He might have sent extra money home after the robberies."

"She's accomplished at lying. It would be easier to talk to Willie." Jack winked at Sara. "He likes you."

"Okay, but I wouldn't be surprised if Ron or Emmet Ant was the third man in the early robberies. I kinda think the Albuquerque bank was Willie's first robbery." She picked up Bug and tousled his ears. "I won't talk to him until I learn more about Crystal's and his childhoods."

"Sounds good. I think I'd better drive to Santa Fe and pick up Emmet."

"Why? The judge yesterday released him from jail while he awaited trial on drug charges with the condition he couldn't leave the state."

Jack scowled. "Do you think that would stop him?"

***

The head mistress of Green Pastures School seemed relieved when she released Crystal's records. She blurted out to Sara over the phone, "We pride ourselves on helping exceptional students. Some because they're too bright and can't fit into a regular classroom. Some because emotional or physical traumas have prevented them from developing appropriate social skills. But our psychologists and teachers never reached Crystal. She did well in classes but never shared herself with others—students or teachers. In one sense, the way she renamed herself Crystal and dressed as a pink fairy during this last year were the most honest things she did in twelve years at the school."

"What was abnormal about her social skills besides being shy?"

The response was rapid. "She wasn't shy. She had no interest in others and seemed to delight in watching animals or other children suffer."

"Please explain."

"Oh dear." After a long pause, "Well, she liked to rip bandages off the skinned knees of other children and then press the wound to see if she could make the wound bleed more. When we corrected her, she said, 'I want to make sure the wound is clean. Bleeding cleans the wound.' Lots of variations, but you get the idea."

"Do you know what initiated her behavior?"

"No. Her mother seemed to be open with us. She admitted when she enrolled Crystal in our kindergarten class that she and her husband disagreed on how to handle Crystal. Her husband thought Crystal needed to be institutionalized because of her abnormal behavior around animals. Portia thought Crystal was just a lonely child who needed to be surrounded by other children. However, Portia filed for divorce within six months after Crystal was enrolled at Green Pastures School."

"Do you know anything about the divorce?"

"Why do you ask?"

"The divorce settlement was extremely generous." Sara paused, hoping the head mistress would say something useful. "The type of settlement that occurs when a husband has made a serious mistake."

"All I know is I never met him. Although Portia came to events at the school, he never did."

J. L. Greger

Time to change the topic slightly. "Is there any chance that Portia had a second man in her life when Crystal was in elementary school?"

"Why do you say that?"

Sara debated how honest to be but decided the head mistress had a more complete knowledge of Crystal's past than anyone else. "Crystal told us that Bodet Harper was soon to become Portia's third ex-husband. We can find no record of Portia marrying more than twice. And Crystal told a friend—perhaps I should say cohort—that Portia's second husband was fun, but we know Bodet and Crystal didn't like each other."

The head mistress sighed. "You'll find relevant material in the notes of the psychologist who initially worked with Crystal. He reported Crystal talked about a 'fun' man who stayed with the family sometimes before she started school. However, after Crystal started second grade, she denied the existence of the man. Later psychologists never could get her to talk much about any of the men around her home. She called the neighbor boy 'Weird Willie' and said his father 'took better care of his sheep than his children.'"

"That's an insightful comment on Willie's father. What did she say about Bodet Harper?"

"Nothing. Portia notified us when she married Bodet. Crystal refused to say his name for two years. When she was in eighth grade, she told a teacher, 'It's disgusting to see Portia and Bodet together.' We checked a bit. None of the residents in their community thought there was anything odd about Portia and Bodet."

Sara was disappointed. "None of this sounds bad enough to warrant keeping Crystal in a controlled environment for another year."

The head mistress cleared her throat. "You haven't looked at the pages of disciplinary actions against Crystal."

Sara had been scanning the files as she spoke. "I see other children were more apt to fall on the stairs when Crystal was around, but no third party ever witnessed the events. Oh, I see Crystal convinced younger children to eat poisonous mushrooms on a field trip in the woods, but she claimed they were confused."

"You get the picture. Other children, especially those younger than ten, were injured if they were near her. Most of her peers avoided her. We installed surveillance systems to watch her more carefully, but she soon discovered the locations of cameras and only misbehaved when not in the cameras' ranges."

"That doesn't jive with notes that we found hidden in her room." Sara gave the first name of the boy who'd sent notes to Crystal.

"Our clinic didn't provide her with contraceptives. Of course, that proves nothing. Besides, the boy you named is only eleven."

"One last set of questions. What did Crystal say about her mother?"

"In the last twelve years, no one ever heard her call her mother anything but Portia. In fact, she avoided mentioning her mother, even when the psychologists asked probing questions." The head mistress cleared her throat. "That's not normal. We've seen this behavior among children when the mother was mentally disturbed or distant. But Portia always seemed normal and interested in Crystal at all events here. Crystal received letters from her mother every week. But she threw many of them away without reading them." A long pause. "One dorm supervisor collected several of the discarded letters. They seemed normal—not preachy, upbeat."

"Is there any chance Crystal didn't believe Portia was her biological mother?"

"Crystal made that claim often. But Portia insisted she was Crystal's biological mother. That's one more of Crystal's traits. She lies well."

"Okay. Crystal didn't bond with her mother." *Sending her away to school may have made it worse.* "Thank you for your cooperation. I expect a forensic psychologist may want to talk to you and your staff more."

Sara emailed the recording of her conversation and all the records from Green Pastures School to the FBI psychologist:

> *Good luck in prying info from Crystal. She seemed to have outsmarted trained psychologists at Green Pastures School for years.*

* * *

Willie walked slowly around the conference room. He ran his hand over the mirror at one end of the room, apparently not realizing Sara sat behind the mirror watching him from the observation room. Then he sat down at the table with his back to the mirror and started to sing, "Here's the church and its steeple. Here's all the people."

Sara assumed he was playing his hand game but couldn't see his hands. She walked into the conference room and interrupted his second rendition of the ditty. "Willie, how do you like the safe house?"

"I miss the fair." He started to sing his ditty again.

First things first. Got to get info for Jack. "Willie, you admitted you drove your sister's car for Art and Vano when they robbed a bank in Albuquerque last week."

He slouched in his chair. "So?"

"Nothing for you to worry about, but I need to get the facts right. Did you ever drive Art and Vano to other locations last year or even the year before?"

He frowned. "I didn't have my sister's car then."

Smart answer to my poorly worded question. "Yes, but did you ever drive those two using Portia's truck or another vehicle?"

"No, I never drove any vehicle but Portia's truck and camper. It makes me nervous to drive other vehicles."

Another smart answer. "Okay, did you ever pick up Art and Vano from a grocery store or beauty salon using Portia's truck?"

"Hmm." Willie studied his hands. "I think Crystal sometimes went on outings with Art and Vano. She would have used the truck. Why are you asking?"

"I was trying to check out answers I got from others." *He's smarter than he pretends. Better distract him.* She handed him a small bag of cookies. "If you help me today, maybe you could stay with your sister. Would you like that?"

Willie grinned. "Maybe I could open my booth in Gallup."

"I doubt that, but we might find a job for you in Gallup. Then you could help your sister and earn some cash."

"I'd earn more selling items from my booth."

"Remember its ownership isn't clear until we determine who killed Portia." Sara smiled internally because the statement had been an excuse when she first told it to Willie. Now it seemed likely Willie could become the sole owner because a murderer couldn't inherit property from the person he or she murdered. "If you help me, we may be able to solve your problem. Think back to last Wednesday night. After Portia found the bank bags in the straw in the stable, what did she do?"

"I told you already. She was angry." He smiled. "But she told me not to worry. She'd fix it."

"Where did you and Portia go next?"

He rolled his eyes. "Told you. Crystal wanted to talk to Portia and told me to 'disappear.' I hate when she pretends to wave a wand at me and says 'disappear.' She thinks she's special in that stupid pink outfit." He folded his hands into the church with a steeple formation.

"I can see why you were annoyed." Sara put her hand on Willie's hand to keep him from singing his ditty again. "What did Portia do?"

"Went with Crystal."

"What did you do?"

"Pretended to go back to our camper." He pulled his hands from Sara's grasp.

"What did you really do?"

"Hid behind a booth and watched Portia and Crystal. I knew Portia was annoyed with Crystal because she lowered her voice and said, 'Crystal, I know life is tough for you.' She always said that when she was annoyed with Crystal. Then she said, 'but,' like she always did."

Willie will take longer to tell me the story than it took to kill Portia. "Tell me everything you heard and saw."

"Are you sure? It might get Crystal in trouble. I told you Portia kept telling me that she, Crystal, and I were family."

Sara wanted to scream but kept her voice soft. "Portia would want you to tell me everything. We can't solve your and Crystal's problems without your help."

He nodded. "They walked to the kitchen of King Art's and went in. The lights were already on. They didn't have to use a key to get in." He folded his hands to make the spire for the church.

"Did you move closer to the kitchen?"

"Yes, because I thought I heard Portia scream and then cry." He shook his head. "But I must have been wrong because I heard nothing but the radio afterward. I stood by the back door until I spotted Art and Emmet. Art yelled at me when he unlocked the back door of the kitchen."

Funny. Art didn't mention seeing Willie. Don't want to interrupt Willie's train of thought.

"I went to Portia's camper. and tried to sleep but couldn't." He started to cry. "I was worried about Portia. So, I went back to watch the kitchen. I watched Ron pack bags into boxes and carry boxes—they looked heavy—to the dumpster behind the stables. Then I spotted Tallulah and decided I'd better split because she would tattle to Ron."

Sara listened to Willie ramble for another hour. As far as Sara could determine Tallulah's, Art's, and Willie's stories were generally—but not perfectly—in sync. Willie's story suggested Ron and Crystal had acted as soon as Portia entered the kitchen and were guilty of murder one—a preplanned murder—not the spontaneous result of an argument—murder two.

He added one detail, which in a weird way pleased Sara. "When Ron came back from one of his trips to the dumpster, Crystal met him at the door to the kitchen with a knife in her hand and said something strange. Something like—you looked as surprised as Portia did."

Don't think it proves much. But it is consistent with Ron's claim that Crystal had pushed Portia back into his knife before she stabbed Portia. She doubted Willie would be a good witness in court. A defense lawyer could easily confuse him.

***

Sara watched Willie from the observation room. He traced his hand along the edge of the mirror as he had before their session Only this time, he knocked on the glass and smiled. Then she remembered he only did his hand routine when he wanted to evade questions.

Willie is a lot smarter than he pretends.

She called the assistant prosecutor. "I want to see Willie's medical records for two reasons. It is a logical part of determining how to charge him with abetting the bank robbery. But the real reason, I want his medical records is it may give me insights into Crystal's behavior. It is likely Willie and Crystal suffered the same early childhood trauma."

The assistant prosector was silent for almost a minute before he said, "Let me think." He hung up.

Sara's phone pinged

The assistant prosecutors whispered, "Get a warrant for Willie Shakes's medical records. Say it's needed to offer him a fair plea deal. No defense lawyer will object. Don't mention Crystal." He hung up before she could reply.

Sara hummed as she wrote the request and crossed her fingers.

CHAPTER 34: Jack's Day Gets Longer

Darn. The last thing I want to do is to drive to Santa Fe to talk to Emmet Ant. Jack thought a second. *I could invite Carolyn to go to dinner. I've never eaten at Sara's favorite restaurant in Santa Fe—Osteria D'Assisi.*

He stopped by the desk of his favorite analyst. She wasn't at her desk. He turned to the other analyst—the one with the poor red dye job. "Please contact Sergeant Miguel Roybal of the Santa Fe police. Tell him to find Emmet Ant ASAP and meet me at the men's dorm. I should arrive in less than an hour."

"Why don't you do it yourself?"

"Because I'm in a rush, and Emmet Ant might try to leave the state. Roybal can get him faster than I can."

The woman flipped her red hair behind her ear and pouted. "I suppose."

"Just do it now." Jack rushed to his car.

Ten minutes later, he was speeding north on I-25. His phone vibrated. It was Roybal.

"What's up?"

"We think the bank robbery in Albuquerque might not have been Art's and Vano's first robbery. Sara and I think Emmet might have been the driver for earlier robberies. We also think Emmet might defy the judge's order from yesterday and try to leave the state."

"That's a guess."

"If you help me, the FBI might take over the charges against Emmet. He and his lawyer made a not guilty plea on the drug charges yesterday in state court. That means you'll end up spending a lot of time with lawyers to nail him with his third possession charge."

"Don't know."

"I'll treat you to dinner at Osteria D'Assisi."

"Done. I'm on my way to find Emmet Ant."

Sara must be right about the restaurant. I'd rather have had dinner with Carolyn but nothing about this case is perfect.

***

The grounds at Las Golondrinas looked sad. All the colorful signs had been removed. The smell of rotting food emanated from a row of garbage bags surrounding the main entrance. Trucks with various trailers had replaced the booths. It appeared some of the booths would be towed away on trailers, while others were being folded up and packed onto the cargo beds of trucks. Men and women were sweeping up the remaining debris which also emitted a sweet but unpleasant odor.

Jack thought he saw Carolyn on her phone as staff packed up boxes in the shed at the entrance. It didn't look like the Chancellery of the Exchequer or a cute candy shop now. It was gray and almost empty except for a few shelving units on one wall.

He was debating how to approach her when he heard the roar of a truck's engine. A blue truck with a crew cab lurched forward. He heard Roybal yell, "Stop! This is a police order."

Two men who had been adjusting the hitch on their truck jumped aside to avoid being hit by the blue truck. Another man flicked his finger at the moving truck. The blue truck at the last second turned to avoid striking him and instead hit the trailer of a third truck.

Jack expected the driver to jump out. He didn't but rather seemed to sink down within the cab. Jack ran toward the truck.

Roybal reached the truck first and tried to open the driver's door. It was locked or jammed. "This is the Santa Fe police! Open up!"

Jack ran to the back door on the other side of the cab as a man with dark hair crawled out. Jack pointed his gun at the man. "Hands up or I'll shoot!"

It was Emmet Ant.

"Why did you run? I only wanted to ask you a few questions about some robberies in Pennsylvania and Michigan last year."

Emmet hardly moved his lips as he growled, "I want a lawyer."

***

The good news was the lawyer who had represented Emmet yesterday on drug charges, agreed to meet Emmet and Jack at the front shed of Los Golondrinas in an hour. In the meantime, Santa Fe police officers charged Emmet with reckless endangerment of others with a moving vehicle.

Jack only partially listened to their discussion as he read Sara's latest email:

> *Willie claims he wasn't the third man on any previous robberies. Seems likely he's told the truth. Makes your discussion with Emmet more important.*

Are you sure Carolyn can't give us more on her grandfather?

Dave went home early. Bug and I are going to give up after we finish with Willie.

That does it. What do I have to lose? He left Emmet with Roybal and two other Santa Fe officers and approached Carolyn.

She was less than eager to answer questions about her grandfather. She replied to his first two questions by saying "I don't know." Her response to his third question was: "Talk to my mom and dad. I don't remember ever being alone with my grandfather when I was a child."

Finally, she sniffed. "You know you make work for me every time I see you. Now I've got to hire a driver to move King Art's kitchen trailer. Emmet was going to drive it today." She glared at him. "At least, I'm told the damage to both trucks is minor and won't prevent them from being driven."

"What do you mean? A condition of his release yesterday was he couldn't leave the state. I told you that detail yesterday." *Carolyn has lied one too many times. I'm through.*

***

Jack pitied for himself as he drove back to Albuquerque with a silent Emmet locked in the back seat of the FBI cruiser. He decided to share his misery and called Dave.

"Sorry to call you at home." *I'm not sorry, but I don't want to sound vindictive.* "I'm bringing Emmet Ant into the ABQ detention center. I already spoke with Emmet and his lawyer. Emmet denied participating in a string of robberies during the last three years, but I can hold him for a day or so in the detention center because he tried to flee the state. But before we both talk to him, you need to talk to Viv."

"What about?"

"Looks like Emmet called Viv on a burner phone Saturday morning. Seems likely he was arranging the hit on Elu and needed Viv's help."

"Viv will never admit that."

"Do you think you could make her angry?"

"What good will that do?"

"I think Emmet might have agreed to split the money recovered from the cemetery if Viv discovered the meaning of the code on Vano's ring from Elu. If you convince Viv that Emmet was going to double-cross

J. L. Greger

her, I think she'll talk. Bet she knows about the robberies Art and Vano pulled off last year. She'll know if Emmet was their driver."

"Got it. I've got to sweat Viv. Pretty sure Sara sent me the data on Art's and Vano's robberies last year. I didn't read it." He coughed. "I don't read most of the crap from Sara until I must. Too many details."

"One more possibility. Crystal might have driven for several but not all the heists."

"I'll start turning the thumb screw on Viv." He coughed. "Don't be like Sara and try to protect him. Put Emmet in the general lock up. It'll scare him more."

CHAPTER 35: History Haunts the Present

Tuesday

"How's my favorite duo?"

Sara turned her phone onto speaker mode as she always did during her early morning talk with Sanders. That way she could tinker around the kitchen as they spoke. "Bug's fine, and I'm hanging on—barely. We've got enough on four people to charge them with major crimes. The assistant DA is a gutless wonder and wants to negotiate plea deals with all of them."

"So, you still think you'll tie up your cases by Thursday. You know that's the day after tomorrow."

Sara pulled two slices of toast from the toaster and slathered them with peanut butter. "I didn't say we've solved the murder, but Bug and I are out of here on Thursday."

As she spoke, Bug sat by her feet. She leaned over and rubbed peanut butter on his snout. He snorted and then eagerly licked his face.

Sara suppressed a giggle as she watched Bug. "So, have you made the arrangements for our trip?"

"I booked flights to Paris and four nights in a small boutique hotel in the Montmartre district. I thought we could be lazy tourists and take the funicular up to *Sacré-Cœur Basilica* and visit the *Musée de Montmartre*. I've never been there, but it appears to have several unique exhibits. Mainly well sample food and wine at local cafés.

Sara smiled as Sanders showed off his fluent French. It was one of his "East Coast snob behaviors." She wouldn't have smiled if he could see her because it would annoy him.

"That sounds great. So, you're willing to endure two eight-hour flights for three days in Paris?"

"It won't be bad. I booked business class seats."

"And you don't think you'll have to attend to business from Thursday morning until Monday evening?"

"I didn't say that."

Sara noted the defensive tone in his voice and said nothing.

"You know I must respond to crises as they arrive." He paused. "But I also thought of an alternate way to splurge and relax. We could wander around small historic towns and seafood places on the eastern shore of Maryland."

"We could take Bug to Maryland."

Sanders coughed. "I thought you might say that. I found several dog-friendly bed and breakfast inns along the shore."

"Which do you prefer?"

"I thought you wanted something luxurious. That's Paris. But I was in Paris less than a month ago for business. The Shore is easier for me."

As Sara drove to work, she thought their preference for the Maryland shore over Paris suggested both she and Sanders were too work-oriented. The bright spot was Bug would get the attention he deserved.

***

Sara started her day at work by settling Bug in her office and studying the results netted from her various warrants. She started with Portia's medical records because they were smaller than those of Crystal and Willie.

Portia hadn't visited a physician for much besides an annual physical, except during her pregnancy nineteen years ago and during a two-year period about twelve to fourteen years ago. During that time, Portia had come to the emergency room of the University of Arizona in Tucson on four occasions. On the first and second occasions, she had broken fingers. The third time she had multiple contusions but refused to name who had beaten her. The fourth time, her leg was broken.

All four times, Portia told nurses, "I'm clumsy." Her responses were probably not true because Portia only visited the emergency room one other time in the previous twenty years.

Crystal's files were lengthy with reports from several consultants. The records indicated Crystal developed normally until about three. Then, although she was potty trained, she started wetting her bed regularly and being aggressive. A variety of consultants documented Crystal's worsening aggression problems. One suspected she was autistic. One suggested she was bipolar.

About a month after Portia's third visit to the emergency room, a child psychologist suggested Crystal would benefit from the controlled environment of Green Pastures School. She was enrolled in its kindergarten program mid-year less than a week after Portia's fourth visit to the emergency room.

After Crystal was enrolled in Green Pastures, her medical needs were handled at the school. Her original pediatrician saw Crystal only one more time. He treated her after she fell from a tree and broke her arm during summer vacation when she was six. He noted in her medical records that he had also treated Crystal's friend, Willie, for two broken legs at the same time. He noted neither child would answer questions about the incident.

Crystal's medical records at the school indicated she was a physically healthy child with an IQ of about 130. However, discipline and counseling did little to improve her aggressive tendencies until she received a variety of medications. Risperidone seemed to be the most effective along with behavior modification counseling.

Sara was exhausted after studying Crystal's medical records. The experts suspected Crystal had been abused and/or seen others—Sara noted the plural—abused during the time she was three-to five-years of age.

***

Sara took Bug for a walk and then called the lawyer who handled Portia's divorce. He was eager to talk now that she had a warrant for his records on the divorce.

The lawyer noted Portia had first consulted with him days after her second visit to the emergency room. "I warned her that her husband would not reform, but she explained he was a doting father to Hannah."

"So, she took no action?"

"Correct." He sighed. "She was a different woman when she spoke to me the day after her third visit to the emergency room. At that time, she feared Herbert might be inappropriately touching Hannah. Her solution was for me to draft the creation of a trust for Hannah and a divorce settlement which included the transfer of all joint properties to her. I counseled she should file criminal charges against Herbert and document Herbert's actions with Hannah. She refused."

"Why didn't she file the divorce then?"

"Don't know. Anyway, she hobbled into my office with a cast on her leg six months later with Herbert in tow. He signed the divorce settlement and the documents creating the trust without saying a word. I never saw him again."

Sara questioned him for thirty minutes. He was adamant. Portia had never shared her suspicions with him "She didn't even say anything bad about Herbert, but she certainly smiled as he signed the agreements."

***

J. L. Greger

It was about ten when Jack emailed her from the ABQ detention center:

Dave and I have talked to Viv and are now trying to get a confession from Emmet Ant. The assistant prosecutor is listening in because I want him up to speed if we need to cut a deal. So, do not confuse him with other requests this morning. The poor guy isn't used to what he called "fast-breaking cases."

Sara emailed back:

Glad someone is making progress.
***

Sara called Willie's sister, Ellie. After a couple of pleasant comments, Sara said, "Willie is probably going to sign a plea agreement today. He's admitted he drove the getaway car for a bank robbery in Albuquerque. It's a federal crime."

Ellie gasped.

"We don't think he willingly abetted the robbery. We're not even sure he fully understood the consequences. Thus, the US Attorney for New Mexico is willing to give him a plea deal. He will be placed on probation for two years. During that period, he will be required to get psychological and career counseling and must gain employment. In return, he must testify in court on cases involving his cohorts."

"What?"

Before the sister could complain, Sara added, "A defense lawyer was assigned to him and believes this is a good deal for Willie. However, there is a problem to be solved."

The sister's voice became hoarse. "I figured it sounded too generous."

"Willie is due to inherit a half interest in business property owned by Portia Merchant."

"You mean his boss. It's sad she was killed. He was fond of her."

"She appears to have been a kind woman. The problem is the will won't be probated until her murder is solved. Willie doesn't want to leave New Mexico without his property, but he has no residence in the state. In essence, the best solution is for Willie to move in with you. He thinks you need help, and he wants to help you. We think we can help him find a job in Grants. Of course, once Portia Merchant's will is probated, Willie will be able to set up business wherever he wishes. He's quite a salesman and seems to understand the basics of the business. The woman who manages

Portia's businesses claims Willie has ordered much of the merchandise for the booth for the last two years."

"I don't know. I'm not well."

"His lawyer is willing to talk to you. Willie deserves this opportunity and your father doesn't seem to want to help him."

The response was rapid. "Dad never helped us kids. Sure, Willie can come live with me."

This is my opportunity. "As I went through the medical records of Crystal…"

"Who?"

"Hannah Merchant prefers to be called Crystal Star. As I was saying, I was reviewing Crystal's medical records and noted she and Willie broke bones falling out a tree when Crystal was six and Willie was nine."

"I think you have the facts confused. Crystal dared Willie to jump from the tree. When he refused, she pushed him off a limb. He was never the same after that fall."

"What do you mean?"

"Willie didn't talk for six months. He hadn't been a good student in first and second grade, but he was hopeless after the fall. He also started doing the weird hand routine."

"You mean the 'Here's the Church' one?"

"Yeah."

"What did your parents do to handle Willie's silence?"

"Mom was dead already. Dad ignored Willie and me. All he cared about was his sheep and making cheese. I doubt he would have taken Willie to the doctor that day if Portia hadn't insisted."

"I'm sorry, your and Willie's childhoods were so rough."

"Funny, we were happy because Portia—especially after the fall from the apple tree—acted like a mother to me and Willie. You know he never did the stupid routine when Portia was around."

"Do you know what triggers his routine?"

"He does it when he's nervous, especially around Dad and Crystal."

Guess I've got to have another session with Willie. Got to try not to make him nervous.

CHAPTER 36: Whittling Down the Problem

Jack looked like death warmed over when he staggered into Sara's office.

Dave looked better than usual. "It worked. Viv bought our story that Emmet was trying to cheat her and talked. The old bat has quite a temper."

Jack dropped onto a chair. "As far as I'm concerned, the whole carnie crew should be jailed for lying to agents and police. I reviewed our interviews as Dave drove us back here. Not one of them has told the truth willingly. I'm used to people omitting facts, but this group has been something else." He reached down and petted Bug. "Dave is right. Viv is vindictive. She finally told the truth more because she wanted her cohorts to suffer than because of the deal we offered."

Dave winked at Sara. "And we offered her a deal she couldn't resist despite the objections of DEA agents."

Sara pulled three cans of cola from the refrigerator under her desk. "What did you learn?"

Jack grabbed one can and handed another to Dave. Then Jack took a long slug of cola and leaned back in his chair. "Vano robbed produce stands in Pennsylvania two years ago."

Dave interrupted. "Seems he'd been doing snatch and grabs ever since he was kid and never got caught."

Jack continued, "But Vano did not understand the operation of Camelot Fair Enterprises. Ron, even before he was the boss, had initiated the business of paying fellow employees for tattling to him. Emmet reported on Vano after the first fruit stand robbery." He chuckled. "Ron was waiting a mile down the road after the second produce stand robbery. He demanded Vano and Viv split the take with him and teach him the tricks of the trade."

Sara blinked. "Wait. How did Viv get involved?"

Dave smiled. "She was Vano's getaway driver for the first and second produce stand snatch and grabs. Ron was mad at her because she was one of his paid stoolies. She knew his rules."

Jack threw his empty can into a recycle container. "To make a long story short, Ron was the driver for Vano's other three snatch and grabs that summer and cut Viv out of the deal. Viv admitted she was annoyed, but she couldn't do anything because Ron could have reported her drug sales to the police."

Sara murmured, "What tangled webs we weave when first we practice to deceive." She regained her focus. "So, what happened last year?"

"Viv was less sure of the details. She knew Ron and Vano together planned robberies in Texas and Oklahoma with Art as the gunman and Emmet as the driver."

"I figured Ron was being a male chauvinist pig." Dave winked at Sara. "But it seems Crystal helped the boys canvas a nail shop and beauty salon in Michigan and got a part of the take. Guess Ron is just as ageist."

Jack groaned. "Stop trying to be funny. Ron is a crook. Anyway, Viv claimed she knew nothing about the bank heist in Albuquerque until she heard Ron and Emmet arguing on Tuesday night." He looked at his notes. "With that info, we started questioning Emmet. His lawyer advised him to cooperate." He stared at the ceiling. "After the assistant federal prosecutor and I negotiated with Texas authorities."

Dave smiled. "Inconvenient, but we have signed plea agreements from Viv and Emmet."

Sara shook her head. "What for?"

"Viv accepted five years for the drug charges against her because we aren't prosecuting her for abetting the robberies in Pennsylvania. We tacked on five more years for arranging the attack on Elu in the detention center. She also agreed to testify in trials against Ron, Crystal, Art, and Emmet as necessary." Dave shook his head. "Like I said Viv is a vengeful, old bat, but that was good for us."

Sara's raised her eyebrows. "You didn't answer my question. What do you have on Emmet?"

Jack looked up from his phone. "Emmet signed a plea for lying repeatedly to authorities and soliciting two crimes: the assault on Elu and the failed plan to kill Ron in the ICU. He'll get twenty years in a federal prison and must testify against Crystal and Ron, but he won't be charged in Texas for bank robbery."

"How did you get him to sign the agreement?"

"He drove the getaway car for multiple robberies in Texas. He and his lawyer thought Texas judges and juries were hard on repeat offenders."

Jack returned to studying notes on his phone while Dave explained more details. "I pointed out to Emmet that he almost looked like a serial killer. He did nothing after he saw blood on Crystal's hands and Portia's body. He hired men to kill Ron in the ICU and women to kill Elu in the detention center." Dave winked at Sara. "Then there's Jack mean streak."

"What?"

Jack didn't even look up from his phone. "I simply noted juries often give life sentences to serial killers. So, when the assistant prosecutor offered the plea deal of twenty years, Emmet took it."

"All because Emmet goofed up Jack's plans for a pleasant evening with Carolyn last night."

Jack cleared his throat and ignored Dave's comment. "Since we were on a roll, the federal prosecutor and I got Art to sign a plea agreement for bank robbery and desecrating a body. He'll be sentenced to fifteen years and must testify in court against Ron and Crystal."

"Will Texas charge him for the robberies committed last year?"

"They signed off because of the federal sentence."

"Wait!" Dave pounded his cane. "Jack's not giving me credit. I got Art to admit he planted the meat cleaver under the fender of Portia's truck because he thought Crystal had cut her finger when chopping Portia's hands. He hoped a lab would find Crystal's blood on the cleaver. It was his ace in the hole. Surprised he was that smart."

Jack looked up. "I apologize, Dave. You're right. It's also why Art got only fifteen, not twenty, years. He gave us real evidence against Crystal."

Appears Dave got on Jack's nerves. Maybe he'll appreciate me more. "You two have had a good morning. Now do you want to hear about my less successful morning?" She didn't wait for them to answer. "A defense lawyer could make a strong claim that Crystal is guilty of murder but mentally ill in New Mexico. Although that plea is accepted in state courts in New Mexico, it isn't accepted in federal courts."

"Let's get lunch before we listen to all the details" Dave smacked his lips. "Something greasy from the 66 Diner on Central. I can pick up the order while you and Jack figure out what to do about Crystal."

***

After Dave had left, Jack groaned. "He makes me nervous. He borders on abusive to suspects." He shook his head. "But it works. The assistant federal prosecutor even consulted with his boss. The prosecutor said, 'Dave is what Jack and Sara need.'" Jack shook his head. "I don't think we're softies." He shrugged. "Then the federal prosecutor told his assistant prosecutor to never close a deal Dave hammered out without a sign-off from us."

"We're not softies. We just think the law should be about fairness not revenge."

Sara pulled out a file and began to summarize Willie's medical and school records for Jack. "His elementary school teachers described him as 'rambunctious' and hypothesized he was distracted by his mother's illness and death. However, after he fell from the tree and broke his legs during the summer after third grade, his teachers described him as 'hesitant and nervous.' They also noted he had developed several obsessive-compulsive behavior patterns." She scrolled through several pages. "Doctors noted his father seemed 'disinterested' in him. Portia brought him to all doctors' appointments and attended all his parent-teacher meetings."

"Stop." Jack stood and began to pace. "Why are you wasting so much time determining Willie's history? The assistant prosecutor is willing to sign the plea agreement with Willie. It's time to focus on Crystal and prepare first degree murder charges against her and Ron."

Sara felt her face flush. "Because the pieces—the motives particularly—don't fit. If Crystal and Ron had argued with Portia for hours and emotions were high, then the stabbing and dismemberment makes sense."

Jack snorted.

"Well in a weird sense, the passion of the murder would make sense. But they killed Portia within minutes of her entering the kitchen. It was a preplanned exercise."

"It was murder one."

"What were their motives?"

"Portia was ready to argue with Ron about involving Willie in the bank robbery. Bodet said Crystal often argued with Portia." He was quiet for a minute. "Perhaps Portia had discovered Crystal and Ron were lovers."

"Tallulah didn't think their relationship was sexual. Something else provoked Crystal into a frenzy."

Jack put his hands on Sara's shoulders. "You're great at deep diving into a case, but this one is simply a matter of two crazy Gen Zer's."

"I was ready to accept that, too, until our best analyst—the young one with dark hair—found a lawyer in Albuquerque who had met with Portia last Tuesday."

Jack gasped.

"You remember I asked the analysts to contact all lawyers in New Mexico to see if they'd seen any of our suspects in the last month."

"Yes, you do that for all our cases, and it's never turns up anything useful. That's why the analysts don't rush to do it."

"Well, it did this time. Seems Portia met with the lawyer last Tuesday morning in Albuquerque. She changed her will and wanted to split her property between her husband, John Shakes, her bookkeeper, John's daughter 'who had the gumption to not stick around waiting to inherit,' and a trust. The split was to be fifty, ten, ten, ten, and twenty percent of the total estate, respectively. The trust was to be split between Crystal and Willie in five years if they had succeeded in finding useful employment and had not been convicted of major crimes."

"What happens if Crystal and Willie don't meet the new will's requirements?"

"The money reverts to the Boys and Girls Clubs of Tucson."

"Did she sign the will?"

"Yes. Portia insisted the lawyer meet her Wednesday afternoon at the Las Golondrinas Museum Store."

"Where's that?"

"Near the entrance to the medieval fair. Most likely, Ron saw her from his office at the entrance. But Willie and Crystal could have spotted her, too." She was silent for a moment. "In retrospect, it seemed strange when both Willie and Crystal presented us with copies of Portia's original will so quickly."

"Do we know why Portia cut Willie out of her will?"

"That's why I spent so much time studying Willie's school and medical records this morning. I talked to his sister, too."

She opened another file on her laptop. "Here's a line-by-line comparison of Portia's new will with Herbert Engel's new will. Pretty obvious he was following Portia's lead. She had the lawyer send a copy of her will to Herbert Engel."

Jack traced his finger down the page. "Wait. You didn't tell me about this." He was pointing to a section in Portia's will.

I fear I have spoiled Willie Shakes and Crystal Star by giving them too much and catering to their whims. If Willie Shakes or Crystal Star, aka Hannah Merchant, have failed to find useful employment or have been charged with a major crime in five years, they will forfeit their rights to the funds in the trust. Then the twenty percent of my estate in the trust will revert to the Boys and Girls Club of Tucson to establish an internship program. The funds are to be used to pay stipends to students while they learn trade skills or to reimburse employers for expenses they incur because of employing novices under twenty-one instead of employing experienced workers.

"I wanted you to read it yourself. Willie is counting on his inheritance from Portia. He would have been as angry as Crystal if he thought he was about to lose his inheritance."

"What's next?"

"We have lunch. Dave should be back any minute. We tell the assistant prosecutor not to sign any settlement agreements with Willie. And we figure ways to ensure Crystal and Ron go straight from the behavior clinic or the hospital to jail."

Jack started to pace again. "Ron's no problem. I can get the assistant prosecutor to formally charge Ron with bank robbery this afternoon. Do you think the Santa Fe police chief and the district attorney of Santa Fe County will care if we also charge Ron with aggravated assault of Tallulah, too?"

"I talked to them, well their assistants, his morning. They're pleased to let us do the paperwork but are willing to be our backup if necessary. For example, they'd agreed with me that state law may be more appropriate for handling the case against Elu."

"Good. The assistant prosecutor thinks it's too early to file charges for Ron's assault on Hank."

Tears rolled down Sara's cheeks. "The doctors told me they can't predict when or if Hank will come out of the coma." She wiped her face.

Jack sat down and put his arm around Sara. "Don't worry. We don't have to rush to charge Ron for his assault on Hank or for murdering Portia. And Crystal's DNA on the meat cleaver guarantees she can be charged with mutilating a corpse."

"But what are we going to do about Willie? He's the smartest one of all. He convinced everyone for years that he was an innocent, retarded man. Except, for abetting armed robbery, we don't have anything on him. However, I think he incited Ron and Crystal to kill Portia. That's why he left the bank bags in the straw where they would be found. But that's not a crime."

"I bet Crystal can give us something useful on Willie. Dave managed to bring out the vindictiveness in Viv. He'll do the same with Crystal."

CHAPTER 37: Greed

"Crystal, I'm not a patient man like these two." Dave pointed at Sara and Jack. "We have enough evidence to charge you with the murder of Portia Merchant." Dave leered at her.

Her lawyer put his hand in front of his lips as he whispered to Crystal.

Crystal tossed her pink hair and pouted a moment. "I told you already. I just watched."

Dave ignored Crystal. "We also are charging you with mutilation of a corpse. Your blood is on the meat cleaver used to chop Portia's hands. That's ten years."

"Art made me."

Dave flashed a broad smile. "The State of Michigan is prepared to charge you with two robberies last summer."

Crystal's lawyer turned pale, but Crystal giggled.

Dave snorted. "Art, Willie, Viv, and Ron have all signed statements that you abetted the robbery of a beauty salon and a nail shop." Dave smacked his lips. "Willie especially liked signing his statement. He thought it was 'repayment' for the way you bossed him around for the last fifteen years. He even claimed he broke his legs because you pushed him from a tree."

Crystal didn't flinch. "Doesn't matter. I was a child. His fall occurred years ago. You can't charge me because it exceeds the statute of limitation."

Sara was amazed how much Crystal knew about the law and how Crystal's lawyer had remained silent.

Crystal flashed a grin at Dave. "I'm not a stupid country girl. I know my rights. You don't have anything that will stick on me."

"Honey, you're naïve." Dave stomped his cane on the floor. "The whole jury will be in tears when the pathologist finishes his testimony on the condition of Portia's body." He smiled. "And that wonderful blood on the cleaver."

As agreed, Sara delivered the punchline. "Ron claimed you pushed Portia into his knife. The pathologist said that wound in the back was not deep enough to be the fatal wound. That means you were standing in front of Portia and delivered the fatal wound to her throat."

Dave chuckled. "We have you for murder. Kinda too bad that we have almost nothing on Willie. Looks like he'll get the whole trust according to Portia's new will."

Crystal's lips formed an "O."

Her lawyer whispered in her ear.

Dave leered at her for a minute. "Yep, we got a copy of the will Portia signed last Wednesday. No wonder you were mad and killed her Wednesday night. You thought Willie was a fool, but he outsmarted you by playing dumb."

Sara handed a printed copy of the new will to Crystal and another copy to the lawyer. "Do you think Willie threw the bank bags in the straw in the stable and tattled on Ron for no reason? I think he wanted to rile Ron."

Dave coughed. "Sara, you know what else? I think he was busy riling Portia while our girl was making out with her 'bad' boy' Ron."

Crystal flushed. "You got it wrong."

Dave winked at Sara. "Doesn't matter. A jury will assume you two are a modern-day Bonnie and Clyde."

The lawyer stood. "I think that's enough."

Dave coughed. "Good. I thought Sara might listen to a plea request if Crystal gave us goodies on Willie. Me, I want her to face the full ire of the court." He stood.

Sara pulled Dave's sleeve. "You're not being fair to Crystal. Agents talked to Willie's father, John. He said Portia was a fine woman and good boss." She crossed her fingers underneath the table and stared at Crystal. "He thought Willie only pretended to be dumb because it made Portia feel guilty for what you'd done when you were six."

Crystal's face flushed. "I didn't push him. I only dared him to jump. Then I jumped, too. We thought we could fly."

Sara thought it would be interesting to explore the weird behavior of the children. *By six and nine, they should have outgrown the fantasy of thinking they could fly.* She guessed it was more useful to enrage Crystal. "But Willie will testify you forced him. A jury is more apt to believe him than you. There are no charges against him."

Dave sat down. "Is there any reason why we shouldn't believe Willie?"

The lawyer leaned over and whispered to Crystal. She listened for a minute and then shook her head. "Willie didn't love Portia. He just fed her ego all these years while I was away. Mainly he wanted to get away from that stupid dairy and go on the road with the booth. On Sunday evening in Tempe, the old fool told him she was going to change her will. She was selling off her fair gear when the season ended and investing the money in the dairy. In her new will, he'd get partial ownership of the dairy with his father and sister." Crystal gave a harsh laugh. "He was so mad he insisted I ride in the camper with him as he drove from Tempe to Gallup. He told me everything and gave me a copy of the old will."

Her lawyer whispered in her ear.

"No, they should learn about the good, little boy. Whenever Willie got annoyed with his father or Portia, he'd grab a barn cat and kill it. He's buried a lot of them behind the sheep barn. No one found them because he butchered—that's the word he used—like his father and Portia did the sheep for meat." She shook her head. "So childish, I stopped doing it years ago."

Sara held her breath and checked her recorder was on. When she realized, Crystal had stopped talking, she said, "That's dreadful. What else did he say and do?"

"He'd heard Portia make an appointment with a lawyer in Albuquerque for Tuesday morning while we were still in Tempe. He was scared." Crystal turned to Dave. "Is that enough to get me a plea deal?"

Her lawyer shook his head as he stared at Crystal.

Dave winked at Sara. "Not for me. Not even enough for a softie like Sara."

Crystal shrugged. "Willie told me he was busy Tuesday until about two but would get a copy of her new will by dinner on Tuesday night." She laughed. "Portia was a fool to let him live in her camper."

"Did you know what Willie was going to be doing until two last Tuesday?"

"Of course." She giggled. "Portia always kept her good, little boy short on cash. He'd do anything for a hundred dollars."

Sara pulled up copies of the old and new wills on her laptop. "Besides arranging for you and Willie to share the truck, booth, and camper, the old will granted you and Bodet Harper the rest of her property." She turned her screen so Crystal's lawyer could see it. "You lost more than Willie when your mother signed the new will."

Crystal yawned. "Didn't matter. I have my trust fund—my ticket away from Portia and her farm. I'd told her I wouldn't go back to Green Pastures School for an extra year and she couldn't make me. The money in the fund is mine when I turn twenty-one."

Got her now. "I guess you hadn't realized your father created a revocable trust. You also underestimated Portia. She contacted your father to get him to revoke the trust."

Crystal's face turned white. She stuttered, "He wouldn't do that."

Sara pulled a document from her tote. "Your father terminated your trust on your last day at Green Pastures School. Here's a copy of the document. The lawyer who wrote Portia's new will said he included this document in the packet he gave Portia when she signed her new will on Wednesday." Sara paused to give Crystal time to think. "That means Willie must have seen this document when he stole the new will from Portia's files in the camper." After another pause, "Are you sure he didn't tell you about this revocation document?"

Crystal trembled and muttered incoherently.

If I push now, I may get the truth. "Looks like Willie played both you and Ron. He got you and Ron to do the dirty work of killing Portia."

Color returned to Crystal's face as she twirled a pink curl of her hair around her fingers for at least a minute. "You're right. Willie almost had to drag Portia to the spot in the barn where he hid the bank bags. Stupid old broad."

Her lawyer winced. "Crystal, don't say more."

She ignored him. "Willie and I wanted Ron to see Portia at her worst—bossy and self-righteous. Then he'd help us give Portia what she deserved."

"So why didn't Willie help you and Ron in the kitchen?"

"He did."

"How?"

"Ron started to vomit as soon as a little blood trickled out of Portia's back. I hit Portia on the head with a frying pan. Willie had thought I might have to stun her before he cut her throat. So, I was prepared. He knew how slit her throat because he'd helped his father butcher sheep many times on the farm."

The lawyer put his hand over Crystal's mouth. "What's the deal?"

Crystal looked angry for a second and then must have appreciated he was right. "I won't accept a murder one charge."

The negotiations went on for an hour. The crime scene became clearer—at least Sara hoped it had. The story was consistent with previous signed statements.

Sara didn't interrupt as Dave goaded Crystal to tell what happened after the murder.

"Ron stood in the corner—like a wuss— and avoided the blood while he called Emmet to get Art from the men's dorm. When they came, Emmet pushed Art inside the kitchen and slammed the door."

Crystal couldn't explain why neither Art nor Emmet saw Willie in or near the kitchen at first. After several minutes of saying, "I don't know," she said, "Oh yeah, Willie left while Ron called Art to get the clean-up supplies and a change of clothes for me."

Dave goaded her immediately. "So, Willie outsmarted you again. He got away and cleaned up before anyone saw him. Doesn't it make you mad?" He stood. "Doesn't matter. I don't believe your story."

Crystal panted a bit. "Willie took Portia's bracelet when he left the camper. The silver one set with pink quartz. Bet he still has it."

CHAPTER 38: Just Desserts

The interview with Ron was a piece of cake. After Dave had outlined Crystal's scenario of the murder, Ron coughed and conferred with his lawyer.

"You don't have it quite right. I said from the start I didn't like blood. I was holding a kitchen knife and standing behind Portia—like I was told—while Crystal argued with Portia. Suddenly, Crystal shoved Portia back into the knife." He gulped. "I didn't know what to do when Portia screamed. But Willie and Crystal did. Crystal struck Portia on the head with a skillet. Willie cut her throat." Ron turned pale. Tears ran down his face. "It all happened so fast."

Sara patted his hand.

"It was terrible. Never seen so much blood." Ron looked at Sara. "Didn't bother Willie. He reached into the blood and pulled a bracelet from Portia's hand. Then he rinsed the bracelet in the sink and used a kitchen brush to clean it like he was preparing a potato for baking as he ordered me to get Art 'to do the butchering.' Didn't say anything else. He locked the door when he left."

Sara handed him a tissue. "What did you and Crystal do?"

"Crystal started hosing the floor and the body with water and flushing the blood down the drain in the center of the kitchen floor. I called Emmet."

Sara hesitated before asking her last question. *I think I know the answer, but I doubt Ron does.* "Why did you drop two bags with body parts in the stables?"

"I didn't. Crystal asked me that question, too." He turned to his lawyer. "Crystal said, 'I was useless. That's why I was so desperate to get away last Friday."

He quickly signed a plea agreement for a thirty-year sentence for the deadly assault on Portia, the deadly assault on Tallulah, and the bank robbery. The assistant prosecutor had agreed to not prosecute Ron for his assault of a federal agent, no matter Hank's outcome. Sara hoped Hank's family didn't feel cheated, but it was the fastest way to get Ron to testify against Crystal. To get Ron's cooperation in convicting Willie, the assistant prosecutor guaranteed that Ron wouldn't be incarcerated in the same prison as Willie.

***

The interview with Willie was even easier. Willie listened stoically—without playing his hand game—as Sara read Crystal's and Ron's statements. "It my word against those of two criminals. I don't have a record. A jury will believe me."

Sara handed him a photo of a heavy silver bracelet with pink quartz insets. "We found it in your backpack this morning. The lab found specks of blood in one of the crevices by the center stone."

The lab had decided the speck was too small to use a quick DNA test, so they were going to use the slower standardized test. Sara lied. "It was Portia's blood."

Willie turned to his lawyer. "I was so patient. I put up with so much from my father, Portia, her first husband, and Crystal for so many years. Working on that farm was hell. All I wanted was to escape becoming my father on that damn dairy farm." He shook his head. "But it wasn't enough. I'll take a plea of murder two. I don't want my sister to hear my crime described in court. Forget anything about the robbery." He closed his eyes. "I guess prison won't be any worse than the dairy."

Sara thought Willie demonstrated how good an actor he'd been. There was no stuttering, hand games, or childish talk during the ensuing discussion. She, Dave, and Jack agreed Willie was someone to be feared and thought he should be charged with murder one and given a life sentence. The assistant prosecutor wasn't bothered by their concerns. He okayed a plea of forty-years-to-life for Willie.

***

While Sara and Dave worked with the assistant federal prosecutor, Jack monitored the negotiations between the Santa Fe district attorney and the lawyer appointed by the public defender's office to represent Elu. She finally accepted a plea of guilty of attempted murder—a third degree felony in New Mexico—but mentally incompetent. She was ordered to receive psychological evaluation and treatment in a state facility followed by a maximum of five years in a low-security prison facility that offered vocational training.

***

After he agreed to Willie's plea agreement, the assistant prosecutor turned to Sara, Hank and Jack. "You three must get me more evidence—something new—on Crystal before I negotiate with her."

Sara gasped.

Jack turned gray.

Dave snorted. "Where do you suggest we look?"

Sara was relieved when her phone pinged. It broke the stony silence.

"I need a favor, but I might have something for you." Roybal cleared his throat. "Bodet Harper has a lot to say about Crystal Star and Herbert Engel. How soon can you get to Santa Fe and help me interview Bodet?"

Sara turned to Jack. "Roybal has an interesting offer. Seems Bodet Harper knows a lot about Herbert Engel. I'd like to know—even if we can't charge him—how he goofed up Crystal, Portia, and maybe Willie so much."

"Why not? We might get the 'new' evidence our assistant prosecutor wants. Dave can stay here and listen to the prosecutor's ideas."

Dave coughed.

Jack really doesn't like Dave. I feel sorry for Dave but it's every man for himself now. She flashed a smile at the assistant prosecutor. "We'll report back if we get the evidence you need."

As they left the room, Sara said, "If you drive, I'll rummage through the material I got from San Luis Obispo Sheriff's office on Herbert Engel. They finally sent his medical records late yesterday, but I didn't have time to study the files."

***

Sara thought Roybal looked more comfortable in a black shirt, tie, and slacks with a camel-hair jacket rather than police uniform, but he seemed nervous as he pulled Sara and Jack into a small conference room at the main office of the Santa Fe police offices.

"Bodet is sticking to his story. He insists he didn't do the heist in Scottsdale. He got the Gorman oil pastel when the thief's usual fence said the art was too hot to handle."

"So, what's the problem? Can't you get him a sentence of five years for fencing art?"

Roybal pulled at his tie. "He won't name the other fence without assurances of a reduced sentence. He's in California. I have no contacts there."

"So? You process Bodet as a fence in New Mexico and hand your data over to California authorities."

"But I won't get any national attention. I need to announce the name of the big-time fence to the press if I'm to leave this police force and become a consultant on art thefts for insurance companies. You know I don't belong in a police department."

J. L. Greger

Jack began to cough violently.

Sara smiled. "Now I get it. Bodet and his lawyer have figured out your not-so-secret ambitions. I don't see how we can help."

"Bodet's lawyer suggested his client could be a valuable witness when Crystal is tried for murder."

"How does he know we didn't already make a plea deal with Crystal?"

Roybal leaned closer. "I asked that, too. Bodet replied, 'I know my stepdaughter. She won't take a plea. She knows she can convince any jury of her innocence.'"

Jack was texting rapidly on his phone. "But why would Bodet want to be involved in a murder trial? It won't help his case for fencing art."

"His lawyer says Bodet wants to get justice for Portia."

Hate to be the cynic. "More likely, Bodet wants the FBI to take over his case and cut him a deal."

Roybal studied his feet. "Just listen to Bodet. I'm bringing him and his lawyer in."

***

"I don't regret much of in my life, but I regret not killing Herbert Engel when I had the chance. It happened about when I had begun to appreciate Portia's many talents." He winked at Jack and Roybal. "You guys know what I mean."

Roybal groaned. Jack kept his face blank.

"It was after a hot day in August. I went out to Portia's orchard and saw an old geezer talking to Crystal and Willie. I snuck up to listen because I thought it was Herbert Engel." He licked his lips and studied Sara and then Jack. "Now I didn't want to tell Portia what I saw because I knew it would rile her." He wiped his lips. "Reasonable woman except when Herbert was mentioned. Guess that was logical. He roughed her up several times. Gave her horrible tattoos which she later had a tattoo artist convert into stars and butterflies." He stared at the ceiling.

Sara cleared her throat. "And what did you hear or see?"

"The old geezer was trying to convince the kids they could fly." Bodet scratched his chin. "Didn't make sense. Crystal was six then and smart. She knew she couldn't fly. Willie was even older. I went off to talk to John Shakes in the dairy. The next thing I knew, John and I heard screams from the orchard. We both ran toward the screams. Couldn't believe what we saw. Willie was lying on the ground under an apple tree screaming. Crystal was hanging onto a big bough. And there was Herbert reaching toward her and saying, "Fly, fly.""

"What did you do?"

"Ran toward the tree. Then the old coot pushed her, and she fell."

"What happened next?"

"John Shakes checked the kids, and I pulled the old coot from the tree. He had the nerve to say, 'I taught them an important lesson. They'll never trust anyone again.' I lost it and started to hit him, but he was stronger than I expected. He put up a good fight." Bodet felt his jaw. "Then he pulled a couple of hundred dollars from his pocket and threw them at John and me. 'Keep it, and don't tell Portia.'" Bodet hung his head and was silent for at least a minute.

Sara saw neither Jack nor Roybal were ready to talk. "What did you do?"

"Took the money and told him I'd shoot him on sight if I ever saw him again. Then John and I carried the kids to the car. Portia took them to the hospital. Neither John nor I ever told Portia about Herbert. Neither did the kids." Bodet started to sob. "Portia would be alive now, if I'd told her. The old coot would have rotted in a mental hospital or a prison."

Sara stood and put her arms around Bodet. "Here's what we can and can't do. In theory, the statute of limitations in child abuse cases is extended until the children are adults. In New Mexico, until they are twenty-four. So, he could be charged with child abuse. The problem is Herbert Engel is terminally ill with metastatic cancer. The medical records I saw this morning indicate he has less than a month. I doubt our assistant prosecutor will want to mount a case against him."

Jack nodded. "But I think they and Ron could sue Herbert or his estate in civil courts. Carolyn said her grandpa often 'tormented' Ron."

Sara shook her head. "I'm glad you didn't tell us your story before we cut and signed deals with Ron and Willie this morning. Your story could swing any jury decision. We also can't withhold your information from the defense in Crystal's case. You may have just helped her get away with Portia's murder."

Bodet laid his head on the table and sobbed. "I'm so sorry Portia."

Bodet's lawyer gulped. "I guess this doesn't help my client make a plea deal."

Roybal cursed and left the room.

Jack patted Sara's arm. "This story might explain Crystal's reference to Portia's second husband as being 'fun.' As a young child, Crystal might not have recognized Herbert when he visited in secret and thought of him as Portia's second husband."

Bodet lifted his head. "I'm sure Herbert never saw Crystal again—at least at Portia's homestead after that incident. Portia and I almost never let Crystal be out of our sight during August and December when she was at home."

"Doesn't matter. This case is way beyond Jack's and my legal knowledge. We'll give the recording I made of your statement to the assistant prosecutor for these cases. He'll have to talk to his boss, authorities in California, and the district attorney for Santa Fe."

As Jack and Sara walked to their car, Sara said, "I bet Crystal won't remember this incident without a psychiatrist's help, but she remembers wanting to fly. Why else would she dress as a fairy with wings?"

CHAPTER 39: Some Dreams Come True

Wednesday

Sara was copied on a flurry of emails between psychiatrists, the lawyers for Bodet Harper and Herbert Engel, the assistant prosecutor, and the US attorney for New Mexico on Wednesday morning. No one asked for her opinion, even after she forwarded a piece of new evidence to Carbonne. She also noted Roybal and Dave were not cc'd, but Jack, Carbonne and the chief of the Santa Fe PD were.

A psychiatrist had determined that Crystal didn't remember the incident in the tree. Crystal insisted—as she had told Sara—she had dared Willie to jump and then had lost her balance and fell. Another psychiatrist determined Willie remembered the details as Bodet had reported.

The assistant prosecutor argued that the psychiatrists' determinations didn't matter. Crystal and Willie knew what they did to Portia was wrong. Hence, they were guilty. He "personally" wanted to try Crystal for second-degree murder in federal court, but he thought it was a "waste of his time to be involved in the art theft investigation."

As soon as Sara read the assistant prosecutor's statement, she emailed Carbonne:

> *Bet you a diet cola, the assistant prosecutor will be reversed.*
> *We're going to have to negotiate more with Crystal and be stuck*
> *with the investigation of the art theft.*

Carbonne responded immediately.

> *I'll take the bet. At least the part about you having to negotiate*
> *more with Crystal or having to investigate the art theft.*

Around three, the US Attorneys for New Mexico, Arizona, and California issued a joint statement. They had "broken a major art theft ring." Three art thieves in New Mexico and Arizona and a fence in California had been arrested. Jack Drum was named as the FBI agent leading the continued investigations, which were expected to result in more arrests. Roybal and Bodet were not named in the announcement.

Sara received a copy of the plea agreement signed by Bodet Harper and the assistant prosecutor. Bodet would receive only a year's probation in return for naming and testifying against the others.

Less than ten minutes later, Sara was summoned to Carbonne's office. A can of diet cola sat on the conference table in his office. Jack and Carbonne were already drinking their colas.

Jack looked at her nervously. "I hope you aren't insulted that I agreed to take over the investigation of the art thefts. Carbonne said you didn't…"

Carbonne winked at Sara. "Need that time sink on your plate. I promised Sanders, I'd get you out of Albuquerque on Thursday. Besides, Jack likes these interstate projects. They give him a chance to meet new women."

Sara tried not to smile. "So, who's handling the charges against Crystal?"

Carbonne leaned back in his chair. "The US Attorney and I agreed Crystal Star would make mincemeat of the assistant prosecutor on the case. He appointed a more senior assistant prosecutor to take over negotiation with Crystal. The new man convinced her and her lawyer to take a plea in less than an hour."

Jack put his can down. "You didn't tell me that."

"I'm telling you and Sara now. You, Sara, and Dave have done a thorough investigation, but the assistant prosecutor on the case wasn't up to the task. Crystal signed a plea for second degree murder with a sentence of forty-to-life after we agreed she could visit her father in the hospital."

Jack shook his head. "That's all she wanted?"

"The new assistant prosecutor made it clear to Crystal and her lawyer that he planned to charge her with first-degree murder." He licked his lips. "Of course, Sara's last lead helped. Remember the boy from Green Pastures School who exchanged letters with Crystal. Sara asked agents in Arizona to interview him several days ago. They finally did this morning. Crystal had promised to help him kill his father in July, but the boy had second thoughts."

Jack stared at Sara. "You told me you'd sent Carbonne one more piece of evidence against Crystal this morning. But you didn't say it was dynamite."

Sara smiled. "I told you I'd wrap up this case in time to get on a plane tomorrow." She took a gulp of cola. "Of course, I didn't believe it." Her eyes got misty. "It's a hollow victory because Hank is still in a coma."

Around five, Sara got the call she'd been waiting for since last Friday. Hank had come out of his coma, and he wanted to see Sara.

Sara rushed into the ICU and found his daughter standing by Hank's bed. She looked drawn and pale. "He wouldn't allow the doctors to medicate him for pain until he talked to you."

Sara grabbed Hank's hand and massaged it. "It's Sara. What's so important that you won't listen to your doctors?"

His eyelids fluttered. His voice was soft. "Ron kicked me and… Tallulah."

She could tell he was struggling to speak. "I know. Tallulah told us."

"Said he had to get away… or Willie and Crystal would kill him…" His eyelids fluttered and he was silent for thirty seconds. "… like they did Portia."

Sara laughed. "So, all my work was unnecessary. All we had to do wait for you to wake up from your nap."

"Some nap."

She squeezed his hand. "I'm so happy to have you back"

"I'm filing for retirement. My daughter thinks it's time."

She squeezed his hand again and started to leave.

"Wait. Maybe you can visit me… after I leave the hospital and tell me how you solved the case."

His daughter followed Sara out of Hank's room. "A young man stopped by this morning and left this note. He said it was written by four of his friends."

To Sara and her man,

Thanks for helping us improve our act.
You were right. We placed the contents of two of Ron's boxes in the stables.
We wanted Ron to get what he deserved.

The Jousters

Thursday

Sara and Bug took an early flight from Albuquerque to Washington. Sanders met them at the airport and whisked them away to

J. L. Greger

the beaches along the Maryland Eastern Shore. There they dreamed of the future together.

THE END

THE SCIENCE AND HISTORY BEHIND THE STORY

Much of the action of this novel occurs at a medieval fair. Many Americans make two assumptions about fairs: Food safety is a problem. and the staff often have shady backgrounds. Here are a few facts.

<u>Food safety</u>

Seven major food-borne pathogens (strains of *Salmonella, Clostridium, Campylobacter, Listeria,* and *Escherichia coli*) caused about ten million illnesses in the US in 2019 (1). An extensive public system involving the Food and Drug Administration (FDA), the Centers for Disease Control (CDC), and the Food Safety and Inspection Service of the US Department of Agriculture (USDA—FSIS) and state health agencies has evolved in the US to control food-borne illnesses.

The efforts of state health officials in monitoring the food safety issues at King Arthur's Feast in this novel are addressed humorously, but the importance of maintaining food safety practices in institutional settings is not funny.

Here's a bit more about the two food-borne infections featured in the novel. Infections with food-borne ***Salmonella*** are characterized by diarrhea, fever, and stomach pains, sometimes vomiting, and go away in a few days (2) They usually are caused by eating undercooked meat or food cross-contaminated with undercooked meat by the food handler. However, they can be caused by poor sanitation after handling infected animals.

Symptoms of ***Clostridioides difficile* (C. *diff*)** infections range from mild diarrhea to severe life-threatening inflammation of the colon. The bacteria used to be called *Clostridium difficile* but recent genetic analyses caused it to be reclassified in 2016.

In the past *C. diff* infections were associated with poor sanitation and the overuse of antibiotics in clinical settings, e.g. nursing homes and hospitals However, recent research suggests pork, particularly improperly cooked suckling piglet, is a major source of C. diff infections (3).

Several features of *C. diff* make treatment and prevention difficult. About 2 to 5% of the population are carriers with no symptoms. Alcohol-based cleaners are not effective in killing *C. diff* bacteria on surfaces. Many strains of *C. diff* are resistant to common antibiotics and treating patients with these antibiotics will worsen a *C. diff* infection because other bacteria killed by the antibiotics are not present to limit the growth of *C. diff* (4). Roasting meat to less than well done does not destroy *C. diff* spores (5).

Stereotyping fair workers

Several characters employed at the medieval fair in this novel had police records. The causes of criminal behavior are debatable. High levels of poverty, unemployment, and population density are associated with increased crime rates (6). Individuals with limited options because of poverty, criminal records, and mental illness are more apt to accept the high-stress, low paying, and transient jobs offered by fairs.

Several of the employees of the fair in this novel displayed aggressive behavior even though they didn't have a "poor" background. (I can't be more specific without giving away the plot.) It's simplistic to classify them as mentally ill. Most individuals with mental illness are not violent. Those who are violent often have a history of substance abuse, antisocial behavior, and anger issues (7).

Childhood trauma is sometimes considered the cause of later aggressive behavior by adults. However, one multi-variate study noted only two forms of childhood trauma were independently predictive of adult aggressive behavior (8). They were witnessing violence and emotional (not physical) abuse.

Science is the key to modern police investigations.

Molecular biology techniques have been refined so a nanogram— one thousandth of a millionth of a gram—quantities of DNA can be identified in mixed samples (9). Although rapid DNA tests are useful for screening data, the slower, standardized tests are more sensitive and are required as evidence in court.

Artificial intelligence (AI) can identify patterns and "hot spots" in complex data sets—such as social media posts—and facilitates the analyses of fingerprint identification and facial recognition. However, codification of methodologies and awareness of biases is important (10).

Although less sophisticated, techniques for identifying blood at a crime scene remain important. UV light (around 365 nm) and luminol are commonly used to identify blood at crimes scenes. However, luminol gives false positive luminescence when it reacts with chlorine bleaches and may make samples less useful for DNA analyses.

                                        J. L. Greger

An alternative to luminol is **DCFDA** (2',7'-dichlorofluorescein diacetate) (11). It is sensitive in six-day old blood samples when diluted a million-fold. It is less apt to give false positives in the presence of chlorine bleach and damages DNA less than luminol.

History pertaining to New Mexico

The bits of history in the novel are subtle but demonstrate that history is an important part of the culture in New Mexico today. The fictional medieval fair in this novel is held at a historic ranch that is now a living history museum—**El Rancho de Las Golondrinas** (12). This ranch was an official rest stop on the Camino Real, which was the major trade route connecting Santa Fe to Mexico City from the early 1600s until the late 1800s.

Portia Merchant, the victim in the novel, is called a *curandera. Curanderas* were major health care providers in the Southwest, especially in rural areas, up to the 1960s. The New Mexico Historic Women Marker Programs has honored them with a marker in Mora, New Mexico (13). Today many herbalists and midwifes in New Mexico market themselves as *curanderas.*

Bodet Harper in this novel tried to sell the art he'd acquired by several different means to galleries in Santa Fe. This is logical because **Santa Fe has been a major art center** since the beginning of the twentieth century because of two major factors. It and Taos were art colonies for "Anglo" artists. The Santa Fe Indian School had a major program in art—the Studio School (14). The famous Navajo artists with connections to New Mexico mentioned in this book are Harrison Begay and R. C. Gorman.

Harrison Begay was trained at the Santa Fe Indian School painted and produced prints of Navajo scenes in the "flat" style promoted by Dorothy Dunn (14, 15).

R. C. Gorman primarily produced prints and oil pastels and is sometimes called the "Picasso of American Indians artists" (16). He owned the Navajo Gallery in Taos for many years.

Gorman's art was the inspiration for the Native American woman on cover of the book.

References

1. Food borne Illness Acquired in the United States—Major Pathogens, 2019. *Emerg Infect Dis* (2025); 31(4):669. https://doi.org/10.3201/eid3104.240913

2. Salmonella. https://my.clevelandclinic.org/health/diseases/15697-salmonella

3. The environment, farm animals and foods as sources of *Clostridioides difficile* infections in humans. *Foods* (2023);12(5):1094. https://www.mdpi.com/2304-8158/12/5/1094

4. *Clostridioides difficile* infection. https://en.wikipedia.org/wiki/Clostridioides_difficile_infection

5. Moist-heat resistance, spore aging, and superdormancy in *Clostridium difficile*. *Appl Environ Microbiol* (2011);77(9):3085–3091. DOI: 10.1128/AEM.01589-10

6. Economic correlates of crime: An empirical test in Houston. *J Criminal Justice* (2024); 95: 102306 https://doi.org/10.1016/j.jcrimjus.2024.102306

7. Mental illness and violence: Debunking myths and addressing realities. *Monitor on Psychology* (2021);52(3):31 https://www.apa.org/monitor/2021/04/ce-mental-illness.

8. Five forms of childhood trauma: Relationships with aggressive behavior in adulthood. *Prim Care Companion for CNS Disord* (2012);14(5). DOI: 10.4088/PCC.12m01353

9. DNA profiling. https://en.wikipedia.org/wiki/DNA_profiling.

10 FBI. Artificial Intelligence. https://www.fbi.gov/investigate/counterintelligence/emerging-and-advanced-technology/artificial-intelligence.

11. A novel method for blood detection using fluorescent dye. Microchemical J (2023):193 https://doi.org/10.1016/j.microc.2023.108987.

12. El Rancho de Las Golondrinas. http://golondrinas.org/

13. New Mexico Historic Women Marker Program. https://www.nmhistoricwomen.org/new-mexico-historic-women/curanderas-women-who-heal/

14. Santa Fe Indian School. https://en.wikipedia.org/wiki/Santa_Fe_Indian_School

15. Harrison Begay. https://en.wikipedia.org/wiki/Harrison_Begay

16. R. C. Gorman. https://en.wikipedia.org/wiki/R._C._Gorman

J. L. Greger

CAST OF CHARACTERS

Law enforcement

    Sara Almquist, science consultant for FBI and protagonist

    Jack Drum, FBI agent and Sara's partner

    Miguel Roybal, Santa Fe police sergeant

    Hank Snow, resident FBI agent in Santa Fe

    Paul Carbonne, special agent in charge (SAC) of Albuquerque FBI office

    Winslow Red Feather, CSI technician for the FBI

    Scott Carpenter, FBI agent and leader of SWAT

    Dave Roper, FBI agent

Medieval fair

    Management of fair

        Ron Engel

        Carolyn Taft

        Herbert Engel, owner of Camelot Fair Enterprises

    Staff in Portia's Potions booth

        Portia Merchant, owner

        Crystal Star, aka Hannah Merchant

        Willie Shakes

    Staff in King Arthur's Feast food stand

        Art Last, head cook

        Back-up cook

        Tallulah Dosela, server

        Elu Dosela, server

        Emmet Ant, server

    Staff in Treasure House booth

        Viv Lorenzo, owner

        Vano Georgescu

        Tony Marin

    Staff in stable

        Earl Scruggs, aka the Red Earl, stableman

        Three other itinerant stablemen

        Alonzo Wilder, local stableman

Other characters
    Bug, Sara Almquist's Japanese Chin dog
    Eric Sanders, Sara's significant other
    Bodet Harper, Portia's husband
    John Shakes, Willie's father
    Ellie Shakes, Willie's sister

ACKNOWLEDGMENTS

I appreciate the efforts of Lorna Collins for carefully editing this manuscript and of Barbara Hodges for creatively designing the cover. Thank you.

None of my books would be possible without the patience and love of my dogs: Bug, Elf, and Star.

ABOUT THE AUTHOR

J. L. Greger is a biology professor from the University of Wisconsin-Madison turned novelist. The pet therapy dog, Bug, in her mysteries and thrillers is based on her own Japanese Chin. She includes tidbits about science, the American Southwest, and her international travel experiences in her **Science Traveler Series**.

The Flu Is Coming. In the first book in the series, a woman scientist traces the spread of a deadly new flu virus among the frantic residents of a quarantined New Mexico community. (New Mexico/Arizona book award finalist)

Murder...A Way to Lose Weight. A dean in a medical school helps police discover whether an ambitious young "diet doctor," disgruntled patients, or old-timers with buried secrets are killers. (Winner of the 2016 Public Safety Writers Association contest; New Mexico/Arizona book award finalist)

Ignore the Pain. A woman scientist learns too much about the coca trade and too little about a sexy new colleague while on a public health assignment in Bolivia.

Malignancy. A woman tries to escape the clutches of a drug lord and accepts a risky assignment as a science consultant in Cuba. (Winner of the 2015 Public Safety Writers Association contest)

I Saw You in Beirut. A woman's past provides clues for the extraction of a nuclear scientist from Iran. The author's experiences as a science and education consultant in the United Arab Emirates and Lebanon are featured.

Riddled with Clues. A homeless man and a woman scientist are targeted by drug gangs after she listens to the strange tale of an undercover drug agent about his war experiences. The edited memories of an actual CIA agent in Laos during the Vietnam War are featured. (New Mexico/Arizona book award finalist)

A Pound of Flesh, Sorta. The police and a woman scientist can't decide whether a package contaminated with the bacteria that causes the bubonic plague is a plea for help by a whistleblower or a threat from gang leaders awaiting trial. (New Mexico/Arizona book award finalist; New Mexico Press Women Communications award)

Dirty Holy Water. A woman who usually serves as a science consultant for the FBI learns there is a thin line between being a victim and being a villain when she becomes the chief suspect in a bizarre murder case. (New Mexico/Arizona book award finalist)

Games for Couples. Did lethal compounds in a cultured meat product—meat made in a test tube—kill a man in a clinical trial? Or did the toxic competition between biotechnology companies and spite of battling couples cause his death? (New Mexico/Arizona book award finalist)

Fair Compromises. Sara Almquist and her FBI colleagues rush to find the culprits who endangered the lives of a hundred attendees at a political rally by poisoning the food with botulism toxin. Their target was a woman candidate for the US Senate. (New Mexico/Arizona book award finalist)

Bungle in the Jungle. The US consular office in Manaus, Brazil, is a "Bungle in the Jungle." Can Sara Almquist and the new acting Ambassador to Brazil figure out how the staff became enmeshed in the illegal international trade of drugs and cultural artifacts? (New Mexico/Arizona book award finalist)

Escape from a Dark Cave. An FBI scientific consultant investigates the murder of a young man near a historic cave in New Mexico. As she reconstructs the victim's final days, she learns the autistic victim found the cave to be soothing. She finds the cave to be depressing. (Public Safety Writers Association award; New Mexico/Arizona book award finalist)

The Man Who Looked for Death. Who can an FBI agent and a scientist trust as they investigate a murder in the ghost town of Golden Gully? The medical examiner thinks the victim was tortured for several days before he was killed. However, the ten residents in this remote town in the Gila National Forest deny knowing the man. The local sheriff's office is less than cooperative. (Public Safety Writers Association best cover award 2025; New Mexico Press Women Communications award)

Crazy Like a Goat. Scientist Sara Almquist and her FBI colleagues investigate the murder of a retired professor. Why did someone poison his booze? Did he know too much about the dark side of a successful chain of senior living centers? Or had he played too many pranks on his friends and neighbors? (Public Safety Writers Association best mystery award in 2025; New Mexico book award finalist)

For Whom the Cranes Call. The wildlife refuge at Bosque del Apache is a noisy but idyllic spot as cranes settle there for the winter. Then the body of a man wearing new, red boots is found on Christmas Day. Investigators soon learn many had reasons for wishing him dead.

Fair Dreams. Fairs are supposed to be fun. However, Sara Almquist and her FBI colleagues find little to smile about as they investigate a murder at a medieval fair in Santa Fe. There are too many suspects and motives.

J. L. Greger also wrote ***Come Fly with Elf.*** In this picture book for children, a tiny Papillon dog called Elf dreams of flying in a hot air balloon. She has written two collections of short stories: ***The Good Old Days?*** and **Other People's Mothers.**

See more at: http://www.jlgreger.com.